THE ELECTRA CONSPIRACY
PART 1

To Nikki
love
Liz

Elizabeth Revill
x

First Published in Great Britain 2012 by Mirador Publishing

First edition: 2012
Second edition: 2019

Any reference to real names and places are purely fictional and are constructs of the author. Any offence the references produce is unintentional and in no way reflects the reality of any locations or people involved.

A copy of this work is available through the British Library.

ISBN: 978-1-913264-03-1

Mirador Publishing
10 Greenbrook Terrace
Taunton
Somerset
UK
TA1 1UT

The Electra Conspiracy
Part 1

By

Elizabeth Revill

For Andrew

Prologue

AN ASHEN, DRAB DAY of interminable grey with no definition between sky and cloud stretched across the heavens. A pack of news hungry journalists were gathered at the stark prison gates outside Wormwood Scrubs in the U.K. They were vying for position to question the prison spokesman who had emerged waving his official statement. He mounted the podium set with microphones. The press surged forward in a questioning babble. Television cameras pushed in and flash bulbs popped continuously.

"Karen Gibbs, Daily Telegraph. Is it true that Carol and Karl Stevenson are to be given new identities to prevent reprisals from their own family?"

"The Home Office considers that the brutal slaying of their parents when they were still children stirred public opinion to such an extent that yes, they will be given new identities and a fresh start."

"Barry Porter, News International. Is it true that the twins have been educated to degree level?"

"Yes, during their internment they studied extensively. They have both achieved first class honours in Business and Accounting, and English Literature."

The barrage of questions continued, unnerving the official who struggled to give the Justice Department's perspective and floundered over its reasons for freeing the twins who were convicted double killers at the age of just twelve. The spokesman knew he had to keep control of this press conference and maintain the lead in the debate so that the newly released inmate, Karl Stevenson, now in his mid-twenties, could make his safe escape quietly and easily from the back exit of the prison, where a car was about to arrive to take him away to a safe house.

The melancholy grey of the heavens began to shed its tears as fine drizzle that lightly drifted down. The official took a gulp of the misty air. He could taste and smell the city dust as it filled his lungs. He jumped as another question was shouted at him.

"Gary Walker, the Sun. Are the twins allowed to have contact with each other or will that be forbidden as in Venables and Thomson in the Bulger case?"

This was a trickier question for the official to answer and he stuttered his reply, looking uncertain. "It was initially thought that yes, they would be forbidden from seeing each other but they have responded so well to therapy and are filled with such remorse that this question is still under review. In the interim they will have no contact with each other but that may not be a permanent ruling and I believe Carol Stevenson's lawyers have already launched just such an appeal against a continued and enforced separation."

The press conference rattled on with more and more questions fired at the now uncomfortable official who knew he had to keep going a while longer until he received a signal from his superiors.

An anonymous black saloon car had arrived and was now waiting at the rear. Security men watched as a lone male figure was quickly smuggled out. The car door opened and Karl Stevenson, dived into the back seat. His twin sister, Carol, was already sitting in the rear. She grinned in delight as she recognised her brother.

"Long time no see," she opened her arms to welcome him.

"Thirteen years, I believe," answered Karl patting his sister's knees.

"Who's counting?" she said devilishly and they hugged. They held tightly to each other; the moment was emotional for both of them. "It's so good to see you," she finally managed to say.

"You've grown up," said Karl admiringly. He studied her slim, athletic build and smooth skin. Her lustrous hair perfectly framed her striking features. His twin sister had developed into a beautiful young woman.

They gazed at each other, hardly daring to believe that they had been reunited. Carol finally acknowledged her brother. She quietly appraised his good looks and fit body and murmured appreciatively, "As have you." The car carefully pulled away unobserved and disappeared into the drizzling mist.

At the prison gates the plethora of questions continued. An elderly clerk scuttled out from the sombre prison and approached the official. He whispered in his ear, and the relieved spokesman announced, "That's it Ladies and Gentleman." The journalists still continued to shout out their questions but the thankful official hurried back to the safety of the prison and the throng began to disband.

A smart looking female television presenter spoke directly to camera. Her voice was efficient and demanded attention, "So, there you have it. In spite of the public outcry at the news of the release of these two vicious young murderers who testified at their trial that they wanted to see what it was like to kill, and selected their own parents for this macabre experiment; they are now apparently rehabilitated and will go on to serve productive lives. In the coming months I am sure there will be much debate over this controversial decision. More on this story can be heard on this evening's six o'clock news. This is Karen James for Channel 5 at Wormwood Scrubs."

Across the ocean in New York, a grizzled prison guard drew the thick curtains across the execution chamber housing the newly executed and apparently lifeless body of murderer, Christopher Lomax. Justice Department's camcorders, which documented the event, stopped rolling. Subdued witnesses and officials, slowly and silently, filed out from the cheerless observation room. The killer's weeping mother dabbed at her eyes with a hankie and the door to the soundproof room clanged shut tolling its announcement that death comes at the end. For Christopher Lomax life was seemingly over.

Immediately, the curtains were closed, the back door to the execution chamber opened, which led into a private corridor and Lomax, now complete with a new intravenous drip, was rushed along it at almost break neck speed by men in white coats. He was propelled into an operating theatre where a thin-faced surgeon and team of specially vetted medical staff were waiting. The surgeon gave Lomax an injection to counteract the effects of the drugs that had reduced him to a temporary death and he restored all the killer's vital signs. The monitor began to bleep as his heart began to beat strongly once more. Lomax took a huge gulp of air and an oxygen mask was placed around his mouth. The surgeon helped by two medics rolled Lomax onto his side and inspected the skin on his back.

One doctor palpated the killer's dermis in the centre of his shoulder blades. His clipped tones announced, "Good. Good. The implant's still secure."

They gently released his body so that he fell back and faced upwards again. A plump nurse replaced the oxygen mask with a tube. The surgeon picked up a scalpel and said, "We'll start with the nose."

The plastic surgeons worked tirelessly for ten hours under the swelteringly hot lights. Lomax's aquiline nose was redefined and made smaller. Harvested fat from his stomach was injected into the skin over his cheekbones; his chin was squared and dimpled like that of Kirk Douglas. The restoration of his face continued until they were satisfied with their work. Lomax's surgically changed face was bandaged and dressed with only his eyes, nostrils and mouth visible. Still unconscious he was wheeled into recovery where foreign nurses fussed around him and where three other people were similarly bandaged.

At the same time, Karl and Carol Stevenson were driven unobserved out of London. The journey was relatively sombre. The twins knew that they mustn't relax their guard and that after their initial greetings they needed to maintain a certain diffidence between them. To reveal any need of each other could possibly compromise their future. They left the city's fog and choking traffic and travelled through the leafy lanes, past green fields to a secluded but large, rambling, military, red brick building in the Suffolk countryside. Heavily guarded, the sign outside read, 'Chemical Core Special Operations Division'. Military personnel could be seen marching with precision and exercising in the yard.

Carol and Karl were checked into the compound by two guards with machine guns wearing bullet-proof protective jackets. Brother and sister exchanged looks and stared at the high fences surrounding the compound, the iron watchtowers and the presence of incredibly heavy security, and surprisingly, they looked pleased.

The twins were ushered out of the vehicle and taken to their quarters after they were each issued with standard uniform and equipment. No one batted an eyelid or took any notice of them. Men and a few women walked blindly past them along the corridors, like automatons, scarcely brushing shoulders with Karl and Carol who had now arrived at their quarters.

The bullish staff sergeant barked at them, "Into battle fatigues and report to the firing range, now!"

The twins entered their sparsely furnished rooms and changed into the required apparel. A taciturn guard waited outside their doors and when they emerged they looked like regular soldiers. They were escorted to the firing range.

The strict staff sergeant was waiting and put them through a rigorous programme of weapon assembly before they were taken to the gallery, where a variety of targets were set up, some fixed and others moving. The officer demanded, "Let's see what you've got."

Under instruction, the twins rapidly assembled and disassembled a variety of weapons until they could do the task without stopping to think about it. They were then commanded to shoot, in various lighting states, at a number of different targets, which were then inspected. The staff sergeant smiled gratifyingly, it seemed that Carol was a crack shot. By the time they left the range darkness had fallen outside and the twins were transported to a night assault course and their rigorous training began again. Their days were filled with learning how to break into and enter houses without leaving a trace, and how to hijack a vehicle without the alarm being raised. They were taught to shoot accurately on command. The instruction was thorough.

Finally, they both underwent an accelerated and advanced driving course. Karl went out on the skid-pan and was taught how to handle a vehicle in a skid in all weathers. They were both taught how to drive at pace and much more. Carol whooped and laughed in glee at the manoeuvres more akin to learning how to be a stunt driver. Weeks later, legal driving licenses were prepared with their new ID's. They were to be permitted to keep their Christian names to avoid confusion and thus inadvertently give themselves away. They had grown up sufficiently that their appearances had changed vastly, so that there was no need for plastic surgery.

In America, a nurse with the medical staff and the surgeon who had performed the operation on Christopher Lomax waited patiently as the bandages were removed from Christopher Lomax's face. His reconstructed looks bore no resemblance to his old identity. The only thing that hadn't changed was the expression in the killer's coldly penetrating eyes.

The surgeon, with his team and the newly healed Lomax left immediately for a private airfield that was out of sight of any curious onlookers and there they boarded a small military jet headed for a minor landing field in Suffolk England. From there they were to be bussed to the same military building as the Stevensons.

Back in the high security building, closed from the public, under armed guard and manned watchtowers, Carol and Karl, and twenty other inmates, all in protective custody, were herded inside after their daily drill. The internees entered a recreation room. There they relaxed. Carol and Karl joined two other subjects at the pool table and began to shoot a few balls. The air smelled strongly of lavender as if to mask any medical odours.

A nurse in crisp whites wheeled a rattling drugs trolley and worked the room around couples that played chess, read, or engaged in a game of cards or something more physical. Everyone took his or her offered medication without any fuss.

Five musical notes were played repetitively in the background, but they were not so loud as to be intrusive, the sound melded into the chatter and again no one paid any attention to them. In the galleried area at the top of the stairs was a glass fronted observation room where the surgeon who had operated on Christopher Lomax was explaining to the doctor, who had assisted him, how narco-hypnosis worked.

"So, the blending of mind altering drugs with careful hypnotic programming and the musical notes alter their brainwaves. We can make them do anything. As long as it's in their psyche to behave in this way we can programme them to kill on command."

"Just like robots," agreed the doctor. "How efficient, perfect killing machines."

"I do however, have my concerns…"

"Don't you think it works?" questioned the doctor.

"Oh, it works. I just worry a little about the ethics."

"Too late for that now," observed the doctor.

"And the money helps me forget," grinned the surgeon.

The two doctors continued to watch, observe and discuss.

In another part of the country in a large upscale hotel in the Isle of Man, a top-secret meeting was soon to be in progress. Members of the Brandenberg Sect, a group of extremely powerful top politicians, ace businessman and other very wealthy, influential individuals, from the West, were arriving. Flash limousines rolled up the impressive tarmac drive that was lined with ornamental trees and nineteenth century antique lamps, and deposited their important personnel. Some entered the hotel with confidence, others more covertly. The public were being kept well away from the venue as some of Europe's and the West's most powerful men who, it was rumoured, controlled the world by engineering and manipulating world events for profit and control, made their way to the plush conference room, with its amazing plaster cast ceiling and wood panelled walls. They settled themselves inside around the magnificent, heavy oak table. The men all wore a distinctive gold signet ring embossed with a lion's head. Conversation was hushed until the meeting was called to order and officially opened.

The camera in the corner of the room faithfully recorded every comment, every gesture of everyone who spoke. No one would escape notice. They would all be observed. It automatically moved and focused on each individual present, staying with the speaker and panning around the table like a third eye.

Everything was always observed – from the CCTV littering the country like confetti, to the security cameras in private homes. They knew everything.

Discussion was quickly underway and a number of topics were debated and decisions made. The room was heavy with tension as the time ticked on. Proposed military operations were discussed in detail all with a view to benefiting the West and giving them supremacy in foreign climes so that they could achieve control in resource rich countries.

They moved onto another item on the unwritten agenda. Andrew Bawden, the US Defence Secretary, a thickset man in his fifties, and a smoker, appeared to take the chair and announced in his throaty tones, "I can confirm that subjects MK7, 9 and 10 are ready."

David Lace, a lean, angular looking man of forty who was the UK's senior advisor to the treasury asked, "And can they be placed?"

"Anywhere, anytime, Lace," was Bawden's terse response.

Scott Francis, a top UK wealthy businessman in IT, leaned forward, to ask, "High powered positions?"

"Not a problem," smiled Bawden. "Any other business or matters arising from our discussions to date before I raise the next item?"

Philip Birchell, a leading UK newspaper magnate fingered his heavy gold identity bracelet, took a sip of water and pressed, "Yes. Ibrahim Khalid's application for British citizenship; are we agreed?"

Lace jumped in and said abruptly, "Refused."

The rest of the table assented. "We'll progress refusal through the proper channels, of course," continued Birchell.

"Of course," Lace concurred. "Shall we move on?"

There were no further comments, no discussion and no dissension. Bawden and the rest of the sect nodded their heads in agreement.

Bawden, sighed and leaned back in his chair, "And now, gentlemen.... Our last item, a tricky one ... Electra...."

There was a pause as the assembled company considered the pop singer and the problems she had caused not only politically, but also worldwide. It was clear from the shifting of feet and disgruntled expressions that she was a veritable thorn in the Sect's side. Lace broke the silence, "Are you saying she has to go?"

Harley Claymore, the president of a major US bank, snorted, "She's just a singer, does anyone really care?"

Rueben Goldberg, a high-powered shipping magnate, expostulated, "You don't break a butterfly on a wheel. She's just a trivial little tart with nice tits."

Lace came back at him, "It'll upset the aristocracy. What about her brother?"

"She's upset them enough by becoming a pop star," observed Claymore.

"Will they really mind? After all ... No more embarrassments..." asserted Goldberg, as he cracked his knuckles. Heads around the table turned to stare at him.

"Still, it's a bit thick doing away with her," said Lace.

Bawden ploughed on, "We have no choice. Our President feels she's more than a petty annoyance. Her views are downright subversive; she's dangerous," he growled.

"So, she's a campaigner, a human rights' activist. No worse than others I could mention," argued Lace and then nervously took a sip of water.

"She cost our country dear with our arms sales, we lost a highly lucrative contract because of her stance on landmines," said Bawden. "She has too much influence, too much sway. She's a dangerous lady."

"And so she is for us, too," admitted Francis. "Especially now that she's dating that playboy, Ahmed Khalid. The implications are enormous." Francis didn't mince his words. He was always prepared to state the obvious.

"Can't we just part them like we did with the Prince?" reasoned Birchell. "That was easy enough, throwing another woman at him."

"It won't work a second time," countered Lace.

"Well, I don't like it," said Birchell.

"Dammit, Birchell. It's not just her influence," he paused before he stunned them with the next remark. "Word has it that she may uncover the triggers, West will explain," said Bawden.

Lace looked aghast, "Christ! How did that happen?"

The assembled company digested this information and listened closely to millionaire Malcolm West, a smart clean cut man in his forties, who was Electra's manager and producer, "It was inevitable. We never intended her to be around long enough to find them."

Lace quickly fired back, "But around long enough to make you a fortune and twice the fortune once she's dead."

West calmly continued; "Always part of the plan, Lace. Her death will treble album sales ensuring greater placement of our triggers around the world, and yes, making several of our members incredibly wealthy."

Bawden interrupted, "Making a profit is never something to apologise for, Lace."

"We have the manpower to make this happen," said West. "And some of us will need to be involved more than we would probably like."

The Sect fell silent as they considered the information before them. West, pressed on, "I'll keep her going as long as I can, but when I get the call, and it will come, then we have to make her a legend. Agreed?"

One by one hands were raised. Birchell was the last. All eyes turned on him and noted that he very reluctantly raised his arm, and was shaking his head in sorry disbelief. His heavy gold bracelet glinted in the afternoon sun, as did the ring with the embossed lion's head.

The camera caught it all, every glance, every statement and every possible hesitation. It recorded every Sect meeting. The captured data would be scrutinised and analysed. Filed and if necessary utilised at a later date.

Chapter One

Prophecy

MOONLIGHT BOLDLY INVADED A cluttered study. Its silver fingers poked through the half open curtains and prodded the blue white light of a flickering computer that mingled with the glow of a low energy saving bulb in an angle-poise lamp. The desk was piled high with papers and files. To the left was an electric desk clock and calendar, which changed its display as each minute passed, marking time. The date changed suddenly to November 8th. as the time clicked forward to 12:01 just after midnight.

A masculine hand wearing a heavy, distinctive gold ring embossed with a lion's head and a chunky gold identity bracelet stretched down to a thick file resting on the comfortable shag pile carpet at the chair leg. The file name emblazoned across the buff cover read, 'ELECTRA'.

The faceless journalist and newspaper magnet opened the file and scrutinised its contents. He thrust the file aside next to a tower of papers marked, 'Highly Confidential' and he began to type. He tap, tapped on the keyboard beginning with the date, November 15th. The Obituary headline screamed, "POP ICON ELECTRA DIES TRAGICALLY IN HORRIFIC CAR CRASH. MILLIONS MOURN HER LOSS."

The journalist sighed as he began to detail the life of the superstar, her humanitarian and charity work, and campaigns against the sale of landmines and weapons of war, and he worked long into the early hours documenting her complex life and many relationships. He read and edited and reworded until he was satisfied with the copy. By the angle of his jaw and the line of his shoulders his unhappiness at the task was apparent.

Across the city of London, two filmmakers were covering a rare, late night concert at the Hammersmith Odeon starring Electra. The auditorium was rocking with fans and devotees of Electra's music. Through the lens of their camera, they recorded everything. The story of Electra's life became an open book, detailing every nuance between them, the audience and the star's life. The air smelled of cordite, the only thing the camera couldn't record, from a pyrotechnic display that had accompanied the dramatic opening where Electra was flown down to the stage into the middle of a fevered dance number.

Thirty-year old Jon Curtis, his long, thick, fair hair flowing, hippy style over his shoulders, was dressed in comfortable baggy corduroy trousers and a roomy sweatshirt. He stood next to his colleague, strikingly attractive Amy Wilde, aged twenty-eight with her lustrous long, dark hair tied back in a ponytail. They were recording the event from the wings and loving every minute of the assignment. They were privileged to be filming and producing a commissioned biopic on superstar, Electra.

Vivacious Amy was laughing happily and she clapped her hands in delight, as the entire audience were whipped up into a frenzy, while Electra strutted her stuff and her distinctive voice, overwhelmed with emotion, managed to touch each and every person there including the filmmakers.

Vibrant Electra finished a heavy rock number, where she sang and danced, surrounded by her band and a team of lithe dancers. The music reached its climax and the drummer beat a funereal tattoo. Electra stopped and bowed. The crowd went wild. She held up her hands and quietened the audience. A hush fell across the auditorium. Two screens rolled down at each side of the stage and as Electra spoke she had the audience in the palm of her hand, "You all know my feelings about capital punishment and about the countries that still practice it. What you are about to see happened in the USA just eight months ago. This next song says it all, The Shortest Day. Judge for yourself."

The lead guitarist led in with a melancholy riff as film footage flickered to life on the screens and everyone observed and listened. A lone saxophone joined the guitar and played hauntingly as a convicted murderer, Christopher Lomax, lean, tall and muscular, walked in slow motion the long corridor to his death accompanied by prison guards and a priest who constantly chanted prayers as he followed the orange jump-suited killer. Lomax showed no emotion, no remorse. His mouth was set in a hard line and his expression was stern. His steel blue coldly penetrating eyes stared unblinkingly ahead.

The audience in the theatre watched in deadly fascination as Lomax was taken into the execution chamber, ordered to lie down and strapped to a gurney. Life support monitoring equipment was attached to him together with an intravenous line. A white-coated doctor flicked the switch that would deliver the first of three deadly drugs to take away Lomax's life and soul. Sodium thiopental was followed by an ultra-short barbiturate and an anaesthetic agent at a high dose. In less than thirty seconds Lomax was rendered unconscious as the man was flooded with the lethal narcotics.

The priest droned on.

The song continued, the sadness in the music echoing the exit of the life force from Lomax's body as he slipped into unconsciousness. The timing was precise and as the song ended, the vital signs on the monitor flat-lined and Lomax's bodily functions ceased. The long beep toned with the saxophone's final note. The reaction of Electra's adoring fans was stunned silence. Even Amy watching from the wings bit her lip, a tear rolled down her cheek and Jon lowered his camera. No one was unaffected, such was the power of the song.

Electra addressed her audience that was gripped by the number and accompanying film. The air was thick with tension, "So, my friends, you can see that capital punishment is just as barbaric as war." Electra's well-modulated voice resonated throughout the auditorium. "No one should play God and take another's life, no matter what they have done, which leads me into the next song and covers another subject close to my heart."

Plaintive notes struck up and Electra's full toned and hauntingly beautiful voice began to sing, as she did this, so the screens changed and film footage from war torn countries stormed across the screens. The visual brutality was a stark, contrasting image against such a beautiful song. Landmines exploded and the images of the suffering of innocent victims, especially children, filled the screens; injured people hopped and hobbled on crutches minus their limbs; children with no arms looked desperately forlorn, and shattered bodies littered the ground. The expressions on the victim's faces revealed lives filled with misery as the corpses of the newly dead piled up in numerous war torn countries. A collective gasp ripped through the audience, while Jon and Amy, standing in the wings, watched in rapt amazement.

"How does she do it?" asked Amy in wonder, brushing away yet another tear. "I must have seen her do this song a hundred times and it still gets me." The camera continued to record her soft voice.

"I don't know," said Jon.

"But it's what we've got to capture, her presence and magnetism. Her sheer power," pressed Amy. "We have to get that across on film."

"Yes, I know," agreed Jon. "To use a cliché, it's a tall order," he said philosophically.

Electra took a final encore and people stamped their feet, cheered, whooped, whistled and applauded. She rushed off stage leaving the fans clamouring for more. Stage staff congratulated her as Jon and Amy, still filming, followed her rapidly along the corridor to her dressing room. Outside her door amongst the melee of backup singers and dancers, en route to their changing rooms, stood Electra's musical producer and agent, Malcolm West. He looked an imposing figure. His eyes scanned the corridor, taking in all the activity. His expression lightened as he spotted Electra moving toward her dressing room. At the side of him was another very tall man, physically fit and clearly alert whom West introduced, "Electra, this is Paul Grayson your new bodyguard."

Electra grasped his hand momentarily. "Hi Paul," and she nodded at the new member of her Security Team before dashing inside her room. The swell of sound from the fans going crazy in the auditorium permeated through to the back stage area. Paul Grayson raised his cold hard eyes at the abrupt introduction and muttered in a thick Brooklyn accent, "I expect I'll meet her at the party afterwards. I'll get to speak to her more fully then."

West answered, "Don't count on it. You don't know Electra. She'll be straight to the studio."

Grayson raised an eyebrow as if to say, 'a pop star not partying?' His fixed expression and hard eyes were captured on CCTV outside Electra's dressing room, eyes that were reminiscent of the ones from the film during the concert.

West took charge, "Wait here, and watch her back." He studied Grayson's face and ordered, "Let no one in. I'll send for the car. When she's ready, you escort her and you drive."

Grayson had his instructions and he waited patiently outside Electra's door until it opened. Electra hardly glanced at him, "Right, let's go."

He accompanied her along the corridor with Jon and Amy in tow. They exited the stage door where fans jostled for a better vantage point; as soon as they laid eyes on the superstar her admirers attempted to mob her. They surged forward and she just managed to escape into the parked limo. Grayson slipped comfortably into the driver's seat. Electra, West, Amy and Jon piled into the back with Jon's camera still running. Grayson started the motor as the fans crowded around.

"Studio, please, Paul, Mal," instructed Electra.

West caught Grayson's stony eyes in the mirror as if to say, 'I told you so.'

The limo continued on its journey as it fled Hammersmith, the pursuing fans and press. West took the opportunity to quickly brief Electra, "Ahmed has called twice, and so has the Prince."

"Call Ahmed. Tell him I'll be working," ordered Electra.

"And the Prince?"

Electra did not respond. Jon and Amy exchanged a look. Electra turned to Jon and Amy, "So, where do you two want to be dropped off?"

Jon switched off his camera and requested, "Jimmy's bar please, I could do with a night cap."

"Me, too," agreed Amy. "It's been a long night."

Grayson followed directions and pulled up outside Jimmy's, an all-night bar, and there he dropped off the two filmmakers who bade the others a quick goodnight.

The limo pulled away. A camera watched it leave and captured them walking into the bar. Jon and Amy trekked in and sat at a booth. A television above the bar was set at a music channel, and currently featured John Lennon in a white suit playing a piano and singing, 'Imagine'. The mood was one of contented but relaxed weariness reflecting Jon and Amy's demeanour.

In the corner of the bar, the security cameras rolled capturing every customer, every drink and every movement. Amy glanced up at the CCTV above them, "Do you realise we are the most watched country in the world?"

"Big brother rules."

"The problem is we are so used to it we don't even notice them, now. They are everywhere even in some taxicabs and buses. All that data squirreled away on a server somewhere in Siberia or Alaska." She alerted the barman with a cheery wave. "Bottle of Shiraz, please, Hugh," requested Amy. "And two glasses."

"No Pinot Grigio?" queried Jon.

"Not tonight... just for you," she smiled back at him.

The barman obliged and brought over the glasses and a bottle. "Run a tab?" asked Hugh.

"Nah! I'll get this," offered Amy.

"Looks like you need it. Bad night?" queried Hugh.

"On the contrary but, it was a long, long night," said Jon.

"But a good one," added Amy and handed Hugh a twenty-pound note.

"Be right back with your change," affirmed Hugh.

Jon took a sip and ran his fingers through his hair, "Mmm, this tastes good, just what I need to help me unwind. And fancy… Shiraz, just for me." He grinned, "What happened to Pinot Grigio?"

"Just a small treat for all your hard work. Next time, you can get me my favourite."

"Fair deal," agreed Jon. "How do you think we did today?"

"Pretty good," replied Amy with enthusiasm. "Look what's in the can already. We've got her early morning routine, a gym workout, her visit to one of the charities and some cracking footage of the concert both front of house and behind the scenes."

"And the piece de resistance, a real coup, a personal interview. But, we've heaps more to do. Can't rest on our laurels now."

"We can work out what else we need when we run through all the footage tomorrow. Possibly we can arrange further interviews with family and friends; like how they see Electra, the person as opposed to the rock star," said Jon.

"Hm, that makes sense," agreed Amy.

Jon yawned, the wine was having its effect and tiredness was taking hold. Amy however, was becoming more energised and fired up. "But, we couldn't get her to talk about the Royals. Really tight lipped about that. She didn't say a thing in the car after Mal's message."

"Probably because she still loves him," responded Jon.

"No, it's more than that. He was a big part of her life, for such a long time, we can't just miss it out," reasoned Amy. "The general public will be interested in that."

"Reporting on that very tricky relationship means it'll probably come down to other people's views on the affair, you know, friends, band members and so on, and what they thought and felt about it. It's the only way around it, if she won't talk." Jon stifled another yawn.

"Maybe. If we could only get her to open up."

"It's no good," admitted Jon. "I can't think. It's late, and I'm tired. You sort it." He stood up.

"Thanks a bunch," Amy muttered and paused slightly, "Come on, Jon... Don't you fancy another drink?" she pleaded.

"Got a home to go to and a cat to feed. See you at ten." He glanced at his watch, "Crikey! It'll take me an hour to get home, and then I've got to upload the film for editing. Ten o'clock will be here before you know it. I'm off!" He pushed aside the remains of his drink and left Amy twisting her glass.

She looked at Jon's departing figure, wistfully, shrugged and poured herself another drink. "Cheers, Amy!" she said sarcastically, as she slugged it down.

She looked around the bar. There was a young couple in a corner totally involved in each other and a couple of lone guys.

Hugh waved across at her, "Everything okay?"

Amy smiled, "I think I had better follow my colleague's lead. Can you order me a cab, Hugh? I believe I can just about manage the last glass."

Hugh acknowledged her and picked up the phone at the bar as Amy squeezed the last drink out of the bottle. Hugh called over, "He'll be here in ten minutes, all right?"

"Great, thanks, Hugh," and she yawned.

"If you weren't so tired I'd suggest you joining me. I get off in an hour."

"Thanks, but no thanks. No offence, I really must get home. Got another busy day tomorrow. Another time, perhaps?" she smiled.

"No worries." Hugh grinned at her and attended to wiping down the counter, which didn't really need it, Amy thought.

The camera in the bar continued its silent work.

Across town dedicated Electra was in studio focused on mixing and remixing her tracks. With headphones on, she was sitting before a myriad of dials and switches; Electra was listening and sliding knobs, playing the songs back, and setting the levels for bass, percussion and rhythm. Grayson had half a cup of coffee in front of him, reading yesterday's news. He looked very sleepy, his head began to nod and he started to doze.

The door opened with a clunk but Grayson still slept as handsome, Ahmed Khalid entered with his new bodyguard and driver, Karl Goodwin. Ahmed dismissed Karl and with a jerk of his head indicated Grayson and ordered, "Get some coffee and take him with you."

Karl nudged Grayson awake and the two exited. Once they had left Ahmed settled next to Electra. He removed her headphones and kissed her tenderly. He whispered gently in her ear, "I thought you were dropping by after the concert?"

"Aw, sorry babe, you know me. It's the last track. I need to finish it before the tour," she soothed, replacing the earphones but leaving one ear uncovered so she could hear Ahmed when he spoke.

"Don't you have technicians for that?" Ahmed queried.

"Course I do, but I need to check…" she stopped. "What the…?" Electra stopped the track, went back over it and played it again. A puzzled expression manifested on her face and she repeated the exercise and then handed a set of earphones to Ahmed. "Listen to that. Can you hear it?"

Ahmed put them on and listened. He shrugged. "What? What am I listening to?" he asked puzzled.

"There's an odd collection of notes," she counted them as they played. "Five. Five notes on strings running under the backup vocals. Do you hear them?"

"So?"

"I didn't put them there. Shit! I'll have to call Mal."

"But it's four in the morning," protested Ahmed.

"That's what I pay him for." Electra picked up the phone and dialled out.

The telephone rang in West's bedroom. He awoke and reached across a beautiful naked blonde curled up next to him. "Yes?" he answered quietly, not wishing to disturb his companion. As soon as he heard Electra's voice, he sat up and rubbed his eyes, "Electra? What? Slow down, you're going too fast. What's the problem?"

As Electra explained, West's face changed. He tried to placate her, "No, don't do anything yet…. Because I said so… Yes, I know you have artistic rights, I'm just asking you to leave it until I see you and I can hear it myself…. Of course, I trust you. Yes. Just leave it, please. We'll sort it. I promise… No, I am not coming there now. Go home and get some sleep… We'll look at it again in the morning… Yes, I promise. I'll see you in studio… Ten sharp… Okay. Ciao."

West replaced the phone and slipped out of bed. The blonde moved and made little noises as she stirred. "Hey, Mal, come back to bed. Please," she purred. She patted the bed with her perfectly manicured hand.

"Sorry, hon. I'll be two minutes." Malcolm West stepped out of the bedroom, ran down the stairs and into his sitting room. He swore under his breath, picked up his cell and quickly tapped out a text message. 'Electra is on to the triggers.' He hit send, then tossed his phone down and made his way back upstairs to where his blonde was waiting. She welcomed him with her superbly toned and open arms and Malcolm West embraced her as they began to make love.

The following day the recording session was in full swing. Jon and Amy in spite of their lack of sleep were enjoying filming the musical episode. Band members joked and Electra displayed her rigorous discipline and perfectionism but without losing her good humour. That all changed when the outside door opened and West entered even though the red light was on indicating recording was in progress. This flagrant disregard for protocol was something that clearly annoyed the pop star.

Electra raised her hands and proclaimed, "Okay, everyone, take five, grab a coffee or something. We'll get going again in..." She checked her watch, "Ten." She waited until the band had cleared the studio. Some vanished into the Green Room, others went behind the studio glass to the booth where the sound engineer was operating.

Electra turned to Jon and Amy, "You too." Jon switched off his camera. They left the room and joined some of the band members on the other side of the glass.

"Just, what the hell do you think you are doing coming in on a red light? You could have ruined the whole recording," snapped Electra.

"Well, I didn't. I listened at the door and there seemed to be a break."

"No one, but no one comes in when recording is in progress, not even you. Get it?" remonstrated Electra.

"Sorry," said Mal ruefully. "No harm was done."

"That's not the point. It could have been. And more importantly, who tampered with the last track? Those notes just don't work. They have to go," she blazed. "My music is important, all my music. It doesn't compliment or caress the melody. It's extraneous and destroys the passion. I want them out!"

West sat down on a high stool. He began to make excuses, "It's not a problem, Electra. We'll sort it. Just get the rest of the tracks down as arranged and we'll work through it together. I have a feeling it was a deliberate addition, a theme to be picked up in another song. No need to lose any sleep over it. Mitch is writing a new song for you, using those notes in the opening riff, like a subliminal text. It's a clever idea and the song is bound to sell."

"Don't patronise me, Mal," Electra raised her voice and those on the other side of the glass fell silent and listened. Suddenly, aware that the sound was still connected from the studio to behind the glass Electra made a cutting gesture across her throat to those in the control booth. A guitarist obliged and muted the sound from the studio so that Mal and Electra's conversation could no longer be heard. It was clear, however, that West and Electra were arguing. Arms were waved in anger and hostile expressions ruled. It would be longer than ten minutes before the session resumed.

Chapter Two

Following Through

CAROL STEVENSON WAS SITTING on the elegant, sage, soft leather sofa in the comfortable lounge in her brother's apartment at the top of a swish, luxury, three-storey block in Kensington. Her long lissom limbs were tucked under her. She hugged a large glass of fruity red wine, took a sip and frowned as she struggled to remember the answer to a question. Karl was taking his job seriously in testing her in readiness for an upcoming exam. "Um… Talk to them and try to keep them conscious."

"Yes. Which is the Universal Blood Type?" Karl asked his eyes boring into hers willing her to answer correctly.

"O."

"Positive or negative?" he quizzed.

"Negative," Carol confidently pronounced.

"Correct," Karl paused and studied Carol's face. "Would anyone have thought that we'd be handpicked to serve the government?"

"Or that it would be such fun!" replied Carol.

"You always loved danger."

"It pays well," she gestured to their surrounds. "You ought to see my place."

"No doubt, I will, in time."

"You bet."

Karl laughed, "Who'd have thought…? Anyway, back to business. What more can you tell me about blood typing in an emergency?"

"If there isn't any O negative, O positive can be used if the recipient's blood is in the positive category … If the person has AB positive blood then they can receive blood of any type. They are called the universal recipient type. … How long have we got together?"

Karl looked at his watch. "Another hour then I have to report for duty."

"What are you doing?"

"Sorry, Sis. Not allowed to say. We're not even supposed to be meeting. You never know if we're being watched or overheard."

"I know, we'll get our knuckles rapped... I just thought..."

"Once this assignment is over we will have time together and we can share our experiences..."

"Before the next one...?"

"Before the next one," affirmed Karl. "Right, back to the test... What do you have to do to put someone in the recovery position?"

Carol went on to describe the action, "Roll them onto their side, the underneath arm stretched up and the other placed across the body. The top leg should be bent and brought across the other like this," and she demonstrated with a small doll figure that had moveable parts. "Next make sure the airways are clear and that there are no obstructions. How did I do?"

"Perfect. It should be a doddle. The only things you need to go through again are muscle groups in Anatomy."

"That's because some of them are confusing."

"Confusing?" queried Karl.

"Yes, with names that sound like something else," complained Carol.

"Like what?" asked Karl

"Gastrocnemius. It sounds like it should be in the stomach not in the leg," explained Carol.

"Oh, yes. It's the calf muscle, isn't it?" remembered Karl.

"See what I mean?"

"Okay, let's go through them just one more time."

CCTV captured the new day and the new events where press and photographers waited outside a top-notch venue in Earl's Court hoping for a glimpse of superstar, Electra who was there to rehearse for her performance at a private party later that day. Journalists shuffled and stamped their feet as they waited. Every car that passed or slowed was virtually assaulted by the paparazzi.

A Bentley Flying Spur drove up close to the entrance of the smart, luxury hotel. A rear passenger door opened and Ahmed stepped out. His arrival was heralded by a burst of popping flash bulbs. Ahmed battled his way through the encroaching crowd and reached the red carpet. He flashed his ID and entered the building. Newspapermen pushed forward but were prevented from following by the heavy presence of Security Officers, and Ahmed hastily disappeared from view.

The prowling press pack went back on watch and were delighted that the next vehicle, to arrive, a deluxe people carrier, was carrying Electra, her chief bodyguard - Grayson, members of her band as well as Jon and Amy. Grayson stepped out first, his eyes scanned the crowds and he ushered Electra through. The pop star was hassled with questions shouted at her and cameramen yelled at her to "Look this way. Electra! Over here!" Everyone was trying to catch her attention. The atmosphere was buzzing with anticipation.

Jon struggled to film the scene of her arrival and a heavy-handed Security guy tried to bar the filmmakers from entering.

"No, mate, get back with the rest of them," ordered a guard.

"I'm supposed to be here. I'm with them," said Jon.

"Yeah!" snorted the guard derisively. "You and the rest."

Jon lowered his camera, pointed at his pass pinned to his lapel. The guard examined it. "Sorry, mate. Just doing my job," he nodded curtly and Jon was admitted.

Similarly, the way was barred for Amy but the guard was a bit more courteous. Amy rummaged in her handbag for her entry ID, which she eventually found and pinned onto her jacket. She was then granted admission and she added, "We're the only official filmmakers allowed into the rehearsal. It should make your job easier."

"Thanks for that," responded the guard appreciatively, as he hurried her inside before returning join the others keeping watch over Electra.

Electra paused on the carpet and granted the press and crowd a dazzling smile before she, too, escaped into the safety of the venue. The crowd roared their gratitude, and yelled for more.

Across town in the studio, Malcolm West was sitting in the sound booth with a technician. They were putting the finishing touches to Electra's album. West waved his hand and ordered, "Play the opening of that last track again."

The technician did as he was asked. West nodded gratifyingly. "Good, hold off on the bass. Keep it low key until the vocals begin. Then hard in. Try it."

The technician replayed the intro and followed West's instructions. He remixed the tracks and ran it for West again.

"Great!" exclaimed West, "That's perfect. Can you burn me a couple of copies?"

The techie emboldened, pressed, "I thought we had to revise part of the backing track of the last song. Electra said…"

West snapped, "You worry about getting your end right. I'll do the rest. I'm not going to do anything Electra wouldn't approve of." Then he relented and smiled, "I wouldn't dare."

The technician shrugged and reached for a blank CD stack. He put one in the console and hit the copy button. West's smile grew stronger as he fingered his distinctive signet ring.

In Kensington, Carol had covertly entered Karl's flat. The siblings were enjoying a coffee together and celebrating being able to see each other, albeit without permission. They rejoiced in spending time with each other again.

"So you passed?" affirmed Karl.

"I did," smiled Carol, smugly and flicked her hair back from her face.

"I knew you would," grinned Karl. "But you couldn't have done it without me," he teased, patting himself on the back.

"I know," she agreed. "But it was a piece of cake. I'm sure exams have got easier." She stopped momentarily and perused her brother's face before asking, "Why can't you tell me about your placement?"

"Orders," he replied. "Honestly, it's safer if you don't know but I can tell you, it's good fun and I am enjoying it. I can't believe it's so easy to put us just where they want us… Besides, it won't be long and we'll be together again, properly. They've promised."

"I know… I shouldn't really be here, but who's to know? I've been very careful."

"As long as they don't have us under surveillance. Just do as you're told and things will work out," promised Karl. "Life will be good again, for both of us."

They were interrupted by the bleeping of Karl's pager. He switched it off. "I have to go. Can you let yourself out? Wait until I have been gone thirty minutes, just in case someone is hanging around. You never know," he warned.

"Right, I will. I'm sure you don't need it but good luck."

"You, too." Karl gave his sister a swift peck on the cheek. He picked up his car keys and flipped them in the air, winked cheekily at her and left.

Carol finished her coffee. She took her cup through to the kitchen and washed it up. She meandered around the flat and picked up a few items, looking for clues, anything to give her a hint of what Karl was doing. She disliked being kept in the dark. She examined the DVD's in the rack, looking at the titles and smiling when she recognised one or two as personal favourites of hers.

She spent the next thirty minutes, rummaging around, looking through Karl's meticulously tidy drawers and cupboards but discovered nothing. True to her word, once the half an hour was up, she slipped out of Karl's apartment and ran lightly down the stairs to the foyer, where the internal CCTV camera was blinking its red light. She stepped out into the street to vanish up the road and into the busy part of town mingling with the throngs returning home from work. She had more than enough time to get home and prepare herself before her shift. A good long soak in the tub would be just what she needed to boost her energy and relax her.

In Earl's Court the security cameras were busy.

Electra and her band had set up all their gear and were doing a sound check. Giant plasma screens had been erected and DVD players and projection equipment waited to be tested. Jon was on form, coming up with a few jokes while filming the whole proceedings, but without getting in the way. Amy scribbled notes for her voice over narrative to be dubbed in later and conversed with Jon as he worked, while Electra tried a few lines of a song and made a face. She called out to her sound engineer sitting at the console at the back of the vast hall, "Chico, just a tad more on the mic." Chico obliged and Electra tried the song again and smiled approval. "Great, that's perfect. Okay, let's try that again from the top. Make sure we've really got it." She took off her cap and shook her lustrous hair over her shoulders, and then replaced her hat; and all the while cameras watched.

Electra burst into song as Malcolm West travelled through the door brandishing a huge bouquet of flowers and a small gift. He waved at Electra and settled next to bodyguard, Paul Grayson, and Ahmed who had recently entered the concert hall with his driver, Karl. Electra acknowledged West with a smile, finished her song, and clapped her hands in appreciation indicating her band. "Brilliant job, guys. Just keep it like that." Then she skipped down the steps at the side of the stage into the auditorium and snuggled up to Ahmed giving him a tender kiss, before she realised she was still being filmed. She shouted across to Jon and Amy and made a 'cut' gesture. "Censored! You'll have to take that out." She laughed then stuck her tongue out at Jon who lowered his camera, and grinned back at her. "Thanks!" she exclaimed and then put her arms around Ahmed's neck and nuzzled his neck lovingly. Jon raised his camera again as she left Ahmed's initial embrace.

Electra whispered something in Ahmed's ear and reached into her bag and took out a sprig of Holly and stuck it in her hat. He laughed and hugged her close.

The cameras continued their silent monitoring. Always watching, never judging.

West watched her and his eyes narrowed before he switched on his most brilliant smile and offered her the bouquet. She accepted and smelled the scented blooms before passing them to Grayson who looked non-plussed at receiving the flowers. She stared expectantly at her manager, "Well?"

"The reception is all arranged. There's a change of clothes in your hotel room. We've got a great guest list. It reads like the Oscars," he said enthusiastically. "Now, we want maximum publicity to promote the tour. It will help album sales. So, be nice to the press, just for the night, please," Malcolm requested.

"Aren't I always?" replied Electra.

"No," said West wryly.

"I'll do what I have to and no more..." Electra stopped.

"But?" quizzed Malcolm West.

"I'm not happy with all these in your face questions about my private life."

"Electra, Electra..." West sighed, "We need the press. Just for the night... big smiles, okay?"

"Fine. But when the reception's over, that's my time. Mine and Ahmed's. Agreed?" Electra extended her hand to West to strike the deal and saw the present, he was holding. "What's that?"

"A preview of your new album, hot off the press. Just for you." West smiled, his jaws grinned like a crocodile.

Electra batted his hand playfully. "Don't grin like that. It looks so predatory like you know something I don't."

"Maybe I do," West paused. "Your album is going to be so big it will make millions."

"Ah, now I understand the smile and the slot machine eyes," teased Electra and they all laughed together but the laughter didn't quite reach Malcolm West's eyes.

"Okay, let me hear the opening and closing numbers and then take a break. You've earned it," instructed West.

Electra bounced back on stage. "You heard the man, let's go. Hit it, guys." Her opening number rang out and Electra's voice filled the room. She began the song and her tone with that distinctive emotional catch that tore at the heart strings reverberated through those watching.

Amy gasped in awe, "She is just amazing. Isn't she just amazing?"

West nodded, a growing smile spreading across his features.

Carol entered the basement foyer of a public building. She crossed to a machine and card rack, removed one and inserted it into the clocking on machine and clocked into work. The time read twenty-one hundred hours.

Her heels clicked in an organised fashion as she walked along the polished tiled floor and she disappeared through swing doors at the back, where others eager to leave work spewed out and approached the machine to clock off. No one gave her a second glance. They didn't need to; the internal cameras had it all covered.

Carol marched on purposefully, toward her station. She double-checked all the equipment to ensure it was in good working order, as was her job. She replenished the dwindling supplies from the store. Then she settled herself at the station to wait for the call that she knew would come. The place was well equipped and she was allowed to read, or pursue any activity she liked. They even had a bedroom and kitchen as well as a shower. The employees' needs were well catered for, with a flat screen TV and X box games console.

Carol changed into her uniform and took out a book from the cabinet to read, while she waited for that very important summons. The CCTV camera at the station swivelled around and watched.

Electra was performing her heart out in the finale of her stupendous hit show.

Jon and Amy filmed with enthusiasm, not just shots of the star, Electra, but members of the audience, their reactions, their delight, and the thundering clamour for 'more'. Jon and Amy afforded each other a grin, knowing it was all going better than they had dared to hope.

Amy whispered, "This biopic could really make us and have people take us seriously. At long, long last; it really is about time."

Jon murmured back, "Or it could break us…"

"Don't be so pessimistic," scolded Amy.

"Only kidding," replied Jon. "You never know, we could be making Cannes next year, the rounds of festivals and then may be our first feature. Wouldn't that be great? You certainly have enough decent scripts that deserve to get made."

"I know. It's always down to the funding. There again, we are gaining friends in high places," said Amy as the audience, as one, collectively gasped in amazement as they watched Electra.

The closing bars of the final number rang out and Electra swallow dived into the arms of six waiting male dancers who then lifted her aloft as glitter tape rained down from the ceiling nets and littered the stage like a myriad of dancing lights. Electra took her final bow, turned and applauded her band, who all took their curtain call and played Electra off stage.

Electra raced away and Jon lowered his camera. He caught Amy's eye and signalled an 'A okay' sign to her, winked and said, "The footage, Amy, I'm sure, will be blisteringly good."

"Fingers crossed," said Amy.

Electra, still in her skimpy stage costume, attempted to beat the crowd that would eventually swamp the exit door and she dashed along the corridor to the outer door where Ahmed was waiting with her coat, which he threw over her shoulders.

Jon chased after her capturing the moment on film. They burst out onto the street. Ahmed and Electra made a dash for the waiting limo its engine idling. Karl was in the driver's seat and Grayson was sitting alongside him in the front passenger seat. As soon as the couple entered the car, Karl put his foot down and the wheels screamed and rubber burned. They tried to flee from the pursuing press and photographers; some of whom mounted motorbikes and chased after them.

Jon and Amy ran to a waiting cab and managed to drive away before the hordes of adoring fans came clamouring around the stage door exit. The heat was on and both vehicles rushed through the busy streets to the hotel to prepare themselves for the ensuing reception that was to herald the announcement of Electra's proposed European and world tour.

Hotel Security was there to meet them. The celebrity and her boyfriend were ushered away quickly through the hotel lobby to her reserved room where she could change in readiness and comfort for the party.

Close on their heels came Jon and Amy who were not greeted with the same deference but they swept into the hotel without any fuss. They waited for the elevator and zoomed up to the sixth floor and into a suite reserved for them. Their clothes, too, were hanging up for them in protective covers.

Amy flopped down on the bed. "Thank goodness I brought this lot here earlier," she murmured.

"You mean, it wasn't done for us?" asked Jon with feigned disbelief.

"No such luck," grinned Amy. "Famous we're not!"

"Would you want to be?" queried Jon.

"What? And have my every move watched, catalogued and everything I say reported on TV or in the papers to come back and bite me on the bum? No thank you."

"Must be nice though to have the attention, get into the best restaurants, get the best seats at a theatre…" said Jon.

"And never have a minute's peace. Can't go anywhere, chased everywhere," added Amy. "No quiet swim at the community pool, no ordinary gym membership, no visiting the local pub…" she trailed off.

"Well, you never know. If this film is a success, we may be in the limelight."

"Hm. Something, I can do without. You know what they say… be careful what you wish for…" said Amy sagely.

"Yes, I expect you're right. Ah well, better get changed."

"I'll grab the bathroom first," said Amy bossily.

"Don't hog it, I need to shower and shave, get rid of this beginning of designer stubble. It itches like hell."

"That's because you're not used to it. I think it looks quite good."

"Do you?" Jon peered at himself in the mirror and shook his head vehemently, "Nah! It's not me. It doesn't go with long hair unless your name's Jesus."

Amy laughed, sat up, grabbed her things and gave Jon a wink as she dived into the en suite bathroom. "Get prepared for a vision of loveliness," she purred and disappeared inside locking the door.

Jon chucked and called out, "And here's me thinking you were just a jeans and sweater girl." He began to whistle cheerfully and unzipped his suit's dust cover and placed it next to his shirt and clean underwear. He undressed quickly donning the fluffy robe provided by the hotel as he heard the shower switched on.

Jon switched on the television and flicked through the channels, eventually settling on a music channel. He yawned, and flopped in a comfy armchair. He was tired but knew he had a long night ahead of him, and so decided to make a cup of coffee; a shot of caffeine was just what he needed to perk him up. He needed to be alert and on top form. In this line of work observation was key and he believed the smallest detail could be vitally important in a project of this sort.

He heard the shower go off. Amy emerged in a bathrobe and her hair wrapped in a towel. For a moment he caught his breath. Flushed from the heat of the water, the smattering of freckles on her nose were more pronounced and she seemed to glow. He firmly put his wandering thoughts that served to disturb his otherwise calm demeanour firmly out of his mind.

"All yours," she announced.

"Kettle's boiled if you fancy a cuppa?" he said before he disappeared into the steamy bathroom.

Amy looked after him. 'What was wrong with her?' she thought. "A relationship with a work partner was not a good idea,' she told herself sternly; especially when it wasn't reciprocated. "Put that right out of your head, now," she murmured aloud and firmly.

The shower switched on and this time Amy was left with her contradictory thoughts.

Chapter Three

Targeted

THE SERVERS IN ANOTHER part of the world slowly filled up with the actions of Electra's life as captured by their servants, the cameras.

The party was in full swing. Gentle background music added to the ambience; the lighting was in soft focus, tables were laid out with nibbles and canapés, crackers of smoked salmon and cream cheese, and more substantial party food and drinks were freely available. Tantalising aromas drifted up from tasty vegetable samosas, hot meat patties, and chili and rice.

Electra was the centre of attention and she literally dazzled. All was going even better than expected. She worked the room flirtatiously; winning even the most hardened reviewers and critics over, such was her passion for her compositions. The fire in her eyes when she talked about her music was inspirational and infectious.

Grayson was never far away, watching his charge most carefully with an eagle eye. He refused to be drawn into conversation or chitchat by anyone. He was professional and watchful.

Karl sat at the bar drinking orange juice and observing the proceedings. He caught a glimpse of Ahmed who spoke happily with his father, Ibrahim. Here was a most impressive man, who although not too tall, had a magnetic presence and exuded power, power that came from money, decision-making and from running successful businesses. The security camera in the corner of the bar recorded the moment that Ahmed steered his father to a part of the room where he hoped they wouldn't be overheard.

"I can't say too much now, father, but after the reception is over and done with we are planning to make a public announcement; it maybe as soon as next week. Of course, we will tell you first and tell you together, probably when we lunch on Sunday." Ahmed spoke quietly, to keep the conversation private. This was to be strictly between father and son.

Ibrahim patted his son affectionately and proudly on the back obviously pleased at what Ahmed had said. He could clearly see the adoration in his son, Ahmed's eyes, as he followed Electra with his gaze. "My son, whatever makes you happy will make me happy, you have my blessing." Father and son hugged unashamedly. Ahmed was more than delighted with his father's good wishes. He had said enough and was sure his father would guess at part of the proposed announcement but not all of it. The rest would be a big surprise; at least that is what he hoped.

The CCTV camera moved from the couple and roved the room. The party was reaching its climax. At West's nod, waiters flooded the room carrying trays of champagne and they immediately ensured every guest had a glass including Karl at the bar. Karl looked at the drink critically, pushed it away and continued drinking his orange juice.

Malcolm West stepped up onto the small dais at the end of the room and tapped the microphone. Chico sitting at the sound console obliged by turning up the volume.

"Ladies and Gentlemen, distinguished guests. Thank you for coming. I'd like you to raise your glasses as I propose a toast to Electra and the start of her new European and World tour."

The guests, as one, lifted their champagne flutes and proclaimed, "Electra." They all took a sip and West continued, "I am delighted to announce that you are indeed privileged; you are about to hear a sneak preview of Electra's new album, Fallen Angels."

There was a ripple of appreciation from the guests. West signalled to Chico and the sound of Electra's glorious voice filled the room with the first song from her new album. Everyone stopped to listen but Electra strode across to the sound desk and stopped the music. There was a murmur of disappointment from some and applause from others. Electra laughingly addressed the party, "Sorry to stop the fun but Mal forgot to say that the album isn't quite finished so don't expect to rush out to the shops and get it tomorrow. Enjoy the night, folks." Electra indicated that Chico should resume playback. The music boomed out and people now more relaxed began to chat again.

The camera changed its focus from the stage and followed Electra who crossed to Ibrahim standing with his son, and she took Ahmed's hand. "Excuse me, Ibrahim but I think it is now time for us to leave and escape while we can and without too many people noticing."

Ibrahim smiled, "Please, go on. I will look forward to seeing you both on Sunday when I believe you may have something to tell me."

Electra shot Ahmed a look, and he pronounced, "I haven't said a word."

"You don't have to, my son, I can see it in both your faces. And I give you my love and blessing." He embraced Electra and kissed her on both cheeks before taking his son by the shoulders, "All I want for you my son, my only son, is your happiness." He hugged Ahmed to him and grinned, "And now, I must try and occupy some of these people so that they don't notice you leaving."

Electra and Ahmed smiled happily as they approached West who said cheerily, "It's the Cinderella girl!" He added wryly. "Are you off?"

"Well, it's gone midnight and that was our agreement."

"Of course, of course," West acquiesced. He removed a small pager from his belt and quietly alerted the car valet. "Have Electra's car brought around to the front, now. Oh, and switch her album on. There's a copy in the player. She's bound to want to listen." He turned to Electra. "The deed is done. I should try and escape without attracting too much attention." He gestured to Chico and the music swelled. Electra and Ahmed discretely exited the room to get their coats. West removed his mobile from his pocket. He dialled a number and exchanged a few words, a satisfied expression settled on his face.

West acknowledged Karl with a look that ordered him to go after them. Karl finished his orange juice and slipped off his stool at the bar. Grayson was already following Electra out to the cloakroom.

The CCTV buzzed and blinked as it turned its attention to the dance floor where Jon and Amy, now off duty, danced to the music and surprisingly didn't notice Electra's departure. Amy took the opportunity to snuggle into Jon's shoulder. She had a huge look of contentment about her. Jon responded with a brotherly kiss on the top of Amy's head. He grimaced at the movement and reached to his collar with one hand and extracted a pin from his new shirt and studied it distastefully. Amy glanced up and giggled at Jon's frown when he contemplated the pin in his hand. Jon looked uncertain as to what to do with it. So, Amy rescued the offending item and pinned it to her dress. Jon smiled and they resumed dancing.

Cameras in the hallway outside the function room watched Electra and

Ahmed gather their coats. Ever the gentleman, Ahmed helped Electra on with her jacket and took a box from his pocket. "First, I want you to wear this," he opened the box revealing a stunning diamond ring, which he placed on Electra's ring finger. "Now that the publicity drive is over, you can wear my ring. I didn't mishear, you did say 'yes', didn't you?"

Electra smiled up at him happily. "You know I did. Come on, we'd better move quickly if we want to beat the press." Ahmed laughed delightedly and kissed her briefly before they sped out. They entered the elevator and travelled to the ground floor where Karl and Grayson waited.

Driver and bodyguard filed out after the couple through the hotel's revolving doors, where a bevy of reporters and photographers were lying in wait, barely held back by Security. The car valet waited patiently outside the vehicle with the door open and the engine running. Electra's CD was playing and strains of her music filtered through the crowd. Hastily, Karl got into the driver's seat, with Grayson alongside. Ahmed handed the valet a good tip and they slipped quickly into the back seat before the press surged through the restraining bodies only to be joined by other newsmen and photographers, who had been attending the function, streaming through the revolving doors. They all wanted to get a shot of the star as she left with her playboy boyfriend. As a result, neither Ahmed nor Karl buckled up their seatbelts as they just aimed to get away as quickly as possible.

Ahmed leaned forward in his seat and instructed Karl, "Drive and get us out of here. As fast as you can, Karl. They'll soon be on our tail. Lose them." Karl accelerated and sped through the thinning night traffic.

Electra and Grayson struggled to do up their seat belts but there seemed to be something wrong with them. They connected them eventually but the belts were in fact unusually loose and Electra's just popped out of its clip.

A number of the paparazzi were in a determined mood and followed; some in cars, and others on motorbikes. They were dogged in the chase and refused to be out manoeuvred or to slow down. On the contrary, the reporters pressed the limo to travel faster and more dangerously. A motorbike drew up alongside the car. The passenger travelling on the pillion attempted to photograph Electra and Ahmed through the window and Karl determinedly stepped on the accelerator.

Camera after camera captured the fleeing vehicle.

The race was on. As the limo was pursued so began an erratic, reckless, and frighteningly dangerous chase. Road signs were becoming a blur as the Mercedes motored past them. Karl swerved violently, weaving in and out of traffic lanes trying to evade those in persistent hot pursuit. Signs whizzed by indicating the approach of a tunnel up ahead that acted as an underpass under the river. Karl thought quickly, he knew they had to take that route home but only at the very last moment did he veer off into the underpass lane and thus managed to shake off a couple of the followers but he knew it wouldn't be long before they caught up with them again.

The CD in the player jumped tracks and the opening riff of the last song with five extraneous notes played. Grayson leaned forward and attempted to tighten his seat belt.

A white Fiat Uno carefully approached the underpass from the opposite direction. It pulled into the tunnel and parked just inside the entrance. The driver switched off his lights, and waited. The hand resting on the wheel was sporting a gold signet ring with an embossed lion's head. The other hand reached into a pocket and removed a mobile phone and dialled a number.

Carol Stevenson's mobile phone began to ring. It rang three times and stopped. Now, in full uniform she rose from her seat at the station where she was reading and alerted Emergency. She left her post and hurried outside to the departure bay and boarded a large white van. She sat in the back of the vehicle and was joined by a white-coated man wearing a stethoscope. She was surrounded by an assortment of medical equipment. Her phone rang again and her eyes glinted glassily as she answered the call and listened, five distinct musical notes played under the message relaying instructions, instructions that needed to be obeyed.

In the tunnel, the limo's headlights picked up the mysterious white car. Karl screwed up his eyes, the vehicle appeared to be parked in their way. Suddenly, the car turned its headlights onto full beam. Karl was blinded he put one hand up to cover his eyes and tried to avoid the Uno. He stepped hard on the brake pedal, which made the wheels lock into a skid and he lost control of the vehicle as all his careful training was forgotten. The limo crashed head on into the tunnel wall. Screams came from behind Karl who was flung through the windscreen shattering the glass and he spun out across the mangled bonnet and into the road.

Grayson was thrust forward and knocked unconscious on the dash. Ahmed hurtled from the back through the windscreen and landed half on the dash and half on the metal mess that had been the hood of the car. The front end of the limo was twisted, tortured metal. The screeching sound of wheels spinning and the acrid smell of rubber burning filled the air. Fumes from a fractured fuel tank wafted up.

Electra was dazed and in shock. She had no visible injuries. She had crouched down in the rear, on the floor, her back to the front seats. She struggled to open the passenger door but it was stuck. The press pack in pursuit stopped cold. One rider was thrown from his bike whilst others skidded to a halt.

A reporter raced to the stricken limo. Filled with adrenaline he found extraordinary strength and wrenched open the rear passenger door, which scraped raggedly, steel on chrome. He helped Electra out and yelled, "Someone call nine, nine, nine." He checked his watch it was twenty-six minutes past midnight.

Fuel was leaking from the petrol tank and pooling on the floor. The pressman tried to make Electra comfortable as she dropped to her knees. He removed his jacket and laid it down. Electra fell back and rested her head on his jacket and he talked soothingly to her, "You'll be okay now, Electra. The ambulance is on its way." He went to stand but Electra stopped him.

"Please, don't leave me," she whispered.

"Petrol is spilling out," he explained. "I'm just going to get your companions clear. I'll be right back." He rushed to the stricken vehicle and tugged open the front door passenger side, released Grayson from his loose seatbelt and hauled him out, gratified that the man was still breathing even if unconscious.

The mysterious white car turned off its blazing headlights, reversed quickly and sped away. Some reporters noticed and gasped as they pointed at the fleeing car. Another of the paparazzi tested the pulse of Karl. He shook his head, sadly. There was nothing he could do. He was already dead. Another photographer went to Ahmed and there was a flicker of life. He shouted, "Anyone here know resuscitation?"

Another vehicle pulled up. The driver ran to the scene. "I'm a doctor, I can help." He began to work frantically at trying to revive Ahmed.

An ambulance with its ear splitting, brash sirens wailing and lights blazing arrived in the tunnel. In the distance was the sound of another siren blaring. The reporter went to Electra and spoke softly, urging her to, "Stay with me, Electra."

Her eyes fluttered open. "Oh, my God!"

"The ambulance is almost here." He helped her up to her feet and she struggled to stand swaying unsteadily and leaned against him.

"…Ahmed?" she faltered.

"Let's worry about you first." The lights of the ambulance strobed into the tunnel and the vehicle pulled up at the crash site. The ambulance doors opened to reveal Carol Stevenson with her arms outstretched ready to help Electra inside. Electra was assisted to lie down on a trolley as an unconscious Grayson was placed on a stretcher and others carried him inside to lie on the bed on the opposite side of the vehicle from Electra. Carol sat in the middle. The door was secured and the ambulance driver and his aide took off. The sound of the siren as it left the tunnel hurt the ears of those waiting only to be joined by more strident alarms when the police, another ambulance and a fire engine entered from behind. The tunnel's camera observed.

Electra was still dazed and had begun to shake and tremble in the rigor of shock. Carol filled a syringe. She flicked it with her finger and prepared Electra's arm and smiled down at her, "You might feel a little sharp prick. Just relax."

Electra reached up and patted Carol's arm and murmured gratefully, "Thank you."

Electra settled back peacefully but as the injection began to take effect, her chest became constricted. Her face suddenly filled with horror as she found she could no longer breathe. Her hand reached out in desperation to Carol. She struggled to speak but only gasped. A momentary flicker of realisation crossed Electra's face. Her body convulsed violently as she thrashed about on the trolley.

Carol smiled down at her as she watched Electra die. When the light vanished from Electra's eyes and she became still, Carol's smile broadened. It was then that the doctor present took over and removed further evidence from Electra's body. The ambulance went on its way, as the doctor worked, taking a circuitous route that took almost one and a half hours whilst surgery was carried out. It eventually arrived at Accident and Emergency at six minutes past two.

Across the city Malcolm West was lying awake in bed. This time he was alone. He glanced at his radio alarm clock the time read 2: 15 a.m. Suddenly, the house phone jangled twice and stopped. West got out of bed and walked to his PC housed in the corner of the bedroom, which was in sleep mode. He awoke it, pulled up his email and selected, 'Compose new email'. He typed three words. 'It is done.' And hit the send button. He returned to his bed and sighed deeply before finally curling up and falling into a contented sleep.

At the hospital, staffing was limited. A skeleton crew was operating not only on the wards but in the labs as well. A white-coated lab technician exited through the swing doors leaving no one in attendance. Carol watched from a side room, wearing whites and surgical gloves. She waited until the laboratory assistant turned the corner at the end of the corridor, and then she slipped out from hiding and cautiously entered the lab. Her eyes scanned the many workstations and she spotted one with a lamp placed close to a microscope that was illuminating one desk.

Carol quickly stepped across and rooted around the collection of different specimens. She examined various phials and test tubes meticulously, before glancing at an adjacent trolley where she spotted a tray of blood samples. She hurriedly inspected the labels until she found what she was looking for. A collection of phials dated and marked, 'Driver'. Quickly, she took a prepared syringe and injected its contents into three of the blood samples and swapped two others. Carol replaced the samples and was just about to leave when to her horror she heard the footsteps returning.

Carol turned and dashed to a darker corner of the lab and ducked down under a desk out of sight of the technician, Mac, who went straight to the workbench and lifted up the tray of samples that Carol had sabotaged. Mac opened the fridge and placed the tray inside. He closed the door firmly and yawned before he moved to his microscope and set up a slide.

Another white-coated technician pushed open the lab door and stood framed in the doorway. Carol hardly dared to breathe. She remained frozen and out of sight. Blood drained from her face and her heart thumped as if it was trying to leap from her body. She waited paralysed in fear.

"Hi, Mac! Coming for a coffee?" asked the other worker.

Mac looked up and smiled stifling another yawn, "Why not? A shot of caffeine is just what I need." He moved away from the bench and left with his colleague and they chatted happily as they walked down the corridor to the lift that would take them to the staff canteen.

Carol seized the opportunity. She ditched the syringe in a bin for surgical waste along with her gloves and left the lab as quietly as she had arrived. Carol was filled with an indescribable euphoria as she made her way out of the hospital. "What a rush," she said to herself. Karl was right, she loved danger and she was loving this assignment.

The following morning Amy was sitting at the breakfast table looking sleepy. Her hair showered her shoulders in complete disarray. She wore an unflattering dressing gown of a fleecy dusty pink, best kept for winter nights when she was at home alone. She was munching on a piece of toast and yawned, loudly. The satisfaction that the noise gave her made her smile. She took another bite. The toast was still crunchy and oozed with melted butter covered with sweet thick cut marmalade. She licked her lips as butter dribbled down her chin.

The front door bell rang. She glanced at the kitchen clock and it read 8:15. She groaned aloud, "Oh no!" Who on earth would be calling at this time of the morning? The bell rang again in a number of quick bursts. Someone was impatient and it was impossible to ignore. She yelled out, "All right! All right, I'm coming. Keep your hair on!" She rose reluctantly and stumbled to the front door and opened it. Jon pushed past her in a terrible, agitated state. He blindly moved down her passageway toward the kitchen. He was so distressed that Amy didn't quite know what to make of him. Not only was she not feeling at her best, she was tired and not prepared, nor in the mood for visitors, not even Jon.

"Haven't you heard?" asked Jon, tremulously as he set down his camera bag.

"Heard what?" grumbled Amy as Jon strode into the kitchen and slammed his hand on the table. "What's going on?" Amy asked again, her former grumpiness forgotten and her curiosity piqued.

Jon switched on the flat screen television positioned so that Amy could watch it while she ate. He fiddled with the channels until he found the breakfast news. A headshot of Electra stared out of the screen. "Electra. She's dead," he said in anguish.

"What?" said Amy stunned. "I don't believe it."

"Last night. A car crash. Listen." Jon turned up the volume. Amy listened to the news report in total disbelief.

'Today a nation mourns the loss of one of its brightest stars. Electra and her boyfriend Ahmed Khalid have been tragically killed in a horrific car accident in the early hours of the morning. The driver who has not yet been named was killed on impact and Electra's bodyguard; Paul Grayson is in a serious condition in Intensive Care. Police are waiting to question him when he regains consciousness. Ahmed Khalid's father is already claiming a government plot, whilst Electra's brother, the Earl of Shaftesbury is blaming the press for their persistent intrusion into his sister's life."

Jon switched off the TV. Amy sat back at her place at the breakfast table and mechanically chewed on another piece of toast. Jon sat and murmured, "What are we going to do?"

"Have a cup of tea," said Amy blankly. "Put the kettle on. Then phone Mal."

Jon rose and like an automaton filled the kettle. He took the teapot, warmed it and laid out the teacups. The familiar action and routine was somehow comforting. The kettle soon began to bubble and he switched it off. He made a pot of tea in shocked stone silence and poured two cups. The normality of the action contrasted sharply with their mood. They sat and sipped their tea, still without speaking a word.

Amy rubbed her forehead. "You had better ring Mal. I don't trust myself to speak."

Jon nodded in understanding. "Christ, Amy. This is horrific."

Amy responded sadly, "I know, someone so vibrant, so alive… I just can't believe it." Her eyes filled with tears. She stood up abruptly. "I'm going to get dressed. Make yourself some toast or something."

"I don't feel like it."

"You need something. You look like shit."

"Thanks, Amy. Why don't you tell me how it really is," Jon sighed heavily through his words.

"You know what I mean. I don't want you going downhill making yourself ill." Amy left the kitchen and went upstairs to shower.

Amy took a hurried shower. This was no time to linger and enjoy the splashing warm water raining down on her. She did what she had to and no more, quickly towelled herself dry and changed into her boot-cut jeans and a roomy cotton top. She dried her hair and studied her face in the mirror, and decided that she looked like shit, too. Grabbing a bronzing powder and brush, she tried to give her face some colour so that didn't she appear so pale and washed out. She brushed on some mascara and dabbed on lip-gloss in an attempt to make herself feel, as well as look, a little better. Amy stuck her tongue out in the mirror and didn't like what she saw, so she took her toothbrush and gave her teeth and furred tongue a scrub, and then rinsed her mouth. She repeated the application of lip-gloss and then ran down the stairs, passing Jon in the hallway who was now talking on his mobile phone.

The television was on, ablaze with pictures but with the sound still turned down. Amy was drawn to the action on the screen. A female field reporter with a microphone in hand was standing by a crowd of onlookers. Hundreds of bouquets and posies were placed near the scene of the accident. She shook her head sadly, tributes were pouring in from around the world and people had turned out in the hundreds lining the streets. The mood was serious and melancholic matching the way Amy felt.

Amy sighed heavily and put the kettle back on to boil and prepared two cups with teabags. She glanced at Jon who was still at the foot of the stairs talking. She heard him mutter, 'goodbye'. He replaced his cell phone in his pocket and walked back in the kitchen.

"Mal thinks we should carry on. Use what we've got as a eulogy to Electra. He thinks we'll have a winner on our hands. He said it could make us a lot of money. If not, he'll still give us our fee and buy what we have and get someone else to edit it for production, if we didn't have the stomach for it."

"Right now, I couldn't give two stuffs." Amy finished making her cup of tea and sat down stubbornly at the kitchen table and stoically sipped her tea. Jon looked on in frustration at the enforced silence and Amy's unresponsiveness.

The pictures on the television flickered in front of them and Jon sat down slowly and joined her at the table. He was just about to begin drumming his fingers on the wood when Amy plonked down her mug decisively and crisply announced, "Right! Let's get cracking. We've loads to do. Electra would have wanted us to finish this, not for the money, not just for ourselves but also for her fans. Let's do it."

"Hallelujah! Where do we start?" cried Jon gleefully. "Action, any action is better than inertia in my mind. I know that keeping busy is a good way of dealing with emotions, emotions, if I'm honest that I'm afraid of setting free. Work will keep us balanced and focused; don't you think so, Amy?" he said as much to himself as to Amy.

Jon set up his camera and attached it to the television and he began editing the latest footage, whilst Amy went online to gather information.

She glanced up from her computer and saw Ibrahim Khalid appear on the TV screen so she stepped up to the television and turned up the sound. He was making a statement to the press.

Ibrahim looked stern as he spoke in heartbroken tones, "It is clear to me that my son, Ahmed and his future wife, Electra's deaths were murder, deliberate and cold blooded, orchestrated by MI6 in collusion with other secret services ordered by more powerful forces and I demand a full and thorough investigation. I will not rest until the truth is out there, even if royalty is involved."

There was a burst of excited questioning from journalists in attendance. Questions flew thick and fast about the inference of it being an assassination and the fact that Government forces were involved and possibly someone in the royal family. Amy turned the sound down once more and returned to her research, her face creased in confused concern and sorrow.

She muttered under her breath, "This is England not some third world country under a dictatorship. I don't want to believe that it was deliberate. That way madness lies."

Carol had arrived home and taken a leisurely bath. She felt good as if she was on a high. She had also tried to ring Karl but infuriatingly she just got his answer service. Unconcerned, for the moment, she picked up her crumpled paramedic uniform from the floor of the bathroom and threw it in the washing basket. She retreated to her bedroom wrapped in a towel when her landline rang. She answered cautiously, "Hello?"

Her face brightened in response to new orders and a proposed job interview that according to her contact should merely be a formality. She scribbled down the address and observed the instructions to arrive, on time, looking efficient but attractive. Carol had no qualms about doing exactly as she was asked and began to get ready. She would need her portfolio of references and her updated

CV, plus her degree certificates in business management and public relations and English Literature.

She took her smart suit jacket from the wardrobe and put it on, teaming it with a contrasting pencil skirt. Carol selected conservative shoes and bag to match. She studied herself critically in the mirror. She nodded appreciatively knowing that she looked extremely elegant and more importantly, professional.

Carol chose a neutral pink beige lipstick from her dressing table and retouched her lips. She attended to her hair giving it a final brush before she gave herself the last once over in the mirror. "Perfect," she murmured. Carol picked up her handbag, and keys. She glanced around her room before crossing to the door, which clicked shut ominously behind her. She was quite surprised that she had another urgent placement so soon. She had hoped she would have been given some time out before they sought her out to work again. But the brief she had received filled her with delight. She was looking forward to it.

Chapter Four

Ibrahim's Grief Meets Further Intrigue

IBRAHIM KHALID, AHMED'S FATHER walked slowly through his son's flat. He was wearing a black tie and armband and was in an understandably sombre mood. He stifled a hiccupping sob. Everywhere he looked he saw memories of his son; photographs, car keys, his clothes, a jacket placed carelessly over a chair, his coin tray for loose change, and a bottle of his favourite cologne standing carelessly on his dressing table with the top off.

A middle-aged, foreign looking maid had just completed dusting the apartment. Ibrahim caught her arm and steered the bewildered woman into the bedroom and pointed at the bed, where there was a coat hanger with a shirt and a pair of trousers laid out as if ready to wear. His tone was anguished as he instructed her, "Rosie, I want it kept it exactly as it is."

"Yes, Sir," Rosie responded with the hint of an Asian accent.

"Even down to these. Understand?" Ibrahim stated firmly.

"Yes, Sir," the maid agreed. "It will be in honour of Master Ahmed."

"Yes. It will be your job to keep everything in order, just as it is."

"Yes, Sir. I will do exactly as you say." She turned to leave.

"And, Rosie?"

"Sir?"

"I will see you will be well paid for this."

"But, Sir," protested Rosie. "You already look after me well. There is no need."

"I insist," said Ibrahim. "Now, leave me."

Rosie politely acknowledged him and left the room. She picked up her coat, putting it on over her uniform and left the luxury apartment. Ibrahim walked, despair making his feet heavy, to the French Windows and stepped out onto the balcony. He gazed down at the busy street below and listened for a moment to the thunderous traffic noise that rose and filled the air around him.

Ibrahim glared up at the sky that was an innocent blue and, for once, completely cloudless. He raised his arms reaching up to the heavens and a terrible cry erupted from the pit of his stomach and tears rolled down his face. "WHY????? GOD, WHY?"

His cry was lost on the wind above the traffic and life continued below, regardless. At that moment he made up his mind. He would investigate the death of his beloved son, Ahmed and his fiancée, Electra, himself. Something just wasn't right. The facts didn't add up. Someone was to blame, of that he was certain. He would find out who was responsible, with or without the help of the authorities. He decided there and then that he had to get hold of the filmmakers who were doing the biopic. He just felt they might have something, something they were not even possibly aware of. He knew he had to get in touch with them as soon as he was able.

In a dimly lit corridor outside numerous individual offices in a high security building run by the British Secret Service the overhead strip lighting was flickering and crackling as if highlighting that something was happening, which was unethical and underhand. The corridor seemed to be deserted and the offices appeared empty of staff. It was late; many people had already left work and yet, the cameras kept their vigil and continued rolling.

Two men spoke covertly, in low tones. One, very tall, aristocratic man stood deep in the shadows. His visits here were few but this was important and needed his complete attention. The man was in reality the actual president and figurehead of the very secret Brandenberg Sect that boasted over one hundred and fifty members. He stayed in the gloom as if it would help to disguise him. He did not want not be recognised or seen by anyone else. He leaned against the wall and fingered his tie. His manner was regal and his hand sported a gold signet ring embossed with a lion's head. He addressed Max Stafford who was the chief in MI6.

"Khalid needs to be gagged," he ordered. His voice was distinctive, full of authority and ultra-correct in his pronunciation.

"But, won't that be dangerous? It will arouse more suspicions, surely?" replied Max carefully. "Especially after what he has been claiming."

"Most normal people will see him as a rambling lunatic beset with grief that has sullied his judgement."

"Maybe, but there are bound to be others that will agree with him. Electra was a high profile celebrity. Are you sure it's right to follow her death so closely with another, especially with two people that are inextricably linked?"

"Not yet. We won't lose him yet. I agree that it's too soon. But in time… in time," murmured the president. "He needs to be watched. This is already in motion."

"We have a placement?" queried Max.

"Already approved. She's meeting with him now. Then, we just…"

"Bide our time," finished Max.

The two men clearly understood each other. Max clenched his jaw as he watched the president of the sect regally walk away down the dimly lit corridor. A pulse beat in his jaw. He believed, in the words of the Billy Ocean hit song that things were going to get tough, very tough.

Ibrahim, still wearing his black tie and armband was engaged in earnest conversation with an expensively dressed young woman in his luxury apartment. His face showed the strain of the last few days and he was trying valiantly to continue in spite of his grief. He sat one side of a large ornate desk. On the other, with her feet neatly crossed at the ankles was Carol.

"So, you see, it's imperative that I have someone I can rely on. Losing my son and his driver," he stumbled over his words as he struggled to speak, "…He was my right hand man… I…" Ibrahim almost broke down as he shuffled through the sheaf of papers in his hand. He cleared his throat. "I haven't time to work through numerous applicants for this position and I need someone now. You come highly recommended. My advisors tell me you have passed all the security checks… Will you take the job? Of course, you would be expected to live in. The position is effective immediately." He rose from his seat and approached Carol who also stood. She extended her hand and they shook hands warmly.

"I would be privileged, Sir."

"Welcome to the team," said Ibrahim with profound relief. "I will expect you here this evening if that is possible?"

Carol smiled beguilingly and began to move to the door, "Of course."

Ibrahim stopped her, "Before you go, may I offer you some refreshment?"

"That would be delightful, thank you," she purred. "Then I must get on, I have to pack and make all the necessary arrangements." Carol smiled again.

"Of course." Ibrahim pressed on the intercom. "Could we have …" He looked across at Carol, "Coffee or tea?"

"Coffee, please."

"Coffee please, Lucy, for two." Ibrahim clicked off and added, "Also, I forgot to ask, is your passport up to date?"

"It is."

"Good, you will need it. I travel a lot." It was Ibrahim's turn to smile. His whole expression changed, "I think this is going to work very well. Very well, indeed, my dear."

Carol's smile grew even bigger.

The following day Amy and Jon were closeted in Amy's flat and working on her iMac. Neither of them felt like going into their office in Premier House. There would be too many reminders. Electra photos were plastered all over the corkboard as an advertising tool. So, they had come to an arrangement. They agreed to work from each other's homes for a while. They already had installed software enabling them to access files from their office PC's so, it wouldn't be a problem. Amy's laptop was also open and sitting on the coffee table. Jon peered over Amy's shoulder as she was completing the final touches to the script to accompany the footage from the last concert. She paused, and looked up, "Gosh, my eyes are getting blurry. I need to find my specs."

"And I always thought you had twenty-twenty vision," mused Jon.

"Sorry to say, I'm not perfect only almost perfect," she stopped and changed the subject whilst she rooted through her bag for her reading glasses, "You know, I'm glad Mal wants us to finish the film."

"Yes. He thinks we've got enough to make one hell of a documentary," said Jon.

"Ha! I bet! Especially, if it coincides with the release of her album. The extra publicity will make him a bloody fortune," agreed Amy, her words laced with sarcasm. "Ah, here they are," she announced popping them on the end of her nose, and peering at Jon.

"Don't be so cynical. I thought you liked Mal," protested Jon.

"I don't know him well enough to like him, but he's a good businessman.

I'll grant you that. And a millionaire, he didn't get there by playing Mr. Nice Guy."

"But…?" Jon pressed.

Amy paused and scrunched up her face as she thought, "I don't know… I think we can do something more with the film, much more," she pondered a moment and Jon waited.

"Like?" prompted Jon, now intrigued.

Amy stopped screwing her face up in puzzlement and it was if a beacon of light had filled her. She continued enthusiastically, "Come on, Jon. Let's add to it… Document how her fans have reacted… Let's try to get to the truth of what actually happened. You must admit it was very bizarre."

"But it was just an accident, a terrifying nasty accident, but an accident none the less."

Amy studied Jon's face carefully, "But was it? I thought so at first but now I'm not so sure."

Jon looked stunned, as the enormity of her words sank home, "No, I can't believe it. I won't believe it. Who on earth would want to kill Electra?"

"I don't know, but someone must be to blame… maybe the press or…?" Amy shrugged, as she was lost for words.

There was a prolonged silence as the two filmmakers scrutinised each other's faces, each involved in their own tumbling thoughts. Eventually, Jon broke the quiet between them, "Do our own investigation… Is that what you mean?"

Amy pursed her lips and frowned, "I don't know…." She perked up and grinned more enthusiastically, "Maybe, yes!"

Jon began to get back some of his fighting spirit and asked, "Okay, supposing you're right, and I'm not suggesting you are, what, for example, is the consensus of public opinion? I mean, what does her fan club say?"

"Let's see."

Amy went to her laptop. She waited for the search engine to pop up. She typed in her request and as pages of related sites flooded before her, she began to scroll through them, whilst Jon took his camcorder and linked it up with Amy's TV to review their newly edited footage. He rewound the film and played it back while Amy trawled through the numerous websites. She suddenly drew a sharp intake of breath and stopped.

"Here, take a look at this." Her voice was filled with urgency.

Jon hit the pause button. He came to Amy's side and peered over her shoulder. She had found an active forum filled with claims from devoted fans that Electra's death had been foretold by Nostradamus. Amy pointed at the screen highlighting the words repeated on almost every comment, 'Conspiracy'. "Look!" she exclaimed, "Conspiracy, conspiracy, conspiracy…"

"Isn't that what Ahmed's father was ranting on about? Her death was a government plot or something," said Jon.

"I didn't pay enough attention to it, but…" Amy trailed off.

"What?" said Jon a note of frustration entering his voice when she didn't finish her sentence.

"This," said Amy pointing at the screen, "This quatrain from Nostradamus could actually be interpreted as foretelling her death."

"Nah. They can be made to mean anything with the right spin," argued Jon.

"But give me a little leeway here, suppose there is more to it? Go on read it," she retorted.

Jon raised his eyes in disbelief, cleared his throat, and began to read aloud the words on the screen.

"Suddenly arrived the terror will be great,

The principal players in the affair are hidden away;

And the lady on the hot coals will no longer be in sight,

Thus, little by little will the great ones be angered." Jon stopped as he pondered the words, "What's that supposed to mean?"

"Think about it," urged Amy. Jon looked blank. "Electra's last album cover?" she prompted.

Jon whistled low under his breath, "My God, I forgot."

Jon crossed to Amy's CD rack and pulled out an album by Electra called 'Gods and Monsters'. He studied it carefully before waving it at Amy. It showed Electra dressed as a bird of paradise walking over hot coals against a backdrop of a volcano and flowing molten lava. "Do you know you may have something there?"

"I told you," persisted Amy. "And, I've been thinking, what about all the change of personnel and not just in Electra's staff?"

"What do you mean?"

"Well, Electra's chief bodyguard had an unusual accident. After his fall from the flies, backstage at the theatre in Birmingham, he damaged his spine so he was pulled off the job. No one really explained what he was doing up there or how he fell. It was just accepted that it was rotten luck and an accident. He was given a golden handshake and retired. So, she gets a new one, chosen by her management."

"Yes, all normal procedure. So?"

"So, then Ahmed's driver is dismissed from his post something to do with theft of a ring. I mean, a theft after years of devoted service and him with a clean record? He always protested his innocence but bang, Ahmed gets a new driver."

"I don't see what you're getting at," puzzled Jon.

"Don't you think it's all a bit strange?"

Jon shrugged, "Coincidence."

Amy responded, "Coincidence? No. There's no such thing in my book. Read The Celestine Prophecy."

"What?" said Jon confused.

"Never mind... Just think about what I said."

"Okay, so let's suppose... just suppose, mind, that what you say is true. It still doesn't explain, why or how these things should happen..."

"Then let's keep digging. We'll have a far more satisfying film at the end if we can corroborate or totally dispute what's being said. These are all questions that need asking and answering."

"Do we keep Mal informed of this?" asked Jon.

"No," said Amy slowly. "We won't let anyone know. We'll just do it, on our own, you and me. If we get it wrong, we don't lose face and we'll still have a film worthy of distribution."

"You hope!"

"Pessimist! We will," said Amy assuredly.

Chapter Five

MI6

MAX STAFFORD WAS PATROLLING his large, third floor office, filled with high Tech gizmos, telephones, monitoring equipment and the flickering screens of numerous computers all run by an anonymous high security team of men and women engrossed in their work and wearing headphones, so that no one agent eavesdropped on another or affected another's work.

Two of his special ops group were enjoying a bit of early morning banter. Jack Burton, the office clown, in his mid-forties, with an engaging personality, was trying to sell some fresh eggs to his colleague, a careworn Claire Williams, a petite blonde who looked as if life was passing her by, while their boss Max was engaged with another worker at the far end of the office. Claire in her late thirties quietly laughed at Jack's antics as he continued to press her to order some of his eggs.

"They're a steal. Free-range. Cheaper than a supermarket," Jack was trying his hardest to persuade Claire.

"How free-range?" she questioned.

Jack scooted his seat across to his monitor and typed in a web cam address and gestured her to look. "Here. They've got the run of the balcony. I'll show you." He clicked on the site, as Claire looked on bemused.

"What?" she said laughingly.

"Burton's own chicken cam," pronounced Jack proudly.

"You've got a web cam on your balcony?" Claire giggled in disbelief.

"I carry ads on the site and make a fortune from chicken fanciers."

"Don't they fly away?"

"The fanciers or the chickens?"

Claire laughed, "The chickens, nutcase."

"Got their wings clipped. They're not about to commit suicide from that far up."

"Whatever," said Claire as she noticed Max striding toward them. She tried to warn Jack with her eyes but he was too involved in his website.

Max crossed to Claire. "I've just received a directive from the top. In the wake of Electra's death, you're to monitor anyone accessing conspiracy sites on the net."

Claire groaned, "Oh, what?"

"I know it's boring but they pay our wages so we do what we're told." ordered Max.

"I honestly believe that for most of the people going online to these web addresses that it's probably no more than idle curiosity and all this talk about conspiracy and murder will eventually die down," sighed Claire.

Max was about to reply when he noticed the chickens on Jack's screen. "Nice chickens. Now get off that web cam and back on the job." He turned back to Claire. "We have to be vigilant. Just in case," instructed Max.

"In case of what?" asked Claire.

"In case someone takes more than a passing interest," added Jack knowingly as he closed his current page on screen.

Max held up a memo and shook it at them, "Ours is not to reason why."

"What's the next line of that?" quipped Jack cheekily.

"Just get on with it," Max muttered brusquely. "Both of you."

Jack immediately conformed and pulled up a number of conspiracy sites and their forums to do with Electra's death and began examining entries. Claire, however, was still puzzled and she threw a wondering look at both Max and Jack. It was clear she didn't understand why they had to do this, or why Jack was more than happy to do it and follow the directive, as he seemed to do with all orders he was given whether they were questionable or not. She sighed resignedly, altered her screen and she, too, began to search the onscreen data.

Back at Amy's flat, Jon and Amy were heavily engaged in their research of Electra's fan sites. They were accessing a page on conspiracy theories and their related links, Marilyn Monroe, J F Kennedy, Martin Luther King, Lee Harvey Oswald, the Iraq war, and more. One appeared before them about the supposedly anonymous and secret group known as the Brandenberg Sect.

"Listen to this," gushed Amy her excitement becoming apparent.

"Brandenbergers, the ultimate conspiracy theory." Jon studied the page as she read, "The Brandenberg Sect, an elite coterie of Western thinkers and power-brokers, has been accused of fixing the fate of the world behind closed doors. As the organization marks its fiftieth anniversary, rumours are more rife than ever," she stopped, "How come we we've never heard of them?"

"Look at the names of those involved," muttered Jon scrolling through a list, "And that's not all of them, just the ones these people know about. They certainly have some powerful members."

"Exactly, an organisation that boasts the top businessmen, and politicians from the Western world, and no one's heard of them. Why?" questioned Amy.

Jon shrugged, baffled.

"This is frightening. A group like that could control the world. It says there are over a hundred and fifty members, this site only names twenty of them, and these people collude to steer the course of human history. Wow, it claims here that even royalty are involved." Amy accessed another page and feverishly continued reading.

In Max Stafford's office at MI6 Claire was downloading the names of ordinary members of the public that had surfed Conspiracy Theory sites and she logged the time the people had spent on them. The list was growing of more than one time users and as they downloaded this information it was transferred to the printer. There were reams of names. She gave a cursory glance through the first page of the list of the highest users before leaving her desk and handing them over to Max. She thought about reiterating that it was all a waste of time but she managed to restrain herself.

Amy was still working on the information from links to the previous site on the Brandenbergers. She called across to Jon now immersed in doing a little investigating himself. "Give my back a rub, Jon. My shoulders are killing me."

Jon rose and began to knead and palpate the muscles in her back and neck. "It's the tension from working on that thing. You need a better chair and to learn to sit properly," he admonished.

Amy relaxed, enjoying the moment, and then groaned in sheer pleasure as Jon continued to manipulate her shoulders, back and spine.

"Ooh, that's heaven," she groaned, the sounds she made were almost orgasmic.

Jon's face changed as he began to massage and stroke her neck with his thumbs. He was tempted to plant a kiss on her bowed neck, and head as the soft skin looked so tempting and inviting but instead he pulled away, patted her back, and ordered, "There, that's it. Enough! Take a break. Go on."

They swapped seats. Amy yawned, stretched and stood up. She moved to the door, rubbing her eyes and rotating her shoulders attempting to loosen them, "Coffee?"

"Please. Black with two sugars."

"As if I'd forget," she flirted.

Amy went and busied herself in the kitchen, while Jon carried on following up Amy's saved links. He suddenly came across a site entitled MK Ultra Mind Control and The Manchurian Candidate. He began reading and became totally absorbed in the content, so much so he didn't hear Amy return. She placed her hand on his shoulder and he jumped, startled. "You nearly frightened me to death," complained Jon.

"Sorry," Amy grinned. "Have you got anything?"

"You have to read this. Now, this is scary, mega scary." Jon fixed the page back to the start of the article and Amy peered over his shoulder and read.

"Manchurian Candidate? Isn't that a Frank Sinatra film that was remade with Denzel Washington?"

"What? I don't know," he answered confusedly before continuing, "Did you know Bill Clinton apologised to the American people for the action of previous administrations who had been performing experiments on subjects without their permission?"

"How did they do that?"

"Used the military, without their knowledge."

"What sort of experiments?"

"Mind control. Brainwashing."

"But, that's impossible, isn't it?"

"Apparently not. The CIA have long been involved in this sort of experimentation, using all manner of drugs and mind altering substances. They have put out cover stories to appease the press and the public, saying this type of research was abandoned long ago but here as you can see, there are documented cases of victims claiming it is still going on."

"Wow! Scary stuff," Amy agreed.

Claire sat patiently at her computer that was still spewing out yet more names of members of the public from all over the country and abroad, who were following the conspiracy theorists regarding Electra's death and all of the related links. She had just about convinced herself she was merely following orders as she printed off yet another sheaf of papers. She sighed resignedly as she passed them to Max. "I'm sure this is a complete waste of time," she murmured.

Max took the proffered list and studied the first page. A name caught his eye and he crossed to Jack. "Run a check on this one will you?"

"Name?" asked Jack ready and willing to type.

"Amy Wilde."

"Address?"

"Four Horberry Mews, South West One."

Jack entered the information. Claire, now very interested and her tiredness forgotten stood behind Jack, next to Max.

The screen in front of them brought up a picture of Amy and her birth date 24th of the 8th 1980. It showed that she was divorced, an only child and that both parents were deceased.

There was a short resume, on which Amy listed herself as a journalist turned filmmaker, who had at a very young age headed a newspaper investigation, which had brought about the demise of a corrupt Lord, politician and writer. This exposé had won her a National award. It listed her as being a partner in Monumentous Films with filmmaker, Jon Curtis. Jack scrolled through the data on the screen, which detailed her current project, a biopic on Electra.

Max barked, "Print off a couple of copies of this." He walked across to the internal paging system and fingered the gold ring on his hand bearing an embossed lion's head.

Max pressed an intercom button and spoke softly, "Patch me through to the President's office." He was careful not to attract the attention of the rest of the people in the office as he waited for a response. Cultured tones came on the line and Max informed him, "We may have trouble." Max continued to talk quietly, unheard by the others. "You'll see the President knows? .... Good." He listened impassively to his orders. "What else do we do?" Max nodded grimly.

He terminated his call and crossed back to Jack, Claire and two others in his support team. "I want the filmmakers, Amy Wilde and Jon Curtis to be kept under constant surveillance. Jack organise a team. I want to know their every move. Everything. Even if they burp, I want to know. The rest of you, try and put them off track, block their research, crash the websites. If things get too hot…" Max stopped, his face looked deadly serious. "Jack, get Biff and Ron to eliminate them." Max studied the face of each and every member of his personnel, who resolutely went to work. The only one who turned away unhappily was Claire.

Max frowned.

Chapter Six

Ibrahim on the case

AMY SAT SURROUNDED BY boy stuff. The desk in the room was cluttered with CD's, videotapes and piles of newspapers and periodicals. The decor in Jon's flat was typically masculine with burgundy flock wallpaper reminiscent of an Indian Restaurant, as Amy had laughingly remarked. And while she ploughed through the gossip columns in the celebrity magazines, Jon was involved in replaying news reports from around the world on Electra's death. They were both completely immersed in what they were doing. The concentration was so intense that when the telephone rang shrilly, demanding to be answered. They both jumped in alarm.

Amy gestured to Jon to get it. "It's your pad, answer it," she instructed and dutifully, Jon went to answer the call. Amy returned to her study.

Rumble, Jon's tabby and white cat wrapped himself around Jon's legs, purring and vying for attention. Jon leaned down to his cat and Rumble jumped up and butted Jon's free hand with his head begging to be stroked.

"Hello?" queried Jon.

"Jon Curtis?"

"Yes?"

"Ibrahim Khalid, I saw you at the reception," he introduced himself and was insistent on the other end of the line, "I think we ought to meet, you, me and Miss Wilde." This was a voice that was used to being obeyed and someone used to getting his own way.

Jon put his hand over the mouthpiece and hissed at Amy. "It's Ahmed's father. He wants us to meet."

Amy stopped what she was doing and looked up curiously, she nodded in ascension, "Okay, but why?"

"Can you tell me what it's about?" asked Jon.

"It's too dangerous on the phone. You heard my declaration to the press?" said Ibrahim.

"Yes?" responded Jon, his interest piqued.

"You must have something of value to me."

"I don't think…"

"Please. This is important," Ibrahim pressed.

"Okay. Where and when?"

"Book into the Hilton, Park Lane this afternoon. I will have a room reserved for you."

"But…"

"All booked and paid for. I'll contact you there. It's safer. Four o'clock." Ibrahim replaced the receiver terminating the call.

Jon looked across at Amy his face troubled and his expression turning to concern.

"Well?" Amy demanded, impatient to know what was going on.

"Get your things together, we're off to the Hilton."

"Oh, what?"

"Not immediately, but this afternoon."

The gap in the bedroom door widened just a little, as Ibrahim had replaced the receiver. He stood looking thoughtfully out of his office window that adjoined his private rooms and stroked his chin. Carol pushed the door fully open dressed only in a bathrobe. She had just showered and was towelling dry her hair. She smiled engagingly and cheekily asked, "Who was that?"

If Ibrahim was affronted at her curiosity he didn't show it, "No one important. Look, I have to go out. Will you be all right?"

"I'll be fine, Sir," she assured. "I still have some unpacking to do and the week's schedules to review."

"Good," Ibrahim answered curtly and moved to exit the room.

"Sir, I'd be happier if you took Mather with you. With everything that has happened, your safety is paramount," she advised.

"Of course," he responded mechanically, but he clearly had no intention of taking Mather or any other form of security with him. "Make yourself comfortable. Get to know the other duty staff. I'll check back with you later." Ibrahim grabbed his coat and went downstairs. As soon as Carol heard the front door close she went to the window and watched him leave the building. She had an inscrutable expression on her face. Carol was uncertain whether to report the incident or not. She finally decided against it. Carol also determined that she would use other means to gain Ibrahim's confidence.

She retired to her room and switched on the television where she heard that the police had arrested all the members of the paparazzi present on that fateful night and she laughed.

Jon and Amy were reviewing, yet again, the film footage from the night of the reception before Electra and Ahmed had left.

"We've been over this a dozen times. There's nothing suspicious, no men in black. Hell! We must have missed something," said Amy in frustration.

"I'm not sure what we're looking for or even if there's anything to find but I'll burn a copy for Ibrahim," Jon replied.

Amy glanced at her watch. "I'm going to try and see the press photographers."

"The ones who've been arrested?"

Amy nodded, "Yes. I know one of them. I'll meet you at the Hilton. Why don't you see if Grayson remembers anything?"

"If I can get past the police," observed Jon.

"You're clever. You'll think of a way," encouraged Amy.

Jon snorted in derision. "I'll have to be very creative. And I need to get to our office to pick up the rest of the research we did for the original film."

"You'll manage," laughed Amy. "Now scoot. I'll meet you outside the Hilton at…" She glanced at her watch again. "What time did he say?"

"This afternoon at four."

"That doesn't give us very long." She made a face, saved her work and closed her laptop. "I'll meet you outside at quarter to. Okay?"

She didn't wait for a response. Amy snatched up her coat and bag, and left. She ran to her car and started the engine. She let it idle awhile as she searched in her wallet for her press pass. She needed to get to the reporters and photographers that were locked up and wondered if she'd be allowed to visit the ones in custody. Amy drew away from the kerb as Jon came out and moved to his own vehicle. He gave her a quick wave before getting in his own car to drive to the hospital where Grayson had been admitted.

Luckily, the roads were pretty good and traffic flowed freely. His temper was even and calm by the time he reached the hospital but then he knew he would become harassed if he couldn't find anywhere to leave his vehicle. He reached the hospital car park and circled around futilely until he found a place being vacated by another visitor and waited patiently as the woman with a small child reversed out of her space and he slipped into it and parked. He grabbed a ticket from the machine and crossed over the walkway. Whistling lightly, he made his way to the central building.

Jon marched in through the hospital's main entrance and along the corridor to the information desk. He waited until the only visible Security Officer was involved with an elderly lady, helping her into a wheelchair and propelling her to the main doors, and then he approached the young female receptionist. He tried to appear distressed and concerned.

"Excuse me, I've just heard my cousin, Paul Grayson has been admitted, after a car crash. The family were told it was serious. Could you tell me which ward he's in?"

The young woman consulted her list, and smiled, "Certainly, Sir. Grayson, you say?" She continued working through the names as she chattered on, "He could be in ICU or Men's Surgical. Ah, here we are...." she stopped. "Oh, I'm sorry, I'm not allowed to give out that information."

"But, I was contacted," blustered Jon.

"I'm sorry, Sir," she repeated.

Jon thumped his hand on the desk, in annoyance. "What am I going to tell my Aunty Mary, his mother? She's laid up at home and can't get out. I promised I'd see him for her."

"I'm sorry," the young woman said. Her name lapel read, Sandra Clarke. She sounded genuinely apologetic. Jon rubbed his fingers through his hair and swung his hands about in exasperation, knocking over a sheaf of papers on the desk, which scattered on the floor. The young lady, bent to retrieve them and Jon swiftly turned the list of names toward him and spotted Grayson's private room number. He turned the list back quickly and bent to help Sandra pick up the scattered sheets of paper.

"I'm sorry, I know it's not your fault, Sandra," he said ruefully and gave her one of his shy smiles.

"I'm just following orders," she grinned. "Look, if you really want to see him..."

"I do…" he asserted.

"Then, if you go up to the sixth floor and see the hospital administrator, Eileen Cheevely Room 604. She may be able to help you."

"Oh, thank you," Jon fairly gushed his thanks. He helped her gather up the last few papers and beamed at her. "Thanks, Sandra. Aunty Mary will be so pleased."

"I'm not promising anything, mind," she continued.

"No, no. But you never know. Thank you."

"The lifts are that way," Sandra said and pointed along the corridor. Jon gave her a mock salute and walked toward the elevators.

Jon pressed the call button and waited as people filed past. He studied the board at the side of the lift listing the floors and wards. He spotted that the Intensive Care Unit was housed on the fourth floor. He just hoped his luck would hold, and with that thought he crossed his fingers.

The doors opened and he waited for visitors and personnel to exit before entering and he began to formulate a game plan in his head.

Jon strode out and moved confidently down the passageway on past the Children's Ward and onto ICU. He leaned against the wall and thought for a moment to consider his options. He watched as a male cleaner opened a cupboard door and replaced a mop and bucket. Hanging on the cupboard door were a couple of different coloured coats including a white medical looking one.

Jon waited for the cleaner to clear the area and he strolled nonchalantly across to the door and yanked it open. He stepped inside and selected the white coat, donned it and stepped out. He hung his press pass around his neck and walked to ICU. Jon held back as he watched a nurse in front of him cleanse her hands. He did likewise and smiled at her. She hit the punch pad and entered the ward. She held the door open and Jon followed in behind her. He stopped to cleanse his hands again, while he assessed the Nurse's Station, the ward and the private rooms. He bent under the pretence of tying his shoelace and observed the nurse and doctor at the desk.

Jon stood and cleansed his hands once more and moved further into the Unit as he saw the doctor and nurse go into a room opposite. Jon hurried to the desk and checked the room numbers. He realised the room he wanted was further along the corridor and he walked on. There was an empty chair outside with a newspaper and pen resting on it. The way was clear and he slipped swiftly into Grayson's room.

Grayson was wired up to a life support machine, which bleeped as it monitored Grayson's heartbeat and other vital signs. He looked in a bad way.

Jon spoke quietly, "Paul? It's Jon. Jon Curtis. How you doing, buddy?"

Grayson's eyes fluttered open and he stared vacantly at Jon.

"Grayson? ... Paul?" said Jon more urgently.

"Who?" croaked Grayson.

"You've been in a bad accident. What do you remember?"

Grayson shook his head, and whispered hoarsely, "I told you, man. I said all I know. Nothing. I don't remember… Nothing." He closed his eyes and turned his head away.

Jon moved to the foot of the bed and checked the chart. He glanced out of the room's glass panelled door and was alarmed to see a uniformed police officer walking back to the chair outside the room. To his relief, a nurse crossed to the copper and directed him across to the Nurses' Station. As the officer walked away, Jon slipped unobtrusively out of the room, and walked back down the corridor, passing the policeman on the telephone. Jon safely escaped unnoticed out of the ward. He heaved a huge sigh of relief once he was safely back in the general walkway. He stepped back to the Janitor's closet and replaced the white coat and headed back to the lift and the exit.

As he passed through the main foyer Sandra spotted him, she waved and mouthed, "Any good?"

Keeping up the pretence he walked across. "She wasn't in her office, so I tried my luck on the wards. I went to Men's Surgical. He wasn't there so I guessed it must be ICU but that was a closed shop."

"Oh, I'm sorry."

"Not to worry, I'll try again and get a letter of authorisation from his mother. They'll have to let me in then. Thanks for all your help."

"You're welcome."

He was soon out of the hospital, and back into his car. He dropped his vehicle off into the community car park near his home and caught a bus to take him to Park Lane and the Hilton.

Amy was not having as much luck at the cop shop. She was becoming more and more frustrated. Nothing she said made any difference. The desk sergeant categorically refused to say anything to her, answer any questions or allow her through. She was stumped. A young male cleaner was polishing the floor and overheard all that was said. As Amy turned to leave he shut off his machine and followed her out of the door.

"Miss, can I have a word?" Amy turned surprised. "You won't get anywhere with Sergeant Bryant. He's a stickler for procedure, he is. But he goes off duty in half an hour. Sergeant Laycock comes on then. You might have better luck with him. But, you didn't hear it from me."

"Why are you telling me this?" asked Amy curiously.

"Electra was a marvel. She did so much good and she shouldn't have died. Something happened and no one's talking. I want to see someone get to the truth," said the cleaner.

"Thanks," said Amy appreciatively. "I'll grab a coffee and come back. Thank you." Amy checked the time and strolled off down the street to the nearest café and ordered a skinny latte and a Danish. "Sort of defeats the object," said Amy wryly when the waitress brought them across to her.

"Aw, it does you good to treat yourself occasionally, love. Besides, you look as if you need it. You could do with a bit of fattening up, unlike me," chortled the plump waitress, name tagged, Betty, whose tummy wobbled when she laughed.

Amy chuckled with her and sipped her coffee. The pastry was delicious and she was tempted to have another but just managed to resist in spite of Betty's coaxing. Amy continued to watch the clock until it was time to leave. She left a tip for Betty and made her way back along the dusty road to the police station. She was gratified to see that the cleaner had been correct and there was someone different on the front desk. He was younger and quite good-looking. She put on her most dazzling smile and approached the window.

"Hi. I hope you can help me...?"

"If I can I will," smiled the young sergeant.

"Good. I really hope so.... One of my close friends and even closer colleague is in one of your cells and I really need to speak with him."

The sergeant frowned. "And who might that be?"

"Mickey Coombes. Look, I know it's not the done thing but his mum is really worried. She wants to know if she can do anything for him, get a solicitor or just, well, anything."

"Hmm. Isn't he one of the press pack on remand for the death of Electra?"

"Yes, but you see. Mickey's mum is in a bad way. She's agoraphobic and Mickey does everything for her, when he's not working. I need to get in touch with one of his relatives to come and help out. I can do some of it but not all. I have to work, too."

"Why can't his mum call them herself?" queried Sergeant Laycock.

"She doesn't have the number. I said I'd try and I'd kind of like to see him and talk to him myself..."

"I'm sure you would, but..." The young sergeant hesitated.

Amy piled on the pressure, "Please..." She looked at him pleadingly.

"Darn. I shouldn't really. But... well... okay I'll give you ten minutes. What's your name?"

"Amy... Amy Wilde."

"Hold on. Come on through and sit in Interview Room Three."

"Thank you, you are wonderful. I really appreciate it, Sergeant...?" Amy gushed.

"Don't thank me yet," he said as he walked to the door and admitted her. "And it's Laycock. Jim Laycock."

Amy could not believe her luck; she just prayed that Mickey would play along. She sat down in Interview Room Three as instructed and waited.

Jim Laycock went out back to the holding cells and called out, "Mickey Coombes?"

The officer at the back, pointed. "Cell six." He returned to his paper work.

Sergeant Laycock unbolted the small window grille and peered through, "Coombes? Someone to see you."

Mickey Coombes scratched his head. "What's this about?"

"Something to do with your mother. You've got ten minutes. Come with me."

Mickey was just about to say that his mother was dead but thought better of it. His curiosity was aroused so he went along with it. "Poor old stick. What's the matter now?"

"You'll find out. Friend of yours is waiting in Interview Room Three. This way."

The sergeant opened up his cell. He gestured for the prisoner to follow and banged the cell door shut again and led Mickey away.

Mickey was nothing if not curious to see who was waiting for him, He opened the door and Amy rose and flung her arms around him. "Oh, Mickey, your mum's been so worried." She whispered in his ear, "Please play along."

"What's the old biddy been up to now?"

"Ten minutes. No more," ordered Jim Laycock.

Amy and Mickey sat down and she quickly briefed him on her cover story to get her in to see him and then began to ask the real questions. She couldn't believe what she heard.

The ten minutes went far too quickly and Amy scribbled down her number. "Call me when you get out, please." She covered his hand with hers and secretly passed the number across. "What did you say, your cousin's number was again?" she bluffed as the door opened.

Mickey nodded and said, "Zero one two zero seven, four six four three double two."

Amy scribbled it down on her notepad. "Great. I'll get onto it, right away."

"Sorry, Miss Wilde. Time's up," enforced Sergeant Laycock.

Amy rose and hugged Mickey again, "Don't worry, I'll take care of everything."

She sped off and parked her car safely in its garage before hurrying off to take public transport to the Hilton Hotel.

The underground trains were fast and frequent and she was soon at Marble Arch. She began to walk briskly into the street. Amy looked up at the dial on the wall outside the exclusive clock shop in Park Lane and checked it against her own. She gasped and put a spurt on, making a dash for The Hilton.

Waiting outside, on the pavement end of the driveway, was Jon clutching his video bag and tapping his feet. He spotted Amy rushing down the street and smiled in relief.

She jogged up and muttered, "Sorry."

"Okay, how did it go?"

"I've heaps to tell you."

"Let's get in and organised, first," Jon requested.

"And let's make it look like we're used to frequenting these sort of places," advised Amy.

They walked smartly up to the entrance, complete with moustached doorman who ushered them through the revolving doors. They attempted to walk sedately to the welcome desk where the female receptionist eyed them inquisitively.

"Ah, Jon Curtis and Ms. Amy Wilde," announced Jon.

The woman, whose name lapel read, 'Brenda Passmore,' didn't bat an eyelid. She engaged Jon's gaze coolly, "There's a suite booked in your name, Mr. Curtis."

Amy couldn't control her excitement, "A suite! A whole suite."

Brenda Passmore asked politely, "Do you have any luggage?"

Jon lifted up his camera bag, "I can manage thanks."

The receptionist smiled, "Sign here." Jon dutifully scrawled his signature and Brenda passed him a key card. She pointed through the lobby, "Eighth floor. The lifts are over there."

Jon and Amy strolled nonchalantly toward the lift. As they moved away from the desk, the receptionist buzzed on an intercom and spoke softly, "They've arrived."

Jon and Amy just managed to control their excitement in the elevator in the company of an elderly lady with blue rinsed hair who regarded them with interest, "On your honeymoon?" she enquired, kindly.

"No!" chortled Jon, vehemently.

"Are you sure?" the old lady continued. "You make a lovely couple."

"We're just friends," said Amy.

"And colleagues," added Jon.

"Well, maybe you ought to think about it. You'd make lovely babies," smiled the old lady.

Amy blushed and, with relief, dived out on the eighth floor, bleating a goodbye to their elevator companion. Jon followed and they checked the room numbers on the doors before bursting in through the entrance of the suite. They gazed in awe at their luxurious surroundings.

"Wow!" exclaimed Amy, clearly impressed. She swept through the apartment while Jon set up his equipment and put a disc in the DVD player. Amy disappeared through another door into a bedroom and squealed in delight when she saw the huge bed and she flung herself down onto it. She lay there a moment and gazed up at the ceiling. She noticed an ice bucket on a stand containing a bottle of champagne, keeping cool. She called through to Jon, "Jon... In here!"

Jon entered and gave a long low whistle, "So, this is how the other half live." He flopped down on the bed beside her.

"I've never seen such an enormous bed... Have you clocked the champagne?" gasped Amy.

"More like a honeymoon set up than a business meeting," observed Jon.

"You said it, or the old lady did," grinned Amy. She rolled herself up on one elbow. "Still, it's a pity to waste it."

Amy got off the bed and went to the ice bucket and stand, picked up the glasses, and pulled out the champagne. She handed it to Jon, who complained, "It's wet! Isn't there a cloth?"

Amy grabbed the starched white tea towel draped over the ice bucket and began fooling around; she swiped playfully at Jon with it. "M'lud."

Jon caught hold of the end of it and pulled. Amy landed on the bed with him, still holding the glasses in one hand. They ended up almost nose-to-nose. Amy gasped involuntarily and moistened her lips reflexively. Jon studied her face. He noticed the smattering of freckles on her nose, her lengthy dark lashes, her full, soft lips and he suppressed a sigh. There was the fraction of a pause while their faces remained unnervingly close. Amy swung away abruptly. Jon, though, was taken by surprise at the undercurrent of feeling between them and so decided to play things lightly.

"Stand back. Give me room! I'm about to pop my cork," he pronounced.

Amy giggled and held the glasses at his side while he struggled to release the champagne cork. It sprang out with a bang and Jon poured them each a fizzing glass, which they raised in a toast. "To Electra and us," announced Amy. "May we find the truth."

"You said you had heaps to tell me," pressed Jon.

"Yes, when I finally got in to see Mickey. Fortunately, he played along but Jon, listen to this…"

"I am, I am. I'm dying of curiosity here. Spill."

"Okay, Mickey was one of the first on the scene. He saw the whole thing. He said a blinding light or explosion or something at the end of the tunnel must have blinded the driver, which is why he crashed."

"Explosion?"

"But, there was no boom, but the light was dazzling. Someone else said a car had deliberately parked at the end of the tunnel and turned its headlights on full at the crucial moment."

"Yes, I remember reading something about that."

"That's not all, Electra was awake but in shock, she was heard to say, 'Oh my God!' She had no visible injuries, none!"

"What? They said she had severe head injuries and was bleeding profusely? One person said she was bleeding from the ears and nose."

"I know, totally contradictory and get this. She was helped out of the car and stood up…"

"She must have had internal injuries," reasoned Jon.

"Why did the ambulance take so long to get to the hospital? Why?"

Jon shrugged; he had no answers.

"Something is clearly very wrong. What was done to her in that ambulance?"

Jon was aghast, "I can't believe it...."

"Oh, I haven't finished yet. Mickey said the seat belts were tampered with," said Amy triumphantly.

"What?"

"The only person wearing one was Paul Grayson and it was very loose. Useless for doing its job. And why was the tunnel cleared and open two hours later? You know how long Police Forensics take at the scene of a crime. It's almost as if they wanted evidence to be destroyed. No one has been allowed to see the CCTV footage and yet there are cameras both ends of the tunnel. Something is rotten in the state of this realm, this England."

"You're mixing your quotes now," accused Jon trying to lighten the conversation. "Hamlet and... what's the other?"

"Richard the Second," said Amy smugly before she changed her tone, "Jon, the papers say it was all the driver's fault. They said he was drunk. We know that's not true."

Carol had put the final touches to her makeup and hair. She was dressed casually in smart slacks and a check shirt. She picked up her handbag; her coat and car keys before taking a cursory look around the luxury two-storey apartment. Her eyes lingered on a framed picture of Ahmed and Electra laughing and looking happy together. She adjusted the picture slightly and traced Electra's smile with her finger. Her eyes misted over and she shook her head vehemently as if chasing away the remnant of a memory.

Carol exited Ibrahim's accommodation and walked down the plush corridor to the lifts. She entered the elevator and travelled to the ground floor lobby where she bade a perfunctory, 'good day' to the Security Guard on the reception desk and made her way toward the lift and staircase to the building's underground car park. Strategically placed security cameras followed her movements.

Carol hurried to her vehicle and checked it for tracking bugs and other surveillance equipment with a hand held scanner she had secreted in her bag. It bleeped at her from underneath the front bumper. Carol felt around and found it. She carefully removed it and placed it on the bottom of the pillar by her parking spot; securing it so it was not immediately apparent. She would replace it on her return. To all intents and purposes her car was still in the car park should anyone be watching or monitoring her actions.

Smiling delightedly, she climbed into the front seat of her new Mini Cooper and reversed out of her space, drove around the garage and up the slope to the electric gates, which rolled up like a portcullis allowing her to escape onto the road.

Carol swore softly as she swerved to avoid a burgundy saloon car following a black van that was pulling out of a parking space. She negotiated the traffic in front of her proficiently and checked her rear view mirror. She seemed to be free from any one following her. She confidently swung out into the main stream of vehicles travelling down the busy shopping street, where people browsed and window-shopped. She didn't notice the black van draw into the kerb in front of her. Carol drove past and the van waited a moment and pulled back into the line of cars two behind her.

Carol drove on unaware that she was being followed. She headed for Kensington and Karl's flat. She parked her Mini Cooper in a vacant bay, exited the car, locked it and marched swiftly to the building where her twin brother lived.

Carol glanced at the door panel hosting the buzzers to the luxury flats. She pressed the button reading Karl Goodwin and waited. Nothing. She pressed again. There was still no response. Carol fished in her handbag and rummaged around for her keys. She tried a number of them in the outer door but all to no avail.

Frustrated, Carol trundled down the steps and stared up at her brother's window. The curtains were half pulled. There was no movement. Carol refused to be put off. She ran up the steps again and pressed another bell. There was no answer. She tried another.

"Hello?" came an abrupt male voice. "Who is it?"

"I'm the sister of the guy in number eight and…" The man cut her off.

Carol took a deep breath and tried once more. This time the intercom came on and the responding voice was female, elderly and quavery, "Yes?"

"Hello, I'm Karl's sister, Karl in apartment eight. I've forgotten my outer door key and I'm supposed to cook dinner for us tonight."

The buzzer went on the door to admit her and she whispered her thanks. Carol ran straight to the elevator, which took her up to her brother's floor. She dashed along the corridor and stopped outside Karl's door and pressed his bell. Nothing. She tried peering through the peephole but couldn't see anything. She knocked softly and waited. Still, there was no response. Finally, she rummaged in her bag for a bunch of keys and the skeleton key tool that would open most locks. She muttered a quick prayer, "Please, God, let it open." She fixed it into the lock and wiggled it slowly, as she had been taught at the Centre, to engage the locking mechanism. After a few moments she was rewarded with a soft click and the door opened. "Thank you, Lord. Thank you, thank you!"

Carol entered softly; she was careful not to disturb anything or to leave any prints behind. She checked for bugs with her electric scanner. The rooms appeared to be clear apart from one on the telephone to monitor Karl's calls, so she felt free to do a reasonable search of the apartment.

The bedroom was neat and tidy, and the bed made. It didn't look as if it had been slept in. Carol checked the bottom sheet. It was pristine. She knew her brother well enough that whenever he made a bed it was always the top of it that looked well made but he never seemed to pull the bottom sheet tight or tuck it in properly. This one was perfectly made. He had not slept in this bed recently, unless he had maid service, then that would explain the perfect bed, she reasoned.

She moved on around the bedroom. Carol checked his wardrobe. His clothes were still there. She rummaged through the pockets but found nothing to give her a clue as to his whereabouts. His new passport was still in his bedside table drawer and she could find nothing untoward in his abode. "Hmm!" she grunted to herself, "Kitchen."

Carol examined the contents of the fridge. There were the remains of a congealed Chinese take away meal, some cheese sprouting spores of mould. She picked up a carton of milk that was turning sour. She suppressed an urge to retch, as she smelled it. This milk had been sitting in there for days. "Something is up," she said aloud. "Something is definitely up! Bugger!"

Saddened and discouraged, she left the flat ensuring there was no evidence of her ever having being there. She closed the door firmly ran down the stairs and out onto the street to find her car. She gave one backward glance at the building as if it might reveal something more to her. The CCTV camera outside caught her shaking her head in disappointment as she crossed to her car. She was so preoccupied she didn't notice she was being watched by something more sinister.

She sped along the road hunting for a public phone box that took coins. In this new age of technology and mobile phones they were few and far between. She didn't dare use her own telephone. She needed to be anonymous for this call. Carol turned a corner and her eyes searched the street. She knew there was a call box somewhere in the vicinity. Toward the end of the road she spotted a BT booth with the lady blowing a fluted horn and skidded to a stop. Luckily, she was able to park outside it.

Carol stepped out of the car and hurried to the call box. She fished in her handbag pulling out her purse and took a handful of coins, which she slapped on the metal shelf, which had once housed a telephone directory. She then rummaged further and tugged out a scrap of paper with a number. She dialled, let it ring twice and hung up. She waited a minute and then punched in several coins, and dialled again. The receiver was picked up.

"Yes?" The man's tone was measured.

"MK 9, here."

"Yes?" A hint of curiosity entered the man's voice.

"I'm trying to reach my brother."

"You know that's not a good idea," advised the male operative.

"He's my brother. He's not answering his phone. I've been to his flat. He's not there."

"How did you…?"

"I rang the bell." She chose her next words carefully, "He's not answering his door. I was careful. You trained me remember? Don't worry, no one will know. Where is he?"

"At this moment, I'm not sure," his voice was educated, slow and deliberate.

Carol was becoming more irritated and didn't hesitate to show it, "Well, you placed him," she said accusingly. "Just who is it he's working for?"

"You know I can't tell you that," the voice replied in those annoying over patient tones.

"I've a right to see my own brother," Carol's voice had begun to rise. "He's all I have left."

"That might be so, but we also know the two of you have spoken, against all the rules and instructions laid down. Your selfish actions could have jeopardised the whole operation. Both yours and his."

"We didn't jeopardise anything. We haven't had any physical contact," she lied, her voice was beginning to sound hysterical.

"Why don't you calm down?" came the stoic voice down the phone line.

"You said I could ring him," she insisted.

"But not meet," the voice continued coolly.

"We didn't," she denied vehemently.

"I'm not so sure," taunted the agent. "That's not according to my information."

Carol's voice became more panicked, "Please. You said after my hit, I could ring him…. See him. I've kept my end of the bargain."

Silence greeted her.

"Never mind," she shrieked and slammed down the phone. Two returning coins clunked into the tray. She scooped them up and angrily went back to her car. She sat in the driver's seat and pounded the dashboard with her hands, laid her head on the steering wheel and began to sob.

Ibrahim had arrived at the hotel suite and he was reviewing the film footage that Jon had taken on the night of the party before Electra had left. Covering the table were newspapers screaming various headlines over the pop star's death. Some blamed the Paparazzi, others reported that it was a complete accident; some claimed it was the fault of the driver who was drunk while some used the word 'conspiracy'.

Ibrahim studied the shots of Karl sitting at the bar, "Karl was drinking soft drinks all night. He had just one glass of champagne. He didn't even finish that. He had just a sip. He couldn't have been drunk. Yet the papers put him at so much over the limit he wouldn't have been able to stand, let alone drive."

"I certainly don't remember him drinking," agreed Amy.

"Neither do I," said Jon. "We were discussing this earlier."

"So, why are they printing lies?"

Jon shrugged, puzzled, "I saw Grayson. He doesn't remember anything, not even his own name."

"How did you manage that?" quizzed Ibrahim, clearly impressed.

"It wasn't easy. I just used a little imagination and a lot of charm," replied

Jon. "But I can tell you, he was uncommunicative and he didn't remember me at all."

Ibrahim paused and studied the faces of the filmmakers and took out an envelope containing a large amount of cash and a cheque. He passed it to Jon. "Consider this a deposit. I'm hiring your services. At the end of this we'll have a film that will tell the world the truth."

"And what if you don't like the truth?" questioned Jon.

"That's a risk I'm prepared to take," said Ibrahim gravely. "Now, let's go through this again and see what we have got."

Amy began to chart the information she'd gathered against the official reports being fed to the public. Jon and Ibrahim reviewed the film of the fatal night once more.

"One more thing," Amy said. "Mickey Coombes, who got Electra out, says she was conscious and able to step into the ambulance. There was no head wound."

Jon and Ibrahim looked at her. "That's not what it says in the press," said Ibrahim.

"I know," muttered Amy. "We have to keep at it, Jon," she said seriously. "There are far too many anomalies."

Ibrahim smiled bitterly.

Jon nodded gravely. "Then let's get to it."

Amy studied her chart. "We have numerous pieces of contradictory evidence, things that need double checking and questions that need to be asked. I'll scan this and give you each a copy and we can work out who will do what..." She tapped the paper. "These blood test results. They don't make sense. Think I'll try and infiltrate the hospital, don a white coat and pretend I'm staff. See what I can learn."

"Yes, I daren't go back there, yet, in case someone recognises me. I'll go and talk to her band. We intended to do that anyway for the film, so that won't arouse any suspicions. Let's see if anyone can shed any light on anything," thought Jon aloud.

Ibrahim nodded in agreement. "But first back to the film. I want to watch it again. There must be something that we missed. Let's go back to the sound check and rehearsal."

They studied the film from the agreed point and Ibrahim called, "Stop! Stop there. Rewind."

Jon rewound to the kiss and Electra calling him to 'Cut' and to remove that particular shot. Jon began to apologise, "Electra wanted me to cut it but I haven't done it yet," he said sheepishly.

"No, not that and anyway, I think you should leave it in. People are saying they were not in love. This snippet proves it. I know they were unofficially engaged… No, it was after that. Put the film at a slower speed."

Jon slowed the film and they watched as Electra stuck a sprig of holly in her baseball cap. "There!"

The two filmmakers looked at each other, confused. They didn't see what Ibrahim was getting at.

"Don't you see?" said Ibrahim excitedly.

Amy shook her head. She was lost for words. Jon, too, just looked embarrassed.

"What do you, English use holly for?" pressed Ibrahim.

"At Christmas time we use it for decoration," said Amy, still clueless.

"Yes, sometimes we put a sprig on the Christmas pudding," said Jon.

"Yes, yes. There you have it," cried Ibrahim enthusiastically.

"Have what?" queried Amy.

"The pudding club. It was a joke. Electra and Ahmed's little joke. Electra was in the pudding club," explained Ibrahim wiggling his eyebrows as if to make them understand.

"What? You mean she was pregnant?" gasped Jon.

"That's awful," said Amy.

"But there's more. That would account for the reason why they embalmed Electra before the autopsy…"

"Because it would remove any trace of a pregnancy," finished Jon.

"Yes! Otherwise, why do it? It's not normal procedure," asserted Ibrahim.

"No, it's not. There are far too many things that just don't add up," agreed Amy.

Chapter Seven

Men in Black

THE CAMERAS IN THE quiet London street, outside the offices of Monumentous Films, run by Jon and Amy, recorded an anonymous black van, appearing like a spectre. The mysterious black vehicle parked and waited a few minutes. Its windows were tinted preventing curious eyes from looking in. Two well-built men, who looked as if they could handle themselves, and carrying canvas holdalls emerged from the rear doors. They looked all around them, scanning the street, making sure that they were not observed. The few people that were out and about presented no problem to them. They were just eager to be about their own business.

The operatives walked up to the building, studied the plaque on the wall outside to check that they had found the correct office block inside Premier House, the home of Monumentous films. Using skeleton keys, they entered the property and perused the board in the foyer identifying the list of businesses that traded there. Monumentous Films was located on the fourth floor. They strolled to the lift and pressed the call button. It arrived empty and they stepped inside.

They soon reached the fourth floor and walked to the office door. A brass sign outside read Monumentous Films. One man kept a look out whilst the other tried to gain admittance. He struggled with three locks before he finally opened the door. They slipped inside.

The agents moved quickly. They each donned thin surgical gloves and set to work. One man opened his bag on the desk and took out a number of monitoring devices. He inserted one into the telephone receiver; another was placed behind a picture and one under the desk. The plant pot holding a huge yucca was also similarly violated. The other man sat at the computer and booted it up. He typed nimbly and at speed installing a hidden programme onto the hard drive that would be disguised and allow all activity on the main PC to be accessed by one of their external computers. The same programme was entered into another desktop machine. The second anti office containing filing cabinets and other equipment and the small kitchen was also infiltrated. Both offices were suitably bugged so no one would be able to sneeze without the surveillance team knowing about it. Not a word passed between the men as they carried out their work.

The one nodded to the other that he was finished. He picked up his bag and waited by the door for his colleague to complete his work on the computers. The second man shut down the PC and collected his holdall from the floor. They exited Amy and Jon's work space as quietly as they had entered, went back in the lift, down to the foyer and out onto the street. No one noticed, and no one saw except for the building's ubiquitous security camera. They stepped back into the van, which started its engine and pulled away leaving the road with just a fleeting shadow of their stealthy visit. The van travelled speedily through the London streets and headed for MI6 offices and disappeared into the large underground car park.

Max Stafford's office was alive with operatives working long into the night. Computers flickered and Claire continued to monitor a number of conspiracy sites set on a tab when a message flashed up on her screen. She called out to her boss, Max and gestured to Jack. "Monumentous Films! Someone's linking from outside into their main PC."

Max grunted in pleasure. "Then our programme's working. Anything to be concerned about?"

Claire tracked the filmmakers' search. "Info on the Brandenberg Sect."

Max ordered, "Stay with it." He leaned over her shoulder and watched the screen.

Amy and Jon were still occupying the hotel suite. Amy had fired up her laptop and blue toothed into the main office computer attempting to access files on her office desktop. She was also searching for more information about the secret Brandenbergers. Jon was following her progress. He sighed and straightened up. "Maybe we're looking at this from the wrong angle."

"How do you mean?" asked Amy puzzled.

"The Nostradamus prediction. What was it? 'The principal players are hidden away.' Just like the Brandenberg Sect... why would they want to get rid of Electra?"

"Because she was difficult politically? Involved with Royalty and then a Muslim?" mused Amy. "It doesn't look good for the Prince."

"But she'd moved on from him. She was no threat to the throne," stated Jon.

"Unless... How would the aristocracy react to her pregnancy?" asked Amy.

"If she was pregnant. We don't know for certain."

"No. What else was there? Why would they want her dead?"

"She campaigned for Human Rights," Jon pointed out.

"A dirty word now-a-days," said Amy.

"But is that reason enough? She had influence, but no more than other altruistic free spirits like Bianca Jagger, Bob Geldof."

"Yes, but they do it differently, through charity and so on," argued Amy.

"But what if she was being used," questioned Jon.

"I don't get it. What do you mean?"

"I'm not sure... it's just the germ of an idea... Think... What's the most powerful thing about Electra?"

"Her music," Amy answered without hesitation. "Why? ... I'm not sure where this is leading..."

"Neither am I... yet," said Jon his face a picture of concentration and confusion. "Keep looking."

Claire's PC screen at MI6 was flashing with messages as Amy continued to trawl through her saved files and began new searches. Max straightened up and instructed, "If they appear to be interested in the contentious material, shut down the sites."

"Isn't that a bit drastic?" queried Claire. "Won't that make them even more suspicious?"

"Or it will put them off," added Jack, but neither Max nor Claire took any notice of him.

"We've got our orders!" exclaimed Max not wanting further discussion.

"Who exactly are we working for?" demanded Claire.

"That's classified," snapped Max.

Claire frowned and continued, "But I don't see why these two filmmakers are so dangerous."

"That's why you carry out orders and don't give them." Max replied curtly.

Jack who had continued watching the interchange decided he would try and be the voice of reason in the argument. "We have a responsibility, Claire. There are some things that it is best people know nothing about. For example, if it were common knowledge that the government were training selected felons for military purposes, imagine the hue and cry."

Claire bounced back immediately, "Even I've questioned the ethics of that."

"But, Claire… these people are now free and living productive lives. If the call comes to send someone to…" he searched and pondered for an example. "Iran, say… to take out Mahmoud Ahmadinejad or North Korea's Kim Jong Un, then who better?"

Claire snorted. "Huh! They've committed a crime therefore they're expendable. No one will give Jack shit about them. Sorry, Jack."

"That's okay. But, listen, we're not risking honest men and true," insisted Jack.

"Yeah, right!" admonished Claire.

Max had been following the discussion with interest and narrowed his eyes. "If you're uncomfortable with this…"

"No, no. Just a bit of healthy debate, Gentlemen. Satisfying my conscience," she protested with a wry smile.

"And is it satisfied?" asked Max a hint of steel creeping into his tones.

"For now," smiled Claire attempting to make light of her outburst. She returned to work and continued to watch the sites accessed flashing up. Suddenly, they stopped.

"They've stopped but we're still linked. No activity but no movement," observed Claire.

Max asked, "What's their position, where are they?"

"Er…" Claire hit a button and a map came up. The Hilton in Park Lane was highlighted, as was Monumentous Film's office in North London.

"Perfect," murmured Max. "Jack, get Biff and the team over to Jon Curtis' flat. Now." He checked his watch. "We have time."

Amy and Jon took a break from the laptop. Amy let the screen go to sleep as she and Jon shared another drink. Amy gestured around the room. "And we've got this place for the whole night?"

"That's what he said," affirmed Jon.

"It's a pity to waste it."

"What did you have in mind?" queried Jon, his curiosity piqued.

Amy smiled brightly. "Dinner would be nice."

"Why not? It's all paid for. Let's check out the menu." Jon crossed to the desk and picked up the room service menu and they perused what was on offer.

"Just reading the menu makes me feel hungry," said Amy.

"I'm starving. Haven't eaten since breakfast," complained Jon.

"Hm. I bet it was a big one, though."

"Fruit juice, cereal, three rashers of bacon, two sausages, two eggs, fried bread, mushrooms and tomatoes, toast and marmalade. Oh, and a hash brown."

"A heart attack waiting to happen. You need to take better care of yourself... I don't want to be a work widow..." she paused while she studied the menu. "What are you going to have?" asked Amy.

"I'll have the soup, beef Wellington and if I've got room, the luxury bread and butter pudding with cream." He rubbed his tummy with a circular motion, "Yum!"

"English through and through," teased Amy.

"What's the matter with that? Good solid dependable English fare. Can't beat it. What are you having?"

"Um, I think I'll have deep fried brie, the sea bass followed by panna cotta."

"Right let's order... and to wash it down?"

"You know me, I'm the Pinot Grigio girl especially as I'm having fish," said Amy.

"You had Shiraz the other night."

"That was just for a change but I prefer dry white, you know that."

"Then I'll have a cheeky red... what do they do by the glass?" asked Jon as they continued studying the wine list, attempting to unwind. "It's a pity we couldn't eat in the dining room," murmured Jon.

"If only we'd known I could have worn my gownless evening strap," Amy joked.

"Wouldn't suit you," said Jon.

"No?"

"No. Definitely a jeans and sweater lady."

"Thanks!" said Amy indignantly. "I do scrub up well though, like the other night. Or didn't you notice?"

"No," confessed Jon.

"Thanks a bunch, again! I do scrub up well, you know. Like at the party. How could you not notice?"

"Hm! Nor would you if you'd hired your dress from the same incompetent pillock I got my tux from."

"You danced in it all right," she accused.

"Yeah! But, I couldn't bloody well sit down!"

Amy laughed, "Well, we'll make up for that right now. Garçon! Let's order."

Carol was lying awake in her bed. She just couldn't settle. She was frantically worried about Karl. If anything had happened to him, she determined that she would have her revenge. She was also curious about Ibrahim's covert activities. She decided that until she had her answers she wouldn't strictly obey all of her instructions. It was then she noticed the click of the latch on the front door unlocking. She crept out of bed and stepped out through the partially opened bedroom door. She glanced over the banisters of the two-storey apartment and saw Ibrahim putting his coat in the hall closet. She slipped back into the shadows as she heard him enter the lounge and switch on the television. She debated whether or not to go down the stairs and join him but decided against it and slipped back into her room and tried to settle. She punched her pillow hard and closed her eyes determinedly. She just wasn't in the mood for pleasantries. She wanted to scream at someone and she was intelligent enough to know that a response like that wouldn't do her any good at all.

Her eyes refused to remain closed and they blinked open. Carol still couldn't sleep. She was constantly thinking and worrying about Karl. There was something else that disturbed her; she couldn't explain the wave of remorse that washed over her when she saw Electra's photograph of when she was alive and well. That was not part of her brief and it worried her. Obeying her orders was one thing but Carol disliked the feelings she was experiencing. It showed that in spite of her programming, in spite of her background that she had a conscience and having a conscience was something she knew could get her killed.

She slammed her head down on the pillow again and closed her eyes firmly. But they sprang open again. "God damn!" she swore softly. She reluctantly threw back the covers and stepped out of bed. She went into her en suite bathroom and rummaged in the cabinet and pulled out a pack of sleeping tablets. It was no good. Her mind would not let her rest. She gulped two down and returned to bed hoping to be rewarded with the thankful bliss of sleep.

The black van was on the move again. It arrived on the street outside Jon's house. Two men emerged wearing official looking electrician uniforms with S.E.E.B. (South Eastern Electricity Board) printed on their backs and sporting ID tags around their necks. They were both in their mid to late twenties and looked as if they could be useful in a fight. They obviously worked out at the gym regularly. One of them, Biff, who had previously driven the van for the job at Monumentous Film premises, checked his artificial job sheet. He pointed to the building and he and the other operative, Ron, stepped smartly across the road and rang the bell. Ron took a few cautious looks down the street as they waited. They were soon rewarded with the sound of footsteps. The door was opened by a lanky young man, Mike, in jeans, with long dark hair who looked like a typical student. He smiled engagingly as he studied the men in front of him.

"Yes?"

"I'm sorry, Sir. We've had a report of an electrical fault in this building and we need to check it out," said Biff.

"Bit late for you guys isn't it?" queried Mike as he opened the door to admit them.

"Tell us about it," muttered Ron. "But at least we're on overtime. That's some consolation."

Mike continued, "There's four flats here but I don't know if everyone's at home. But, Mr. Blight downstairs has spare keys in case of an emergency. He's a sort of caretaker and live in landlord."

Biff pretended to study his sheet. "Says here the owner thinks it's flat four."

Mike thinks for a moment. "I believe that's the film guy, Jon. Don't think he's in at the mo."

Biff skated over his comment, "Not a problem, the owner," he consulted his list again, "Mr. Carstairs has furnished us with a set of keys."

"But not one for the front door?" asked Mike.

"No, not one for the front door." Ron grinned, "Think he wanted to be sure someone was on the premises to let us in."

"Yeah," laughed Biff. "In case we rifled the flats." He noticed Mike's look of consternation, "Only kidding, mate. I assume it's upstairs?"

"Yes, second floor. If you want anything give me a shout."

"Cheers, mate. Come on, we'd best get on. Don't want to be too late for dinner," concluded Biff and made for the stairs.

The two agents, took the stairs two at a time until they found flat four. Biff looked about him while Ron tried a key from his collection. Three twists and clicks and they were in. They closed the door firmly behind them and set to work.

"I'll take the hall, first bedroom, kitchen and bathroom," asserted Ron.

"Check," affirmed Biff as he began to unpack his surveillance equipment and post listening devices in strategic places in the living room. He then settled himself at Jon's iMac, shooed Jon's cat, Rumble, off the PC desk, booted up the computer and began copying files and other data onto a flash drive before implanting a spy ware and retrieval programme to 'eavesdrop' on Jon whenever he used this computer. Rumble sat on the mat watching them curiously.

Biff was obviously a technical wizard like the man, Alan, who had inserted a programme in the office computer at Monumentous Films who was currently operating in the back of the black van with his partner, Steve. Biff spoke back softly to Alan through a hidden chest mic as he tested the spy ware, "Are you getting this?"

Alan came through on Biff's earpiece, "Oh yeah! That's perfect."

"I've copied everything. Do you want to do a final sweep, in case I've missed something?"

The two continued to exchange notes until both men were satisfied.

The remains of a sumptuous meal lay on the table. Amy flopped onto the sofa. Her wine sloshed in her glass and she giggled.

Jon started to gather his things together and Amy watched him with a hint of regret and innate sadness in her face. "Well, I suppose I ought to try and get to the hospital and see what I can glean on the lab results."

"That's if anyone's talking," observed Jon. He sat back down and looked earnestly at her. "Better munch some peppermints or gum, if you're going to the hospital. We don't want them thinking you're a lush," he advised. "And be careful."

"Am I ever?" She paused and looked at Jon with an indeterminate twinkle in her eye. "Are you sure you don't want another drink?"

Jon shook his head, swallowed down the remains of his wine, pushed his chair back and put on his jacket. He hesitated as he saw Amy lying provocatively on the bed.

"I know, you have a cat who needs you," murmured Amy sorrowfully.

This jolted Jon into action. "Yes, poor little beggar and he hasn't been fed today, or been out. I have to go." He picked up his things and exited the hotel suite.

Amy sat for a little while and finished off her drink. She glanced around the suite. "Such a pity, leaving all this. Ah well." Amy began to collect her things and sang softly to herself. It was one of Electra's songs.

The two agents, Ron and Biff continued to work quietly and efficiently. Ron was standing on the coffee table trying to insert a small camera in the main light's lampshade. There was a knock at the door. They both froze. Ron swiftly pocketed the camera and jumped down. Biff moved cautiously toward the door. Ron assented with a jerk of his head, "Who is it?"

The muffled reply came through the door; "It's me, Mike, from downstairs. I've got you some tea."

The operatives exchanged exasperated looks. Ron mouthed, "Let him in," with a gesture of frustration. Biff opened the door and revealed the student, Mike, standing there with a tray of tea and a plate of assorted biscuits.

"Thought you could do with a cuppa working late an' all. Never know how long you're going to be." Mike took the opportunity of scrutinising his surroundings, which did not go unnoticed by the agents.

"Er, thanks, mate," said Ron.

"Mike," he corrected. "Have you found it?"

"What?" asked Biff.

"The fault," replied Mike.

"Oh, not yet. Still looking, and then again, it may not be here at all," returned Ron. He glanced at his watch. "We better get a move on, don't want to be here all night."

"Yeah, right. I'll let you get on. Just pop this lot back outside my door when you're done, Flat two." Mike took another good look around the room and smiled at Biff and Ron. "See ya!"

"Right you are."

Mike left and Ron closed the door after him. They hurriedly finished up, planting a listening device in the landline telephone. Ron picked up his tea and slugged it down. He wandered to the window and looked out as Biff swallowed down his tea in haste.

A black taxicab was pulling up outside in the street. Jon got out and leaned in the driver's window and paid him.

Ron urged Biff, "Hurry up, Curtis is back."

The men took a cursory look around, nothing seemed out of place. They picked up their things and the tea tray and hastened to the door. They slipped out onto the landing. Rumble seized the opportunity and made his escape from the flat, too. They closed the door firmly and started down the stairs.

Jon entered the building and began making his way toward his floor where he met his cat followed by the two 'electricians'.

"Rumble! What are you doing out?" The cat jumped into Jon's arms and made a fuss of his master as Biff and Ron passed him on the stairs.

Biff called out in a perfunctory manner, "Good night."

Jon was puzzled but responded automatically, "Good night."

The agents dumped the tray outside flat two, as requested, and made their way outside.

Jon reached his flat and opened the door. He looked around but everything seemed in order. The cat jumped out of Jon's arms as Jon bent to dump his bag. Rumble ran to his empty food bowl and mewed. Jon crossed to his PC and touched it. It felt warm. He looked around suspiciously. His eyes focused on Rumble. "If you've got cat hairs on my PC again, Rumble. I'll have you for gloves!" he exclaimed. Jon started up the iMac and checked his files. Everything appeared to be fine. He shrugged and went online to access the Internet. As he waited for his virus scanner to finish he went to feed Rumble who gave one of his huge rumbling purrs.

Outside in the street, the two operatives raced back to the black van. "That was a bit too close," muttered Biff.

"Damn and blast," swore Ron as he felt in his pocket. "I forgot to place the last camera."

"No matter, we've done enough," said Biff.

"What about the student?" asked Ron.

"Silly sod. He'll have to go," decided Biff.

"Shame, but we can't risk it," said Ron.

"Park around the corner. You may have a wait. I'll sit in the pub. With a bit of luck, he may come in. If not, I'll get back to his flat. Do the job there, but it's not ideal."

Ron nodded in agreement and climbed in the driver's seat and started the engine. Biff pulled off his SEEB boiler suit, threw it in through the window and Ron handed Biff his jacket. In the coat pocket the tools of their trade could be seen with the bulge of a revolver. Ron scrabbled around in the glove compartment and pulled out a shielded syringe and a pack of tablets. He passed them to Biff who secreted them in his inside pocket.

Biff patted the side of the van. Ron pulled away from the kerb and Biff crossed the road and made his way to the pub, The Lazy Landlord. He stepped inside and marched up to the bar where he purchased a drink and a packet of crisps and settled at a table by the window overlooking the street, where he had a clear view of the building housing Jon's flat. He saw the lights shining in both Jon's lounge and in the one belonging to the student, Mike.

Biff glanced back at the landlord, Greg, and observed the man's behaviour. Each drink ordered went into a fresh clean glass even when a customer brought his empty glass to the counter it was removed and washed. That was good. Biff turned his attention back outside to the shared house he'd previously invaded. He was prepared to wait as long as was necessary.

Biff checked his watch. He drummed his fingers and tapped his foot in time to the music playing in the bar and waited. He hoped he would not have to sit there for too long. He stared across the road and noticed that the lights were now extinguished in Mike's flat. Biff watched the building all the more closely.

Inside Jon was sitting at his iMac and he typed into the Google Search Engine, 'Electra Conspiracy' and a number of items immediately popped up on his screen. He selected one, but as he began to read the information on the screen, the file deleted before his eyes. He tried another related site but access was denied. Jon chose yet another website from the list and received the message that the page could not be found. Frustrated, Jon hit the refresh button and received the same message. Infuriated he tried another from the Google search but that file was also inaccessible. Annoyed he slammed his hand on the table.

Across the road from the flat, the student Mike who had admitted the 'electricians' left the building and crossed to the pub. He entered and strolled cheerily to the bar. He glanced about him and saw an acquaintance at the pool table and raised his hand in acknowledgement. He noticed Biff at the window table and smiled. Biff nodded and turned away. Mike had recognised him.

'Shame, he was a nice bloke,' Biff thought. 'If he hadn't have known me. I could have let him be. It would have been risky … But now the student's fate was definitely sealed'.

Mike stood at the bar patiently, waiting to be served. The landlord grinned, "Usual, Mike?"

"Please, Greg" answered the young man.

The landlord poured a pint for Mike who fished in his pocket for some money. He took a good swig, wiping the froth from his lips with the back of his hand. "Got any fifty p's?" asked Mike indicating the pool table with a jerk of his head.

The landlord changed a fiver. Mike walked to the pool table and slapped his money down by the coin slot indicating his intention for a game with the winner when the other players had finished.

Biff drained his pint. He returned the glass to the bar placing it next to Mike's pint. Biff loitered while the landlord served someone else and ensuring he was unobserved he dropped a tablet into Mike's pint, which instantly dissolved and then he left.

Mike returned to the bar and downed the rest of his drink. He ordered another to take with him to the pool table. The empty glass was immediately whisked away by the landlord and washed, and another pint was poured.

Mike strolled to the pool table and gestured a greeting to a short tubby guy who had won the last game of pool against one of Mike's friends. Suddenly, he stopped and his throat became constricted. He clutched desperately at his neck as he gasped for air before finally buckling at his knees and collapsing on the floor. The customers looked on, frozen in horror as they watched the young man writhe and convulse. He began to froth at the mouth. Blood started to weep from his eyes and nose. A young woman fainted unable to pull her eyes away from the shocking sight in front of her.

"Someone call an ambulance," shouted the tubby man. "Quickly!"

The barman, Greg managed to move away from the scene playing out in front of him and he ran to the bar, snatched the receiver and with shaking hands dialled nine, nine, nine.

"Ambulance, please, now. There's a man. It looks as if he's dying."

Chapter Eight

Fast Happenings

JON WAS BUSY WORKING on his PC when he heard a siren. He rose and looked out of his window to see an ambulance draw up outside his local pub and two paramedics rushed inside. He looked on curiously as someone was carried out on a stretcher from The Lazy Landlord and into the back of the waiting ambulance. Jon noticed that the person was completely encased in a body bag and so, presumably, must be dead. He murmured involuntarily, "Poor sod."

Jon heaved a huge sigh; his concentration was broken. He rubbed his forehead and dropped into an armchair. Rumble leapt up onto his lap and began to purr and knead his leg, "Ouch! Claws like needles you've got. Settle down." The cat turned around twice and curled into a ball and Jon stroked his beloved pet. His mind was working overtime and he picked up a pad and pen at the side of him and began to make notes. He listed the known facts, cross matching them with what had been officially reported. He made another list of the information they had discovered for themselves. It was becoming a fascinating picture of contradictory evidence.

He stopped and chewed the end of his pen and murmured aloud, "I wonder how Amy is getting on?"

Amy was dressed in a white lab coat complete with an ID badge. She sat with an auburn haired nurse in the hospital canteen stirring her coffee. The conversation was easy and it wasn't difficult to steer it around to the events surrounding Electra's death.

"I was such a fan," gushed Amy immersed in her role. "I don't suppose you were on duty that evening, were you?"

"No such luck," replied the woman whose voice revealed that she was Irish. "I would have liked to have been in here that night. Some people are making a fortune telling their stories to the papers about what went on."

"You'd sell your story?" said Amy feigning shock.

"Huh, on my salary I'd take anything I could get," responded nurse, Gillian Brown.

"I know what you mean. I have to take everything on offer, whether I want to or not until I get a permanent position," mused Amy.

"I'll bet. I think that sucks. It does, truly."

"Ah well, that's life. No job, no money, no money no food, and no roof over my head. I have to take what I can," said Amy philosophically. She paused and took a sip of coffee, "So, who around here could give me the goss?" Amy asked.

"The what?"

"Goss… gossip. Someone round here must know. It would certainly improve my street cred with my friends," Amy added laughingly. "There must be more than is being printed in the papers, I'm sure of it." She studied the nurse quizzically.

"I don't know about that but if you're that curious you should talk to him." Nurse Brown pointed across at a young man who had just entered and grabbed himself a coffee.

"Why? Who is he?"

"Mac works in the labs and he was on duty that night. He had to deal with all the blood samples apparently." She glanced at her watch. "Gosh, I'd better scoot. I'm already five minutes late. The sister on my ward is an absolute tartar. She'll do anything to humiliate me. Good luck with your quest. Catch you again!" And the Irish colleen that was Nurse Gillian Brown hurried away to her duty.

Amy studied the young man before picking up her coffee and crossing to his table. She indicated an empty seat. "Mind if I sit here?" she asked politely.

"It's a free country," replied Mac absently and then he looked, really looked at Amy. He was surprised that someone with Amy's looks should want to sit with him and immediately became suspicious. These suspicions grew when Amy began to talk.

"I hear you've had all the exciting work on the Electra case," she said boldly deciding it was better to speak straight out rather than dodging around the subject.

"What's it to you?" Mac questioned in an offhand manner, designed to close all further conversation.

"I'm a big fan," Amy enthused. "Aren't you? I bet you've had all the press around?"

"One or two," admitted Mac ignoring her first question. He was unused to any attention from a female and definitely never from anyone in Amy's league.

"Is it true what they say in the papers? About the driver… Karl Goodwin?"

Mac studied Amy's face before replying, "You're very well informed, Miss….?"

"Call me Amy," she asserted.

"Just what do you do around here?" quizzed Mac. "I've never seen you before."

"Oh, I belong to an agency. They sent me."

"To do what?"

"I'm a psycho pharmacologist." Mac raised his eyebrows with renewed interest his guard beginning to slip. Amy pressed home her advantage, "A locum. I'm only here for ten days."

Mac softened his expression and became more affable. "They'll get their money's worth out of you, I'm sure. He looked at her huge eyes and began to warm to her. "So, you're an Electra fan?"

"Isn't everyone? … So, tell me, what really happened? I won't say a word. Scouts' honour!" Amy persisted and smiled at him engagingly, raising her fingers in a mock scout salute.

Mac felt himself smiling back, "I can't tell you much. She was D.O.A. Dead-on-arrival. The driver and Ahmed Khalid were dead, too. From what I understand they both died instantly in the crash."

"Oh? I had heard that a doctor worked on Ahmed and had tried to revive him?"

"May have done. I don't know." It didn't look like Mac was about to say anymore.

"The papers say the driver was drunk…" Amy continued to pump the young man.

Mac leaned forward conspiratorially and lowered his voice. He glanced about him to ensure no one else was in earshot. "What I can tell you is that the results of our tests don't tally."

"How?" questioned Amy drawing closer to him to listen.

"The blood samples revealed he was three times over the limit, but…"

"But…?" prompted Amy.

"I shouldn't really be saying this…"

"You can't stop now… I won't breathe a word, honestly."

"Well, when we did the autopsy, the stomach contents didn't correlate with the blood samples. His liver was clear and healthy. One we catalogued as that of a non-drinker or someone who had just the odd one. It didn't add up."

Amy leaned forward to whisper and Mac took this as a sign of interest in him. He picked up two sugar lumps for his coffee and also leaned forward into Amy. She asked, "No trace of alcohol?"

"None in his stomach, bladder or on the cells inside his mouth but the blood samples showed that there was alcohol present, a lot of alcohol and more than that I found carbon monoxide. Just like a suicide. Like someone had got drunk to give himself the courage to top himself." Mac paused a moment and requested, "But, please, keep this quiet. There's a press ban on this. I could lose my job." He dropped the sugar lumps into his coffee from a height with an attempt at being suave. The sugar plopped in and the coffee splashed up into his face breaking the moment. Amy struggled not to laugh.

Mac grabbed a serviette and mopped his face, embarrassed. He tried to regain some composure, "If you ask me, the samples were contaminated or switched. They have actually scheduled more tests."

"Wow," said Amy acting suitably impressed. She glanced at the canteen clock, "My, is that the time? Darn, my break is over. I'd best get back to work…er…" she pretended to search for his name.

"Mac. My friends call me Mac. Maybe I'll see you later."

"Maybe. I'll look forward to it." Amy rose and Mac beamed.

"I hope so. Take care now." Mac sat back and lifted his coffee cup for a sip and watched Amy's well-shaped legs walk her out of the canteen. She looked back and gave him a little wave. He leaned back in his chair and grinned, "Well, all right!"

Jon's flat was looking chaotic. Paper had spewed out from the printer and littered the floor. His PC was covered with 'post it' notes of names with question marks: Karl Goodwin? Paul Grayson? Chico Towns? Malcolm West? And many others involved in Electra's life, her band and even the studio technicians whose names he knew. He was immersed in checking the history of all Electra's known associates in the production team, management agency, as well as the current band and previous band members. He had accessed 192 records online and paid to register so he could examine the corresponding electoral rolls.

Jon inserted a new search in Birth, Marriages and Deaths for Karl Goodwin born between 1978 and 1983. Not knowing the man's birth date, he had to guess and allow himself some leeway. The search pulled up five possibilities. He bookmarked the pages and scrawled the information on his notepad, just to be sure. He didn't want this information to be deleted before his eyes. He then typed in the name of Paul Grayson, and guessing again at a date of birth, he entered born somewhere between the dates of nineteen fifty-nine through to nineteen sixty-four. Although, with this search he wasn't too certain as Grayson was an American, or at least that's what the man's accent told him.

Jon waited for the search to do its job and sat back in his chair and rubbed his shoulder, which was aching from sitting tensely at his PC. He sighed heavily and studied what he had discovered so far. He grabbed a red marker pen and crossed off some of the names, which had obviously checked out as legitimate.

"That's me done for the moment, Rumble. I'm bushed." The cat looked up at him and mewed as Jon stretched and yawned. He shut down his PC and stood up. Rumble followed him to the bedroom and jumped on the bed, purring and waiting for Jon to retire for the night.

Max Stafford talked in low tones to someone standing just outside the doorway of his office. Max turned back into his workspace as footsteps moved away. The distinctive metal tips on his heels punched a hole in the silence. Max wandered around the office checking his agents' work. He stopped by Claire and Jack's desks.

Jack was scrutinising a pile of paperwork and correlating his findings with phone records and information fed to him by Claire. Every detail, every fact had to be checked and double checked for accuracy.

Claire was studying her computer screen. She was still engaged in monitoring the numerous conspiracy sites in multiple windows on screen and accessing the identities of those using them. She sighed heavily. It was tedious work.

Max crossed back along the office and firmly closed his door. He instantly marched over to Claire and Jack, "Things have moved up a notch." Claire and Jack turned to Max and looked at him questioningly. "It's getting a little messy."

"What do you mean?" asked Claire.

"There was a witness, a student, a guy. We had to get rid of him."

"Bloody hell!" blurted out Claire.

"I don't like it any more than you do," growled Max. "It had to be done."

"And orders are orders," said Claire sarcastically. "That was someone's son, brother, boyfriend..." She stopped, feeling exasperated, but Max just ignored her.

"These filmmakers," continued Max. "Would anyone miss them?"

"What?" exploded Claire, unable to contain herself.

Jack picked up a sheaf of papers and glanced through them pulling out two sheets. "The woman's not a problem, no relatives, nothing. The guy's a bit more problematic."

"Now, hold on," interrupted Claire.

Max stopped her with a glance, "It's just a precaution. Until we find out how much they know, or are likely to know, whether they are aware of what they know or not." He drew himself up to his full height and ordered, "If necessary, wipe their ID's. Leave them nowhere to run. Then we move in."

"Then what do we do?" cut in Claire, "Brainwash them?"

"It's a possibility. But for now, we need to get at Miss Wilde's laptop," asserted Max.

"Why?" Claire asked.

"Currently, we can track all the company's activities except what she does on that laptop. We need to cover everything. Jack, sort it."

Jack nodded his head. "I'll get Biff and Ron onto it."

"Do it now," ordered Max.

Jack obliged and patched himself through to Special Ops on screen. Biff's face filled Jack's monitor as Jack explained the assignment.

"So, we're to put Miss Wilde under surveillance?" confirmed Biff.

Max broke in, "Yes, watch her twenty-four seven. We need to get into her laptop."

"We'll get away, then, Horberry Mews isn't it?"

"It is. Check in when you've something to report. Otherwise, every two hours."

Biff acknowledged and the screen went black.

From the subterranean car park underneath the Security Building, the black van emerged like an avenging demon. The rubber on its wheels squealed as the van hurtled around the corner and along the street. It made its way to Horberry Mews.

The team would take it in shifts to watch, record and monitor all of Amy's movements that they could, right down to every twitch of an eyebrow. They would stay on her until they had her daily routine timetabled to the minute, even her loo stops! The night was long. There was no movement in Amy's flat, at all. Hours passed, and operatives changed.

Biff and Ron were on the morning shift. Amy had been seen opening her curtains and sipping something from a bright yellow mug as she walked past the window. The zoom on the camera revealed the mug had a smiley face.

Minutes later Amy emerged unaware of the barrage of camera shots taken in quick succession. She was carrying her laptop and walked briskly toward the corner coffee shop, Chatterbox.

Biff alerted the central office and spoke into his mouthpiece, "She's out. Morning run to the coffee shop."

"Stay with her."

Biff listened to further instructions through his earpiece. "Right!"

In a seedy basement tech lab, Max and Jack were in conference. The cameras in the corner of the room were ignored, just like the plastic chairs.

The team knew they only had a small time frame to try and appropriate Amy's laptop. Jack, the office clown, and Max were enthusiastically engaged in childish banter that Claire was uncertain about, not knowing whether she should join in or not.

Max affirmed, "Her laptop's never out of her sight. She rarely works at home."

"Starbucks shop writer, I know, she thinks she's JK Rowling," said Jack.

Claire attempted to chip in, "A little more 'Sex in the City' don't you think?"

"I'm never up that late unless I'm working... like now. Right through the night," Max replied.

"Chick TV," continued Jack.

"Okay, back to business. Ms. Wilde's laptop," ordered Max.

"Model?" asked Jack.

"Apple MacBook Pro, titanium case," confirmed Claire.

"Stylish," said Jack. "Not very single mother there."

"What do you mean?" asked Claire, puzzled.

"She's a driven career woman," said Max.

Claire raised an eyebrow. "Ha! Being a single mother's probably driven more careers than you'd imagine."

"Hmm, you've got me there," said Jack. Then his tone became more business like, "Download time is about thirty seconds for the trace programme." He paused and his brow furrowed in concentration.

"Be creative. Think," instructed Max. "How do we get that laptop from her? Thirty seconds is a long time."

"Steal the laptop...?" said Jack questioningly.

"And accidentally drop it thirty seconds later on, down the road?" muttered Claire sarcastically.

"The casing is pretty tough... What about if I steal the laptop? Then you come along as a 'have a go hero', wrestle me to the ground, retrieve it and return it?" Jack beamed at them both.

"In the coffee shop?" questioned Max incredulously.

"You can chase me out of the coffee shop," continued Jack.

"Hm. She's the kind of woman who would run after you herself. It's too risky," said Claire dismissing the idea.

"Then that's where you come in..." rallied Jack. "You can be choking on... NO! You can be a pregnant woman. Your waters break and she'll stop to help while I run off with it," said Jack delightedly. He was obviously pleased with his suggestion.

Max shook his head trying to rein in Jack's enthusiasm and creative input. "No, Jack, no. Simple. Keep it simple," sighed Max.

Claire looked askance and ordered, "Jack, make yourself useful and get me an Apple catalogue."

Jack meekly obeyed and picked one up that was lying on the top of a bag of 'Layers Mash' chicken food standing in the corner of the office waiting to be transported back to Jack's flat. He brushed some fine powder off it that had escaped from the packaging and handed it to Claire.

"What have you got in mind?" asked Max.

"I can't remember off-hand but I think it's got an infra-red port for a modem. Set me up with another laptop in the coffee shop and I can pretty well email it to her." Claire smiled gratifyingly.

Max became efficient, once more, "What do you need?"

Claire turned to Jack, "I'll need some Jack style antics while I send an input signal."

"Will she have to be online?" asked Max.

"Maybe. But that's something Jack can do; remote dialling and all that. Get us a couple of laptops, same model as hers. We'll pull them apart and come up with something."

"I'll set up some sort of distraction," affirmed Max.

"Not too subtle, eh? This one likes to think she's seen everything."

"So, what are we going to do?" asked Jack.

"Put our thinking caps on, Jack. Put our thinking caps on," asserted Max. "We must be vigilant and keep up the good work. I will have to draft in more men. It is Electra's funeral tomorrow. We will need a heavy presence there. And then, when Ms. Wilde falls back into her known routine, we can strike."

Claire glanced at Jack whose face was furrowed in thought. He caught Claire's eye and immediately went into a Bruce Forsythe pose of leaning over to the side with his fist on his forehead.

Jack straightened up. "Good game, good game," he muttered, before snapping his fingers. "I've got it! This'll work!" and he grinned broadly at Max and Claire. He stopped, "No, too crude…" He paced around and thought some more, "What about? ... Nah! It's been done…" Claire and Max watched him with mild amusement, "Okay," he said slowly, "This could work, if…" he stopped and looked at his boss and colleague, "Say, I'm getting plenty of ideas, what about you?"

Max rolled his eyes and was just about to speak, when Jack shouted out loud, jumped in the air and punched the air above him. "Yes, yes, yes!!! This will work and I guarantee she won't have seen anything like this. Nor will either of you," and he grinned triumphantly.

Max and Claire exchanged a glance and waited for Jack to enlighten them. He licked his lips in anticipation; he was going to enjoy this. He knew it would be successful. They were going to have to coax the idea out of him. Oh yes, he'd enjoy it.

Security CCTV outside the church filmed every action, every thought crossing the faces of the attendees and monitored the crowds. Cameras behind the tinted glass of the black van took shots in rapid succession of all those present, capturing every movement, every nuance of body language. It would all be carefully scrutinised later.

The street outside the church was packed with people, lining both sides of the route the hearse had taken from Electra's house to the church. A screen had been erected in the square for mourners and fans to follow the service that was being taken inside. The way was strewn with flowers. Bouquet upon bouquet piled up outside the cemetery gates adjacent to the church. Electra seemed to have fans from all walks of life and of all ages, some openly sobbed into handkerchiefs, while others with eyes downcast looked the epitome of misery. The security guards were stunned at the overwhelming response of the mourning public.

Droves of people, politicians, royalty and stars filed out from the church. Police were there in force holding back the watching crowds as press photographers vied for position to record on film, photos of the rich and famous. Television reporters from all channels were covering the proceedings whilst only the BBC was allowed access inside the church.

Malcolm West, members of Electra's band and studio technicians appeared at the close of the service. They all looked serious and solemn. They were followed by Jon and Amy, who walked with their shoulders drooping, miserably. Ibrahim, Carol wearing a hat with a veil, as a mark of respect, and Paul Grayson, his arm in a sling, who was now out of hospital, came next.

The cameras caught it all, the melancholic mood; and the bright sunshine seemed out of place on this day of sadness. There wasn't a cloud in the sky and strains of Electra's hit songs filtered outside to the waiting crowds, who shuffled their feet and waited for the final procession to the cemetery.

Malcolm West narrowed his eyes as he watched Ibrahim approach Jon and Amy. They exchanged a few words. Ibrahim glanced around and almost caught West's eye but Mal looked down as if it was of no consequence. The three engaged in further conversation before shaking hands warmly and proceeding to the cemetery and graveside reserved for close friends and family. The camera shutter clicked.

The Earl of Shaftesbury comforted his weeping mother as they followed the coffin for the internment and the milling throng, pressed forward to the cemetery gate eager to gain a glimpse of Electra's friends and family. This, too, was recorded.

The cameras even caught Biff and Ron who were on duty scanning the masses of people for any supposed threat. The black van was parked on the roadside, almost totally surrounded by ordinary members of the public. But its presence could be felt. The vehicle appeared to have a life of its own, as if it was a sinister character in a suspense thriller. The risen antenna with its spy-ware continued its surveillance.

Amy turned as she was entering the cemetery, and another picture was taken. She noticed the black monster and a feeling of dull foreboding ran through her. In spite of the heat of the sun, she shivered. She brushed the feeling off as being a result of her saddened state.

Amy tucked her arm into Jon's, as she needed human contact and the warmth of another close to her. Jon looked down at her and gave a half smile as if in understanding and to reassure her. The contact served to heighten her emotions and a tear tumbled down her cheek. She sniffed back the tide that threatened to flow and wiped her eyes with her free hand.

Jon and Amy pushed through the throng as the press strained forward trying to single out the celebrities and aristocracy for scoops for their morning papers. A hush rippled through the crowd as word spread that the Prince was on his way out through the church with other members of the royal family.

Jon and Amy hurried away.

"Where to?" asked Amy sadly. "I don't want to go home and I don't want to go to the wake."

"We'll be expected there," said Jon curtly. "We ought to put in an appearance or it won't look good."

"I know. I just don't feel up to it," sniffed Amy struggling to hold back her tears.

"Let's just go for half an hour, you can manage that can't you?" said Jon putting his arm protectively around Amy.

"I suppose," said Amy blowing into her hankie.

"I promise, we won't stay long and then you can come back to my place and unwind. We still have work to do." He pulled Amy into him, "Hey, you're freezing. Sod the underground, let's get a cab."

"If we can find one in this bedlam," murmured Amy.

The two filmmakers reached the end of the street, which had been closed off to all but essential traffic and briskly walked toward the main thoroughfare. There were black cabs a plenty and Jon successfully waved one down and they made their way to the Dorchester Hotel in Park Lane.

The CCTV witnessed the black van, like a phantom from hell, following at a discrete distance.

The couple were amongst the first to arrive but didn't accept the proffered champagne and canapés. They acknowledged some of the other guests, who had begun to enter, with an incline of the head and a wave of the hand.

"Have something, Amy. Come on," pressed Jon. "Just in celebration of Electra's life."

Amy nodded dully and reluctantly accepted a glass of champagne, "The problem is that once I start drinking I won't want to stop. I feel like going on a complete bender."

"I promise you, we'll just pay our respects and leave," Jon promised.

Amy acquiesced and crossed to a corner of the room. She sat hugging her glass and looking miserable as more people began to come into the room.

Malcolm West was the first of the advance party to arrive along with Chico Towns and Electra's band members. He raised his hand to Jon in acknowledgement, grabbed a glass of champagne and crossed to them both.

"Sad day, sad day," said West shaking his head. He paused before pursing his lips and asked, "How are you getting on with the movie?"

Amy was about to speak but Jon answered, "We're still sorting out the footage we have got and we are trying to create a eulogy to her by involving some of her fans. It will take a while and we haven't much heart for it at the moment as you can imagine."

"Of course, of course," said West perfunctorily.

Amy watched the interaction curiously and looked from one to the other as Jon described what they were going to do regarding the film. Eventually, Jon came to a halt and smiled, "So, now you are in the picture."

"Yes, don't forget to keep me in the loop... I thought I saw you talking to Mr. Khalid," probed West.

"Yes, sharing our commiserations, nothing important," said Jon.

"Yes, well he has got some rather wild ideas," mused West.

"Yes, crazy. That's what we thought," said Jon warning Amy with his eyes. "It was an accident, pure and simple. Tragic, yes, but an accident, none-the-less," continued Jon.

Malcolm West inclined his head in agreement. He turned his gaze on Amy who felt compelled to speak, "Sorry, Mal. I don't know how long I can stay. I am just too upset. I think I might get back home, if you don't mind. Have a long soak in the bath and guzzle a bottle of wine. It will do me good."

"I understand," said West. "I'll make your apologies."

"I'll come with you," said Jon sympathetically. "Can't leave my partner at a time like this. As you can see, Mal, she needs looking after."

"No problem," said West. He smiled engagingly at them and raised his glass. "To Electra's film. May it be a winner."

"To Electra's film," Amy swallowed down her champagne and rose. "Sorry, Mal." She walked to the door and exited through the growing party of people arriving.

Jon shrugged at West, as if to say, 'Women!' He placed his empty glass on a tray and followed Amy.

Malcolm snorted derisively and watched Jon Curtis leave before crossing to the Earl of Shaftesbury who had just arrived. He gave his commiserations, "I am so sorry for your loss." The Earl accepted the sympathies expressed. West continued, "The world has lost an exciting and vibrant star. For such a cruel accident to eclipse her wonderful life, it is more than shocking. I had plans for Electra, big plans."

The Earl paused and studied the producer's face, "She will still make you money, Mal. Probably even more now she's gone."

"But, I'd rather have her here with us," he gushed.

"Maybe, maybe not," the Earl said.

If Malcolm West felt uncomfortable, he didn't show it. "Now, now, that's a bit harsh."

"Rest assured, Mal, someone is to blame and I intend to find out who caused this crash."

"Good luck with that. I heard you were gunning for the press," probed West.

"I feel they are mainly to blame. If they hadn't persisted in chasing her everywhere she went and harassing her every time she went out; the accident wouldn't have happened. She wouldn't have needed to flee."

Malcolm West nodded, "I can't deny it. You have something there."

West spotted one of Electra's band and apologised, "If you'll excuse me, I need to have a word with Brett Lane." He was keen to escape and work the room and crossed purposefully to Electra's drummer.

West glanced back uneasily at the Earl as he endeavoured to speak with Brett Lane. He saw the Earl's thoughtful expression change as he helped his mother to a seat where they sat and watched the guests coming and going. Relieved that there was to be no more drama West focused on Electra's drummer and asked Brett about the whereabouts of some of the recent rehearsal tapes. He knew the drummer was in possession of some try outs of new material for a future album.

Suddenly, a fracas broke out behind him. West turned to see the Earl rise in anger as two press photographers entered and attempted to join the wake. They had foolishly come into the room complete with cameras. West saw the Earl stride furiously toward them shouting, "You are not welcome here nor are you wanted. How dare you have such a flagrant disregard for my family at this time of mourning? Get out! Get out, now, before I call Security."

Malcolm West excused himself from Brett and hurried across to diffuse the situation. He steered the Earl away who was now on the verge of tears. West jerked his head to Paul Grayson to accompany the photographers out of the room. West felt that this outburst was bound to be reported in the papers tomorrow. 'Good,' thought West. It would serve his purpose very well. The publicity would be excellent for sales; any publicity in West's eyes was worthwhile.

Amy sat on Jon's sofa in her funereal black, her eyes red from crying. Once she had entered the flat she had completely broken down. Jon attempted to comfort her, and Rumble, not used to such miserable company was rubbing himself around Jon and Amy's legs trying to show his love for his master and his friend.

Their work was scattered around them and even more 'post it' notes were stuck on his PC. "Why did you say that to Mal?" quizzed Amy.

"What?"

"All that eulogy stuff."

"Well, as discussed before, we don't want anyone knowing what we are really doing. That's for us and Mr. Khalid, only. You looked as if you might spill the beans."

"Well, I wouldn't," said Amy.

"You weren't thinking straight and I couldn't take the chance. No one else must even get an inkling of what we're doing," said Jon sagely.

Jon leaned back and Rumble took the opportunity and jumped onto his lap. The cat began kneading Jon's thighs before turning around to settle down to sleep.

"I agree. I don't trust anyone anymore," continued Amy.

"I hope you trust me," laughed Jon.

"Of course," smiled Amy batting him gently with her hand. "Jon?"

"Mm?"

"Do you think we're being followed?"

"One way to find out." Jon put Rumble down who complained with a loud mew and jumped up onto Amy's lap. Jon moved toward the window and tried not to make his movements noticeable by anyone that happened to be outside. He peeped through the nets and saw a sinister black van parked across the road from his flat. "I'm sure I've seen that van before," he murmured.

Amy rose and carried Rumble to join Jon at the window. "It was at the cemetery," she said convinced of the fact.

"But, there were so many vehicles there," observed Jon. "No, I've seen it somewhere else."

"I'm positive I've seen it before, too."

Jon wrinkled his forehead as he struggled to remember. "One night last week, there was a black van parked in the same spot. The same night I came home and Rumble was out… When some poor sod in the pub got stretchered out."

"Could be a different van or perhaps it belongs to someone living opposite," Amy suggested.

"Could be… but a black van… they are not as common as white vans."

Amy leaned forward and pulled at the curtain a little to get a better view. She studied the van. Yes, she had seen it. But where? She tussled with her memory. "I have seen it, Jon. I'm sure it was at the cemetery gates."

Across the road, Biff and Ron saw the slight movement of the drapes in

Jon's flat. "They've spotted us. Drive around the block, Ron. We can walk to the pub. There's a good enough view from there. The boys in the back will keep tabs, come on." He glanced through to the back of the van where there were two more agents, Alan and Steve, with headphones monitoring all the conversation in Jon's flat. They nodded back at him to show they were on the case. Ron started the engine.

Amy and Jon continued watching through the window. "It's pulling away," observed Jon. "Now, is that because they've clocked us watching?"

"Are we paranoid, or what?" mused Amy.

"Too many conspiracy sites!" Jon replied.

"So, do we get back to work?"

"Day off," responded Jon. "Besides, I have…"

"I know, a germ of an idea," finished Amy.

Jon looked surprised and then grinned. "That's right! But, it can wait. Right now, I intend to get drunk, very, very drunk. Care to join me?"

Amy smiled. "Don't mind if I do," and she threw him a look that said, only this time you can't run out on me. "Definitely, yes. But first, I'm just going to backup all my files." She popped Rumble back on the floor, but the cat continued to pester her for attention.

"You really are paranoid."

"No, just cautious." Amy used two memory sticks to copy her hard drive. "From now on, I'll backup everything we do separately, just in case."

Jon rubbed his hands together. "Right let's crack open the wine."

Rumble leapt back into Amy's arms. "I'll get the glasses," said Amy putting Rumble down once more. The cat mewed in complaint.

Jon marched into the kitchen followed by Amy. "Pinot Grigio on ice, waiting for you, and a lovely little Rioja for me. And to go with it…" Jon hunted in the cupboard. "Hm… beans, eggs or a tin of corned beef…."

"There's nothing in the fridge either," said Amy putting two glasses on the table.

"Then take away it is… Pizza, Indian or Chinese?"

"Um, I quite fancy an Indian," said Amy.

"Give me a tea towel and I'll see what I can do?"

"Tea towel?"

"For a turban, I don't have any ornamental knives but a carver from the cutlery drawer might do."

"You're mad, do you know that?" laughed Amy.

"It's good to see you smile again," said Jon.

"Why? Did you think I'd forgotten how?" asked Amy.

"Nope. But you look prettier when you smile."

"Do I?" flirted Amy.

"Anyone does. Do you realise a baby can recognise a smile from fifty feet?"

"And what's that got to do with anything?"

"Nothing. A piece of information that may be useful on a quiz night."

But Amy had stopped listening she was studying the take away menu. "So, do you fancy something hot and spicy?"

"I do."

"Then I'll order a yashmak to go with the curry."

"A yashmak? Oh, I see to go with the turban. Better get seven veils, too."

"Why?"

"For the dance of course. You do dance, don't you?"

And so, they continued with more banter, more jokes and drank more wine.

Ibrahim poured a large glass of champagne for Carol and passed it to her. He turned to her and lifted her veil from her hat, took her by the shoulders and looked deeply into her eyes. "I don't know what I would have done without you today."

"All part of the job, Sir," replied Carol softly as she removed the hat and tossed it aside.

"No. I think you've done much more than your job, much more." His eyes burned into hers and Carol edged closer.

"Call me Ibrahim, please."

Carol whispered, her breath gently caressing his face, "Ibrahim... or Ib...? Ibby?"

Ibrahim smiled, "Ibby will do fine." Their faces drew closer, as if drawn by magnets. Their lips met and they kissed. "I need to unwind. I am going into the Jacuzzi. Would you care to join me?" Ibrahim breathed seductively through his words.

Carol moistened her lips and nodded shyly. "I'll get changed."

"Do. And take the champagne," sighed Ibrahim. "Please, light the candles. I'll be up in a short while. There's a long match lighter in the cabinet drawer."

His authoritative voice appeared to thrill her. He was a powerful man and he felt that she loved that. She ran lightly up the stairs and into her room while Ibrahim crossed to the large picture window and stared out at the night. He took a sip of his drink and his eyes filled with tears. He swallowed hard trying to dislodge the very physical lump that had manifested itself in his throat and he murmured, "Why? Oh God, why?" He downed the rest of his drink as he heard Carol exit her room and move into his.

Ibrahim turned and walked from the lounge, up the stairs and into his bedroom, where he disrobed. He put on some bathers and donned a fluffy bathrobe.

He stopped at his desk and picked up an album of photographs and press cuttings and opened it. It fell open at a picture of Ahmed, Electra, Karl and Paul Grayson. He lovingly traced his finger around Ahmed's smiling, handsome features. Sadly, he tossed it onto his bed with a sigh. It remained open at the same picture. Ibrahim moved into his luxurious en suite where the Jacuzzi was bubbling away. Carol was already in the tub and she smiled welcomingly at him. He removed his robe and stepped into the water. He settled opposite her and they gazed at each other.

Ibrahim pressed a button on the control pad and soft music filled the room. Numerous scented candles flickered around the bathroom creating a romantic mood. An ice bucket on a stand contained the open bottle of champagne. The crystal flutes rested on the top shelf of the spa.

Carol slipped across to him and moved away the lock of hair, which had fallen across his eyes. Ibrahim traced his finger down the side of her face and sighed, "Carol, Carol, Carol, Carol."

"That's me!" exclaimed Carol huskily. She playfully tapped his nose covering it in a mass of bubbles and she giggled. Ibrahim's eyes locked onto hers and he kissed her tenderly. He felt her respond with fervour and desire.

"I meant what I said. I don't know what I would have done these last few days." His voice was low and filled with an undercurrent of passion.

"Ibby!" she protested.

"No, let me finish! My world had fallen apart. I'd lost my only son... and Electra – I had hoped that she and Ahmed..." He struggled to contain the tears he felt rising again, ready to flow.

"Ssh!" Carol put her fingers onto his lips to quieten him. Then, she covered his face with kisses as he continued.

"Then you… You… came and…"

"I know."

"You're my saviour. I'm so lucky."

"I'm the lucky one," said Carol. "I've never known anyone like you. And I feel as if I have known you forever. It's crazy that it's in such a short time. For the first time in my life I'm with someone I really care about and who I feel cares about me."

Ibrahim drew closer and Carol helped him out of his bathing shorts. She kissed him more passionately and wrapped her legs around him as their kisses became more urgent. Carol's naked body pressed against his and her lips parted for another searching kiss.

A sheen of sweat began to glisten on Ibrahim's face, not with the heat of the tub but with the heat of desire. Ibrahim, sighed, "Oh, Carol."

"Not just Carol, your Carol."

Ibrahim entered her. She threw back her head in ecstasy. Passion and need drew them together. His eyes widened, "Carol, you are… you're a virgin."

Carol smiled and nodded. "I wanted my first to be special and there's no one more special, than you, Ibby."

"Then you are now my responsibility, it is our way. I will look after you, I promise."

Their bodies entwined and they luxuriated in the power of love and need. Ibrahim was now Carol's total focus as she pleasured him instinctively. Her inexperience mattered not as he guided her gently, nurturing the growth of her climax until she exploded in shuddering delight.

"I feel alive," she breathed as she arched her back and thrust her ample breasts into him, and rubbed them against his chest. "More alive than I have ever felt."

Ibrahim kissed her eyes, her nose and held her face in his hand. "No one will ever hurt you. I will see to that. I promise you."

Carol knew that his words were sincere and her feelings on this assignment were causing her great confusion but for now, she would enjoy what she had. She nuzzled his chest hair and murmured, "I love your chest. Please hold me."

Ibrahim wrapped his arms around her and held her close. Carol's eyes filled with tears, she didn't understand it.

"What is it? What's wrong?" asked Ibrahim his face creased in concern.

"It was all so beautiful," she sighed. "I never expected it to be like that."

Ibrahim felt desire course through his veins again and Carol welcomed him into her body and into her heart.

In Jon's flat, Jon was slumped on the settee holding an empty glass with Rumble sleeping at his side. A couple of empty bottles were at his feet. Amy hopped around trying to retrieve her shoes from under the table, where the remains of an Indian take away lay congealing on the plates. She moved to the window and peered out. The street seemed clear. There was no sign of the black van.

She heaved a sigh of relief and moved into the kitchen and took out her mobile phone, scrolled through her contacts and selected one. She hit the call button and waited, "Hello? Taxi...?" she whispered, not wanting to disturb Jon. "Yes, Wilde. Er... 07967 889242... Pardon? ... I'll wait outside the building, 44, Clifden Road, nearly opposite The Lazy Landlord Pub... Ten minutes? ...That's fine."

Amy tiptoed quietly around the flat gathering her belongings. Her jacket was half under Rumble and she tugged it gently. The cat's eyes opened wide at this intrusion and he gave an involuntary mew. Amy put her fingers to her lips. "Shush, you'll wake Jon," she whispered. Jon stirred and muttered in his sleep and Amy froze. She hurriedly tidied herself up and moved to the door where she turned and looked back at Jon with an expression of longing on her face. Unable to help herself she crossed back to the settee and placed a gentle kiss on the top of his head, and then retreated to the door to quietly let herself out.

At the click of the latch Jon stirred again. "Amy don't go," he murmured. Amy stopped. She wanted to stay but she wouldn't, not like this. When the time was right and Jon was stone cold sober; then, then it would be different.

Carol entered Ibrahim's bedroom from the en suite and picked up the album from off the bed. She studied the picture, her attention arrested by Karl's smiling face, and a look of fear crossed her features.

Ibrahim entered looking relaxed as he tied up his robe. He eyed her questioningly as he saw her with the album. "What are you doing with that?"

"I couldn't help noticing," she paused trying to keep her voice level. "Tell me, who are the others in the picture?"

Ibrahim pointed at each in turn, "That's Paul Grayson."

"Electra's bodyguard?"

"Correct," Ibrahim nodded.

Carol took a deep breath and in a tentative whisper asked, "And the other?"

"Karl Goodwin."

"Karl...?"

"He was Ahmed's driver and bodyguard."

"Is he the one who...?"

"Yes, he was driving."

Carol returned the book to Ibrahim and turned away, her face told its own story. She struggled to contain her tears and to still her trembling lip. She forced a smile, "I'll just go and dry my hair."

Carol left Ibrahim browsing through the rest of the album. She didn't trust herself to say another word. Carol knew now that she really did have no one. Ibrahim was to be more than an assignment, more than a lover that is if she could keep control.

Carol retreated to the safety and darkness of her room. She drew the curtains shutting out the lights in the street and the little moonlight that usually pushed through the window and pooled on the floor.

She curled up in a foetal ball and cried, struggling to keep her sobs under control but at that moment she knew. She knew that Karl's death wouldn't go unpunished and that she would play games with those in authority as they had played with his life. The old adage, 'Revenge is a dish best served cold,' sprang to mind. Carol determined that she would, indeed, have her revenge. As she made her decision, the tears stopped flowing and she was able to settle into a dreamless sleep.

Chapter Nine

Café Chaos

CLAIRE HAD SEATED HERSELF in Amy's favoured early morning café stop, Chatterbox, on the corner of the main road and street from which Horberry Mews was located. She was taking full advantage of the free wi-fi they had on offer. She had a large cappuccino and cherry muffin. Her MacBook Pro laptop was open and she appeared to be absorbed in her work over breakfast. No one gave her a second glance.

She received a warning through her earpiece from Max, "She's on her way." Claire continued to type and study her sheaf of papers. She glanced around at the other customers; there was the usual pre-work traffic, a couple of businessmen, a young couple and an older woman surfing the net on her Acer.

The café door opened and Amy entered with her laptop in hand. "She's nothing if not predictable," said Max's voice again into Claire's ear.

A middle-aged chirpy waitress came across to Amy, "Usual love?"

"Please," replied Amy with a smile. Her eyes looked better, not so puffy and red.

"You feeling better now, love?" asked the waitress, whose name lapel read, 'Rita.'

"Yes, thanks, Rita. I went on a bit of a bender, yesterday. Must have done me good. I slept like a baby."

"Good, I'm glad. I didn't like to see such a pretty girl as you looking so peaky. Oh, I know you had good reason but well, life's for living isn't it? I'll just get your order." The waitress walked back to the counter with her notepad and called out the back, "Scrambled eggs on brown, please, Jeff." She called across to Amy, "And a pot of tea?"

Amy nodded as she took out her laptop from the bag and opened it up. She waited for it to start up and selected a desktop file and began to add to the script on which she was working.

The waitress picked up a small teapot and filled it with hot water and swished it around as the café door opened.

Jack entered with a pet basket containing several chickens. He moved to a window table and placed the basket on the floor. Once the noise of the hot water from the machine had stopped Rita heard the squawks and clucks from the other side of the counter. She walked around and looked suspiciously at the clucking hens. "I don't know if you can bring them in here."

Jack looked up at her with an engaging smile. "It's only while I grab a snack. They won't be any trouble, I promise."

Rita sniffed. She walked back to the counter and called out the back, "Here, Jeff... What do I do about this?"

Jeff, a big burly man in a large white apron appeared behind the counter. Rita indicated the basket of chickens with a jerk of her head. He walked into the café area and studied the container, then said begrudgingly, "As long as they stay put."

Rita shrugged and went to get Amy's tea.

Claire waited on tenterhooks waiting for the right moment.

Jack blustered on, "Got to sell them on. Can't keep them in my flat anymore. Not enough room."

Jeff went back behind the counter. The waitress returned to Amy's table carrying a pot of tea for one. "Scrambled eggs won't be long, love."

"Don't suppose, you'd like to keep them, would you? Free range eggs for the café on tap," asked Jack cheekily.

"No, thank you," muttered the waitress and tutted to show her disapproval, as she stepped out from behind the counter.

As Rita deposited the tea, Jack surreptitiously removed the pin holding the basket door closed and when the waitress walked past his table to the counter, he nudged the basket with his foot, which caused her to trip and the door to fly open. Suddenly, there were chickens squawking, flapping and scurrying everywhere. There was absolute chaos.

Claire took this opportunity, as everyone, including Amy, was distracted. They were all trying to catch the birds. Out of the corner of her eye Claire couldn't help but see Jack as he dived on the floor and slid along the polished tiles after a particularly handsome Rhode Island Red, the hen however was not to be captured and pecked at Jack's hands. He shrieked and let go of the fowl's leg, which fluttered away scattering feathers as it shook itself. Claire kept typing fiercely. She struggled to contain her laughter at Jack's antics, which she couldn't fail to notice. She hit send and the machines were connected.

One chicken hopped up onto a chair and Amy removed her jacket and sneaked up on it. She threw her jacket over it. "I've got one!' she called excitedly.

"Hang on to it," ordered Jack as he ran after a sprightly white chicken with feathers down its legs. "Come on, Spats. Here, baby, come to daddy."

Claire succeeded in downloading the trace to Amy's machine. She closed her laptop and gathered her things as a chicken flew onto her table turned its bottom around and deposited a message with a plop on her chair. Claire edged her way to the door dodging chickens and clutching hands and escaped onto the street. She looked back through the window and watched Jack for a moment before hurrying away to the van.

In the café Jack had now stood up and he waved his arms about. "Have we got any corn or bread? They'll gather around the food and be easy to contain."

"Why can't we just shoo them out of the door?" asked Rita.

"I'd never catch them then," wailed Jack. "They might get run over and die."

Rita disappeared out to the kitchen and returned with some bread, which she scattered in small pieces on the floor and the hens came clucking around.

Jack orchestrated the rest of the customers to encircle the birds and one by one he caught each one and shoved them back into the basket before finally relieving Amy of the one in her charge.

"Why thank you, Miss."

"No, thank you. That was the funniest thing I've seen in a long while and did me more good than you could imagine." Amy continued chuckling as she returned to her laptop, which had put itself to sleep. She restarted it and continued writing her script narration for the documentary film.

Rita frowned as she fetched a broom to sweep up the breadcrumbs. The other customers were also laughing and everyone chatted together.

"That was just crazy," said the lady on the Acer. "Wait till I tell my friends."

"They won't believe you," joked another man. "I mean to say, chickens in a coffee shop," and he roared with laughter again.

Jack spoke again, "I don't suppose there's any danger of me getting a coffee and toast here now?"

Rita glared at him and pointed to the door, "No way. Out! Find someone else to terrify. Try Starbucks down the road."

Jack picked up his basket and apologised to everyone before fleeing the coffee shop. He hurried down the street to where the black van was parked and hopped into the back where Claire was sitting, and the vehicle drove away. The operatives, too, were chortling at Jack's antics from the camera link and microphone on the pet carrier. "It would make a great scene in a film," said Steve.

"Nah! No one would believe it," added Alan.

"I don't know," said Jack. "They say truth is stranger than fiction."

"Talk about Comic Relief, I'd have paid to see that," grinned Steve.

"Me, too," added Claire. "It really was an absolute hoot."

"Now where?" asked Alan getting back to business.

"You need to get me home so that I can release these little beauties. I don't want them going off lay," instructed Jack.

The van did a U turn in the road and began to travel back the way it had come. Jack couldn't stop grinning as he replayed the scene like a video in his head. But, then things became quiet and serious, once more in the mobile surveillance unit.

After, dropping Jack back at his flat with the chickens the van continued on its way to MI6 and the subterranean car park. Ron alerted Max by phone and confirmed, "Claire has done it. I repeat Chicken Run was a success." He glanced across at Claire and winked and she returned his grin.

Max was alone in the office and he sat at his computer and following Claire's instructions he was able to log into Amy's PC and access all her files. He downloaded the script for the documentary on Electra and began to read it.

Max skimmed through the first few pages and found nothing untoward but as he read on something caught his eye and he read more avidly. "Oh, no," he groaned. "No." He continued examining the text and slammed his hand on the desk in frustration, "God damn!"

Max left the workstation and crossed to the external operating system that dialled out, connected him straight to the Home Office and the direct line to the Senior Advisor to the Treasury, Lace. Max hit a button and heard the refined tones of Lace, "Max, what have you got?"

"You're right. Their investigation is bordering on discovering the truth."

Lace's tone altered dramatically and became more like granite, "Get rid of them."

"Is that necessary?" queried Max.

"We cannot take the chance. Take their ID's first, freeze their bank accounts, close their office, then officially they don't exist. They can be killed with impunity. It will be open season."

"But…"

"You have your orders." Lace terminated the call and the line went dead.

Max rubbed his already furrowed brow and sat down heavily at the desk. He sighed, and then tapped a key. A screen in front of him flickered into life. The face of Biff filled the space. Max instructed, without a smile and without any pleasure in his voice, "Biff, Operation 'Check Mate', it's on." He closed the screen and cursed, "Bollocks!"

At the offices of Monumentous Films Jon was definitely looking the worse for wear after his night of binge drinking. His eyes were bloodshot and his face was pale. Amy was giggling as she told the story of the chickens in the café while she fired up their office PC's.

"You should have been there. There must have been half-a-dozen chickens flapping about. It was hilarious."

Jon stood behind her and picked a chicken feather from off her back. "It must have been." He sat at his own PC with a heavy sigh and went to mail, "I'll just check my emails and then we'll get started."

Amy smiled and said wisely, "Why don't I make you a good strong coffee and give you a couple of Paracetamol? And don't thank me, take advantage of the offer, I won't always play nurse maid, especially when it's self-inflicted."

Amy wandered, into the kitchen area and set the kettle onto boil. She called out, "Do you mind if I put the radio on? It helps me to think."

"Okay, but not too loud! Ouch! My head hurts," grumbled Jon, as his voice reverberated in his skull.

Amy laughed, "Then I won't sing."

"Better not!" warned Jon, and he managed a smile as he emptied his spam folder into trash and cursorily checked his business and private emails. "Nothing much here, a few forwards and funnies. Oh, wait a minute; the Cannes entry form has come through. That's good. The south of France here we come!"

Amy trotted back with a glass of water and two tablets. "Here, get these down you," she ordered and waited with arms folded like a primary school teacher.

Jon pulled a face as the pills began to dissolve on his tongue. "Ugh. They're horrible."

"All the quicker to get into the blood stream, my dear," admonished Amy.

"You sound like the big bad wolf," grumbled Jon. "What are you going to do next? Blow the house down or eat me up?"

"Who's mixing up their stories now?" laughed Amy.

"No, I'm not. The three little pigs rules. It was my favourite when I was a kid," protested Jon.

"Sounded more like Little Red Riding Hood to me," argued Amy. "With the three little pigs thrown in," she grinned.

"Enough already! You're doing my head in," complained Jon.

Amy laughed and returned to her laptop and began to edit her script. Every now and then a little giggle escaped her, which did not go unnoticed by Jon, who was trying very hard to ignore her, but not very successfully.

The cameras continued to collect their data, send it to the servers, where the information was assessed and key players found... And followed.

In the relative quiet of the office Claire was attempting to do a little hacking of her own. She knew she had to work fast and was trying to break into Max's personal files unobserved. She had finally cracked the security code and was now struggling with the password. She stifled a victorious shout as she found her way into files of an acutely sensitive nature, one of which she sent to the printer. She ensured no one was watching and stuffed a printed sheet into her trouser pocket, then returned to her desk and cleared her search history. She looked around and once she was certain that no one had seen what she was doing she continued to access more classified material.

She opened another file on screen and proceeded to study it. It contained more information on the Brandenberg Sect and Claire was becoming more alarmed at what was unfolding before her eyes. She was so absorbed she didn't hear the office door open. It was Jack's laugh that alerted her to Max and Jack's presence in the office and Claire hurriedly exited the programme but not before Max caught a glimpse of her screen.

Max came and stood behind her and said coldly, "Moonlighting, Claire?"

"Just doing a little research," she responded.

"On what?" he demanded.

"I'm trying to get some answers that no one around here is prepared to give," she replied tartly.

Max asserted his authority and a pulse began to throb in his cheek as he laid down the law. "I decide how much you need to know. For Christ's sake, Claire, even I don't know it all," he remonstrated.

"Then why have you sold me the line that everything we do is in the interests of national security?" questioned Claire.

Jack chipped in, "Because it is, isn't it?"

"That's crap, Jack and you know it," said Claire, her temper rising.

Jack naively turned to Max for verification, "Max?"

He remained silent and Claire pressed him further, "Well, Max?"

Max was stuck and in measured tones churned out the official line, "It's our job to help preserve the West's supremacy, economy and way of life…"

"Very noble," said Claire sarcastically. "But in truth the Brandenberg's main tenet is not in preserving our society… It's more interested in creating political instability. So, we can go in as peacemakers to control third world economies, steal their resources; that and helpful assassinations along the way, which by the way help to create fortunes… like Electra. And what did that poor sod of a student do? Tell me that!" Claire was becoming more and more fired up.

"He saw what he shouldn't…"

"And so, he's taken out…" Claire turned and faced Max. Jack looked from one to the other.

"You have a right to be angry, but you need to understand…"

"Understand? I understand all right."

Max grabbed hold of her arm and Claire tried to shake it off, "Let me go! I need some fresh air. It's beginning to stink around here." She got up abruptly from her PC, snatched her coat and stamped out of the room. Max looked across at Jack who was stunned by the outburst.

"Watch her!" Max ordered gruffly.

Claire ran from the office, hurried along the corridor and took the lift to the ground floor. She exited the building, and pulled her coat around her trying to stifle back her tears. Without so much as a glance behind her she didn't notice that Jack had slipped out to follow her.

Claire gauged the traffic on the street and hurried across the busy road, traffic camera, shop cameras, CCTV picked out her frantic journey. A few cars honked as she dashed out. She headed for a phone booth. Claire reached into her pocket and pulled out the printed sheet she had hidden away and she fished in her coat pocket for some coins. She studied the list of names and numbers in front of her, selected one and dialled. It was answered almost immediately. "Mr. Birchell? We need to talk."

"How did you get my number? Who are you?" queried the cultured tones of Birchell.

"That doesn't matter for now. Listen. I know about Electra and a lot more." Claire's voice was becoming more urgent.

"Just what are you saying, young lady?" asked Birchell a note of suspicion entering his voice.

"Please, this isn't a joke. Can we meet?" asked Claire.

"How will I know you?"

"I'll know you."

"Where? And when?"

"Now."

"I don't know if I can …" Birchell stalled for time.

"The park. There's a bench on the grass near the entrance to the ICA."

"But…"

"Be there. Otherwise I can't guarantee the safety of any of your operations."

She glanced about her, looking up and down the road, but she didn't spot Jack watching from a doorway. She spoke for a few moments more, stuffed the paper back in her pocket, replaced the receiver and moved away.

Jack took this as his opportunity and came running up, "Claire, Claire!"

Claire stopped and turned. A flicker of alarm crossed her face to be replaced by a smile, "Jack?"

"What got into you back there? Come on, let's go back, please."

"I'm sorry, Jack. I know I shouldn't have blown my stack. I just hate being played for a sucker," Claire replied trying to appear calmer and more normal.

"You're not," placated Jack.

"Oh, yes, we are. We're being lied to." Claire felt her anger rising again. She bit her lip.

"Don't you see? You start making waves and you'll make yourself a target. Let it go," pleaded Jack.

Claire decided to back track and humour her colleague. She knew how dangerous her stand could be. "You're right," she said meekly. "Perhaps, I'm just being hasty. Give me a few minutes and I'll come back." She paused for a moment and added softly, "Tell Max that I'm sorry."

Jack's expression immediately lightened. "Of course."

"I just need to cool off for a while. Do you understand?" Claire smiled lamely at him. "That was some chicken trick."

"It was, wasn't it? I better get back, okay?"

Claire nodded.

"See you in a mo?" he queried sheepishly.

Claire managed a smile, and sounded more confident than she felt, "Sure thing."

"Okay, don't be long."

"I won't." She watched Jack retrace his steps to the office. Once he appeared to enter the Security Building, she waited a minute then, turned and made her way to the public recreation area and hurried off in the direction of the park. She was careful to check behind her every few yards to satisfy herself that she wasn't being followed.

Claire hesitated nervously at the park entrance but believing the way to be clear she pressed on. She settled on a bench overlooking the duck pond where a small boy and his mother were busy feeding the ducks that quacked and gathered around them, much to the child's delight.

A tall, well-built man with an imposing manner walked toward the pond from the other direction and Claire shaded her eyes. She swiftly looked forward, as Birchell crossed to the bench. He sat at the other end. He unfolded his newspaper. His gold ring and bracelet glinted in the sunlight. He shook out the paper and appeared to be engrossed in it. He spoke quietly but distinctly, "How did you know where to contact me?"

"I took a printout of the names, addresses and phone numbers of the Sect."

"Very resourceful. But, why call me?" he asked.

"You're listed as suspect, not to be trusted. It appears you are to be watched."

"Am I, indeed?" asked Birchell. It was clear that this was news to him.

"There are those who believe you are not working for good of the Sect."

"And how do I know you're not a part of this?" he questioned.

"You don't. You have to trust me."

"And why should I do that, Miss Williams?"

"How do you know my name?" said Claire shocked.

"There's not much I don't know. I am well aware of who works for us, Miss Williams."

Claire gasped, and blurted out nervously, "I know about Electra."

"I repeat, and I'll ask you again, tell me why should I trust you, Miss Williams?"

"Because I'm offering to help you and no one else is. You are against this as much as me."

"Meet me tomorrow, at two," Birchell ordered.

"Here?" asked Claire.

"No. The Art Gallery, ICA. I'll find you." Birchell folded up his newspaper, tucked it under his arm and strode off.

Claire remained on the bench staring thoughtfully into the distance. Her stomach churned, she knew there was a possibility of discovery but strongly felt that for the common good that she was acting ethically and responsibly. She muttered aloud as if to convince herself, "I'm doing the right thing. I know I am." She began to breathe deeply trying to calm herself until she was ready to return to work.

Jack had stealthily followed Claire, dodging into doorways each time she turned around and he had observed the entire encounter. He was standing back, hidden in the trees. As soon as he saw Birchell had risen and walked away Jack hastily made his way back through the park and into the main thoroughfare leading to MI6.

Jack hurried back down the tree-lined street and ran into the office. He took the elevator to the third floor and reported to Max, safe in the knowledge that he hadn't been seen by Claire or Birchell whom he had recognised.

"She met someone didn't she?" asked Max. Jack nodded. "So, who was it?" Max demanded.

"It was Birchell, I'm sure of it," Jack blurted out.

"Was it, be damned?" murmured Max. "Then, we'd better put tabs on Miss Williams. See to it," ordered Max. "Now why would she want to make contact with him?" he mused softly. "Just what does our Claire know?"

At that point, Claire entered. She spoke softly to Max, "Sorry, Max. I don't know what came over me," she apologised. "I just... Oh, I don't know."

Max softened his tone as if to appear understanding, "I do... It's difficult to separate our ideals from our work. We've all been through it, Claire. You have to realise the work we do is for the common good. We're not just some organisation out for our own ends. The methods we use to keep order are necessary, sometimes difficult but necessary."

"I know, but I just hate that innocents get caught up in the mess," she protested. "Like that poor student."

"I understand. We all hate that, Claire. We all do. It's a necessary evil."

Jack watched tears fill Claire's eyes as she became more upset. He could see that she was struggling to keep a lid on her emotions. He swallowed sympathetically, trying to dislodge the lump in his throat as he felt her distress. He caught his breath as he heard her say, "Why? Explain to me, why, please?"

Jack looked at Max. There was no answer forthcoming.

Chapter Ten

Outside Help

JON CURTIS WAS ENGROSSED in reading a report from Mercedes who had complained that they had been refused access to examine the vehicle involved in the crash. He was just about to call Amy over when a flashing alert came up on the screen over the online report. "YOU ARE BEING WATCHED." It continued to flash. Jon called out, "Amy, get over here. Look!"

Amy stopped what she was doing and hurried over. She read the message and looked out of their office window. The black van that they had seen before was parked outside. She turned back to Jon, "Jon our..." but he silenced her with his hand and put his fingers to his lips. Amy crossed back and saw another message pulsing on the screen, "OFFICE BUGGED, CAREFUL WHAT YOU SAY."

"Coffee's nearly out. We'll have to put it on the shopping list."

Jon and Amy exchanged looks as another message lit up the screen, "ATTACHMENTS SENT – COPY TO DISC AND DELETE THESE FILES." Suddenly the screen went blank. Amy grabbed a disc and handed it to Jon. His email account popped up and Jon clicked on his inbox. A mail from an unknown source filled the screen. It had attachments. Jon downloaded them to disc.

As Amy spoke, she started looking around the office for bugs. She spotted one in a wall light and pointed to it. She struggled to sound normal and pointed at the email and then the printer. "The script's coming on really well, but I think we need a hard copy for proofing."

"Good idea," responded Jon. He hit the printer button and the printer began to type.

In the black van, Biff with two other technicians and more henchmen were listening to the conversation. One of them, Steve was monitoring the filmmakers' computer activity.

"They're downloading files," Steve exclaimed.

"Where from?" questioned Biff.

"I'm not sure. It could be the Brandenberg stuff."

"Shit! Can we stop it?" asked Biff.

"I'll try," said Steve, as he typed wildly on his keypad.

"You'd better," asserted Biff as he pulled a gun from his waistband. "Or we'll have to go in."

The printer in Monumentous Film Offices was spewing out paper, which Amy was gathering. Jon removed the disc.

Amy prompted Jon, hoping that he would understand what she meant, "Have you got rid of the cookies?"

Jon nodded as he caught her meaning, "On it." He deleted the attachment files and email as Amy checked the street outside the window. The van was still there. She watched as Biff climbed out of the van with Ron. Biff was seen stuffing a weapon in his trouser waistband. Both of the men were armed. They ran toward the office building. She saw them disappear from view. They had clearly entered the foyer.

Amy jerked her head toward the back door and fire escape. "Fancy a breather? It's getting stuffy in here."

"Why not?" replied Jon as he removed the disc and grabbed the rest of the sheaf of printed files, which he stuffed into his briefcase.

Amy grabbed her laptop, and said more urgently, "Come on! The fresh air will do you good." She looked out of the window again as more armed men left the black van and headed for their office building.

Jon ran toward the front door to their offices and listened. Amy stopped. They both heard the sound of the lift in action and descending to pick up whoever was in the lobby. Amy dashed to the safety door at the back of their office suite, which led onto the rickety fire escape. She pushed the bar hard and it opened. As she fought with the heavy curtains covering the door an internal alarm went off with a high pitched peep. They stepped out onto the ridged ironwork platform and secured the door behind them and the bleeping alarm stopped.

The PC inside the office was still rapidly deleting the selected files.

Amy and Jon travelled down the fire escape as quickly as possible. Amy was looking incredibly nervous and breathing heavily. Not just because of the situation but because of her long-term fear of heights. She regretted wearing such high heels to work. However, necessity spurred her onward and she struggled to keep her trembling anxiety under control.

Biff, downstairs had called the lift, in case Jon or Amy were inclined to use it. Ron had taken the stairs. He sprinted up the steps two at a time and barged past a woman on her way down. She was rudely thrust aside and shouted, "Manners!" after him as he made his way to the third floor.

The door to Monumentous Films was shouldered and splintered open with a crash. Ron, followed by Biff, both with weapons drawn, thoroughly searched the office suite. Suddenly, Biff's attention was attracted to the busy PC screen efficiently deleting attachment files. He hurtled to the computer in an attempt to halt the job. He reached it just as it completed its task. He cursed and slammed his hand on the desk in frustration.

Ron discovered the fire escape door hiding under the curtains. He pushed it open and the alarm began peeping again. He glanced down to see Amy, carrying her laptop, disappearing from view. He took out his radio and alerted the rest of the team. "The back of the building. They're getting away."

Biff dived back out of the main door and raced back down the stairs. Ron gave chase down the fire escape. Flakes of corroded and flaking metal rained down as his feet made contact with the fatigued metal. Something of an athlete he sprinted down the iron staircase and like a free runner catapulted himself over the iron rail to the ground landing softly like a cat.

Amy pulled off her shoes. She and Jon ran down a dusty back alley, past refuse bins with overflowing rubbish. Amy wrinkled her nose in disgust as her foot slipped on some rotten vegetables, which released a putrid smell. They raced to reach the main road where they slowed down amongst the many shoppers. They glanced back over their shoulders and saw Ron and Biff, weapons now hidden from view, pushing through the throng in pursuit.

Jon grabbed Amy's free hand. He ignored the pulsing tingle, which shot up his arm. They ducked swiftly around a corner and in through the revolving doors of a stylish hotel. Jon dragged Amy to the desk and asked breathlessly, "Do you have a room, any room?"

The effeminate male receptionist raised one eyebrow and exchanged a look with his female colleague as if to say, 'My, they're in a hurry.'

The receptionist, however, was not to be rushed and said politely, "We only have a suite left at five hundred pounds a night."

"We'll take it," Jon snapped back. All the while he kept his eye on the hotel doors.

Amy was flabbergasted, "What?"

The receptionist who thought he had seen it all replied coolly, "How would you like to pay?"

Jon fumbled in his wallet and took out the cash, which he thrust down. The receptionist again arched his eyebrow, and turned to the pigeonholes behind him housing room keys and messages. He mouthed to his female colleague, 'Money not a problem, then.' He took a key and picked up the registration card and placed them on the desk. "Suite Eight. If you could just fill out the registration card, Sir."

Jon grabbed the card and proffered pen, "We'll do it later." He dragged Amy hastily toward the lifts as she struggled to replace her shoes.

The receptionist called after him, "Sir, your room key."

Jon slid back across the polished floor of the lobby and snatched up the key.

"I take it you haven't any luggage?" he asked imperiously.

Jon shook his head, raised his briefcase and raced after Amy now entering the elevator waiting on the ground floor.

The receptionist mused as he watched them, "Hmm... I wonder how she likes her eggs in the morning? Fried or scrambled?"

"By the look of her," replied his female colleague, "I'd say fertilised."

The co-workers both hooted with laughter.

Biff and Ron pushed through the growing crowd of shoppers and searched frantically for their quarry. They stopped outside the hotel and Biff slapped his hand against his side in anger as he puffed, "We've lost them." Annoyed, they began to make their way back to the black van.

At one forty-five that afternoon, Claire made an excuse to escape the confines of the office. She stretched and stood up. "Phew, I need a breather. Wow, Jack, just look at the time. I haven't stopped since eight-thirty this morning. I need a loo stop and coffee break. Do you want anything?" she asked Jack, smiling sweetly.

"No thanks, I've just got back from lunch," replied Jack.

"Lucky you, I've had nothing, but I am about to put that right." Claire grabbed her jacket and shopping bag. "Tell Max I'm on lunch. See you in an hour," she said and gave him a quick wave as she left the office.

The expression on her face changed to one of gritty determination as she left the office and checked the time. She walked briskly down the corridor and chose the stairs instead of the elevator and ran down them quickly and out into the street. She took a huge intake of breath and proceeded as fast as she dared to the ICA. Every now and then she would check about her for someone loitering behind her or following. She seemed to be in the clear. With a sigh of relief, she headed toward the gallery entrance. She snatched a last look about her and scurried inside.

Claire walked around the gallery, pausing to reflect on the varied pieces of artwork on display. She stopped at a strange modern piece that looked like pieces from a jigsaw puzzle. She twisted her head around to try and make sense of it. Birchell stopped behind her at the same picture. "Don't turn around. Keep looking at the painting. Were you followed?"

"I don't think so," she whispered.

"But you're not sure?"

"Can we ever be sure?" She glanced up at the camera in the corner of the gallery.

"Point taken... I'm going into the café. Pick up a tray and meet me at the counter."

Birchell walked away and headed for the café area while Claire continued to peruse a few more pictures. She then followed Birchell toward the cafeteria's entrance. She looked around again to see if she could spot anyone likely to be following her. She felt reasonably confident that she was safe. As she walked into the café she saw Birchell at the counter studying the cakes and pastries. She picked up a tray and stood next to him. He placed an A 4 brown envelope on her tray. She placed her hand on it and he covered it with his own. "Your journalist filmmaker friends may be interested in this, as you will be. You have to warn them. They're marked people now. In reality they no longer exist. No one will notice if they lose their lives." He removed his hand.

"What about you?" asked Claire warily.

"I know my time will come. How and where… that's the mystery. And you?"

"I don't feel too safe myself."

"Good, then that should keep you on your toes," said Birchell.

"Where do you stand in all this?" asked Claire curiously.

"Let's just say that corruption has moved in to destroy what were once commendable ideals. Things are now out of control. Electra was a step too far."

"And?"

"I feel a duty to stop the rot. And you, Miss Williams?"

"I no longer blindly follow orders. I have begun to question and I don't like the answers."

"You have what you need in that envelope. Now, I suggest that you had better leave. If you're seen with me…" he stopped.

"The whistle blower will be blown…" Claire finished his sentence.

"Exactly."

She picked up the envelope and left the café area and moved to the front door. All the time she was watched by CCTV, which swivelled onto Birchell as Claire went out through the door.

Birchell placed his tray over Claire's then picked up a pastry and collected a coffee. He paid for both and sat at a table looking thoughtfully ahead.

Cameras on the street picked up Claire's progress. She was completely lost in her own thoughts as she walked back through the park.

Claire was plotting how she could help the filmmakers. Yes, she could provide them with the information they were seeking, she could also organise ways of helping them to get a new identity. Money would be a major problem, she knew. They would find their bank accounts frozen. They would also need a different vehicle. It wouldn't be long before any car they might own would be tracked. Claire thought some more. 'Hm! There is a way. I will need to visit ballistics. A small explosive device and detonator might prove to be very useful, very useful indeed.' Smiling at her solution she stepped out more briskly.

In the luxury hotel suite Jon and Amy were studying the printed papers in their possession that had come from the attachments. They could not believe what they had been reading.

"It's a programme to produce efficient assassins," said Amy incredulously.

"No consciences," affirmed Jon.

"And who better than convicted killers and terrorists?" Amy remarked.

"But, look at this, Amy, many of the subjects they have used are already dead. This is so frightening."

"They're expendable, so who's to care? With new identities no one will miss them," observed Amy.

"Look at this," said Jon thrusting out two sheets. "Do you remember this case?"

Amy examined the papers in front of her. "Karl and Carol Stevenson. Twins. Didn't they murder their parents for fun?"

"When they were twelve years old. They were released last year." Jon paused and scrutinised the pictures. "Look at the photos... I wonder..." Jon stopped as he considered the information.

"What?" pressed Amy.

"I wonder if there's some way we can scan them into your laptop? Then we can use a photo app to enhance the pictures and age them to see what they might look like today, what do you think?"

"Call the front desk. Order the software, after all you paid five hundred for the suite. You can give them their registration card then," she grinned and winked at him, "Go on."

Jon picked up the telephone.

Claire had now left the park. She stuffed the envelope into her voluminous bag and stood in the Mall outside the ICA with a worried look on her face. She gave herself a stiff talking to, "Breathe, Claire, breathe. You can do this. What's that saying? Cool calm and collected. That has to be you." She continued to try and convince herself that she was doing the right thing. 'Right, to my car, then Ballistics and back to work,' she told herself.

Standing on the park side of the water was a lean man with a saturnine face, dressed in a dark raincoat and hat, smoking a cigarette. He removed the nub end from his thin lips and threw it to one side and ground it out viciously with his heel. His eyes narrowed as he watched Claire hail a taxi. He waited until the cab pulled away and then purposefully entered the ICA.

Birchell was just draining the last of his coffee from his cup. He saw and recognised the man approaching him and retreated to the café counter. He pushed his way behind the counter and forced his way into the kitchen where he caused a stir. A pastry chef crossing to his workstation, who had picked up a rolling pin, jumped out of his way as Birchell ran in front of him. A kitchen hand dropped a tray of cutlery, which clattered metallically to the floor and a trolley laden with plates was overturned as Birchell fled through the back and escaped into the street.

The man swore under his breath as he saw Birchell disappear and he swiftly headed for the front door and the Mall. He ran out into the street looking this way and that but couldn't spot Birchell who it seemed had vanished.

Claire was now alighting from the cab outside a big multi-storey car park. Her eyes scanned the area for anyone who looked suspicious or for any vehicle that appeared to be lingering or watching her. To her relief there was none.

Claire entered the stairwell and ignored the lift. She mounted the stairs. She was puffing a bit by the time she reached the top floor. She hurried to a vehicle and unlocked it safely stowing the envelope in the boot. She got into the car and started the engine.

Jon and Amy had purchased a scanner and the photos from the documents are on the screen of Amy's laptop. She had used a computer programme to age the child killers, the Stephenson twins. Now, they had completed the task on the boy they saw Karl Goodwin's face staring out at them.

"Oh, my God! Ahmed's bodyguard," said Amy, softly with disbelief. "He seemed so nice."

A long look passed between the filmmakers until Jon broke the shocked silence. "Try the girl."

They applied the same technique and pulled up a picture of Carol. "She looks a little familiar, maybe she was at the funeral," muttered Jon. "But I could be wrong."

"I don't know her," said Amy confidently. "Mind you I was in no position to recognise anyone on that day."

"No, I think you're right. Just save it to desktop, you never know."

"After that, I'm hungry," announced Amy. "Let's get room service." She shut down her laptop and put it back in the bag.

Inside the black van, one of Biff's henchmen alerted his boss, "She's been using her laptop."

"Where is she?" demanded Biff.

The operative homed in on the signal on the map, which he enlarged. It was clear enough to see the street and the hotel. "Got her! They're only around the corner from their offices," he said in glee.

"Great stuff! Let's go."

Ron started up the engine and the van cruised out into the line of cars and buses. He expertly manoeuvred through the heavy traffic. They drove back to the side street at the filmmaker's offices, parked in safety and hopped out. They walked around the corner and down the street to the smart hotel with the revolving doors.

Inside the hotel suite, Amy and Jon were finishing the remains of a room service meal. Amy wiped her mouth and threw down her napkin. "Now what?"

"Well, the way should be clear for us now, surely?"

"We can't go back to the office. And we can't stay here."

"Let's try my place," suggested Jon.

"Won't it be watched?"

Jon shrugged his shoulders. "That I don't know."

The two filmmakers fell silent when there was an abrupt knock at the door. Jon and Amy froze and looked at each other. Neither of them knew what to do. Jon rose from his seat and peered through spy hole. He immediately recognised the two men who had chased them from before. He whispered, "It's them." He looked around him in confusion. "Now, what do we do?"

"Bugger!" cursed Amy.

The knock on the door became more persistent followed by a shout of "Room Service."

Amy hurriedly snatched up her laptop and Jon picked up all the printed reams of paper and shoved them in his briefcase. He signalled to Amy indicating the balcony and opened the French Windows to it. He stepped out onto the balcony and tossed his briefcase onto the adjoining balcony and clambered across. He reached across for Amy's laptop and took it from her.

Amy firmly closed the French doors and climbed up onto the balcony rail and made the mistake of looking down. She froze, "I can't do this." Paralysed with fear a thin film of sweat broke out on her forehead and upper lip. She gulped and began to tremble as her heart pounded loudly in her chest.

"Come on, take my hand. Hurry," urged Jon, starting to panic himself. "Don't look down," he ordered.

"I already have... No, I can't Jon. I really can't." Her voice came out as a squeak, her mouth was dry and the terror was apparent on her face.

Amy was stuck stock-still, rigid and unable to move. She heard the men banging on the door and shivered.

"Trust me. Please, Amy, come on," insisted Jon. "Please. I can't leave you. You have to do it, come on." He stretched out his arms to her and their fingertips were tantalisingly close. She swayed dangerously in her insecure and profoundly unsteady position.

Suddenly, Amy awoke from her stupor startled by the sound of a gunshot as the suite's lock was blown to pieces. This spurred Amy into action. She struggled to keep on top of the rail. She was in imminent danger of falling off as she tried to step across to the adjacent balcony. In her panic her foot slipped and she gasped. She was balanced precariously, but knew she had to move. Taking a deep breath, she attempted to leap but missed her footing and dropped over the side just managing to grab and cling onto the opposite rail. She squealed tearfully. Her grip was tenuous and she was nearing hysteria but Jon finding abnormal strength from somewhere with a rush of adrenaline caught her by her wrists and hauled her to the safety of the opposing balcony. She crumpled to the floor with a hiccupping sob. Jon gently lifted her to her feet. He cupped his hands around her face, and whispered gently, "Come on, Amy you have to move."

Amy nodded, "I know, I know." She stood up, still shaking, and entered the suite, whose French doors were luckily ajar. Jon tried to still her quaking limbs and thundering heart. He carried his briefcase and her laptop bag.

They both disappeared into the plush lounge area, and tiptoed across the thick shag pile carpet, uncertain whether the suite was occupied or not. They didn't want more trouble landing at their feet.

Biff and Ron had burst into the filmmakers' hotel suite and searched all the rooms, under the beds, inside the closets anywhere that someone could possibly hide. Biff's eagle eyes rapidly scanned the living area, for something, anything, any clue that would reveal Jon and Amy's whereabouts. Biff noticed a small swatch of net curtain protruding from the balcony windows trapped in the door. He opened them and looked outside.

Jon and Amy tentatively proceeded through the occupied suite. As they approached the bedroom they heard a couple in bed making love noisily. The door was partially open.

"Oh, yeah! Give it to me, Baby. Yeah!" grunted the male stud.

His female companion was equally enthusiastic, "Oooh, mmm, aahh ...oh."

"Come on," whispered Jon. "They'll never notice."

As they passed the room, danger momentarily forgotten, Amy's curiosity was piqued and she peeped in. Fascinated by what she saw, a most unusual position, she stopped and stared. Jon came back for her and grabbed her arm. Amy was dumbfounded, she murmured, "How do they do that?"

Jon rolled his eyes and dragged her toward the entrance door, which he opened a tiny fraction. The corridor seemed clear. They made a decision and ran for it. Amy tripped and hobbled on, almost losing her shoe in the process. They hurried to the back of the building and down the service stairway to the delivery yard and paused for breath.

"We're stuck, aren't we?" said Amy in defeat.

"No, we just need a plan," proclaimed Jon.

"Here, let me carry the laptop. You can't manage the lot," said Amy practically. "Where can we go?" She slung her laptop bag across her shoulders and front.

"I don't know... Anywhere. Let's catch a bus or something and think this through. Come on." Jon pressed.

"That all sounds a bit random, let's get back to your place."

"My place? You didn't like that idea a minute ago. What if it's watched?"

"We'll find a way. These guys can't be everywhere."

"Okay, and I do need to see my cat," agreed Jon in a measured tone. "But keep your wits about you and let's travel through the back streets. Follow me. I think it will be safer. Ready?"

"Ready," Amy agreed.

They made their way out from the delivery yard and into the street. Jon took Amy on something of a mystery tour backtracking and dodging in and out of alleys and at the back of people's houses.

"If anyone sees us, they'll think we're up to no good, or that we're a couple of perverts," warned Amy.

"Or a courting couple trying to find some privacy," replied Jon.

Amy looked at him trying to gauge his mood and he looked deeply into her eyes, unnerving her still further. The intensity of his eyes made her gasp. She wasn't ready for this although she had wanted it for a long time. He gently caressed her cheek and inside she melted. She closed her eyes waiting for the kiss that never came. Jon jolted her back to reality grabbed her free hand and they hurried down yet another alley.

Carol was alone in Ibrahim's luxury two-storey apartment. She had Ibrahim's photo album on her lap. It was open at her brother's photograph. She gazed at it sadly and sniffed. She closed the album with a snap, replaced it on the dressing table and rose, wiping away an escaping tear.

Her anger bubbled to the surface. She knew she had to do or say something or she would explode. She steeled herself, picked up the phone and dialled. The phone rang twice. She cut the call and redialled. It rang several times before it was answered and Lace spoke, "Carol?"

She responded quietly, "Yes. About Karl…"

"Sorry, Carol. Karl's dead."

"Yes, I know," she answered numbly. "I wanted to hear it from you."

Lace continued, "You want retribution, Carol, Carol Stephenson, listen." Electra's song played in the background behind Lace's words. "Follow these instructions." Five distinct notes could be heard repeating in the music.

Carol's eyes glazed over and then she became alert as she listened to what she was being asked to do. Lace gave her a name and location. "Can you get out?" he asked.

"Yes, is he the one?"

"He is. He took Karl's life. He caused the accident."

"Then he's a dead man."

Carol replaced the receiver.

Amy and Jon had succeeded in making their way back to Jon's district unobserved. They hid in a doorway on the opposite side of the street and stared across at Jon's flat. Amy glanced down the road. There were no mysterious black vans in view or anything else that looked sinister.

"I know it was my idea but I don't like it," Amy complained.

"There's no alternative. I can access the office PC from my home computer and retrieve all the data. Besides, I need to get Rumble."

"We can't take a cat with us," Amy pointed out.

"Maybe not. We'll see. Just wait in the pub. You'll be safe there. No one would dare to attack you there, in public view. Go on." He gave her a little nudge and she turned to go. Suddenly, filled with indescribable emotion he caught her arm and pulled her into him. They gazed at each other, their eyes locked and Jon's lips came down on Amy's soft and yielding mouth and they kissed. The kiss was prolonged and became more urgent and passionate. He broke it off. As Amy came up for air, she was stunned and touched her burning lips.

"Now go. And be careful," warned Jon. He passed her his briefcase. "And Amy?"

"Yes?"

"If I don't get back in twenty minutes, take off."

Amy nodded and stepped out from the doorway and strolled seemingly nonchalantly toward 'The Lazy Landlord'.

She entered warily, still carrying her laptop and Jon's briefcase and studied the customers. She moved to the bar and ordered, "A large Pinot Grigio, please and a large Shiraz."

"Bad day?" asked the landlord, Greg being friendly.

"Something like that." Amy smiled wanly and paid for the drinks.

"Both for you?"

"No, I'm not that much of a lush, yet. I'm expecting someone."

"I'll bring them across, save you a trip," he said indicating her bags. "I've seen you before, haven't I?" he asked.

"A couple of times. I've been in with Jon, Jon Curtis."

"Ah yes. Haven't seen him this week. Is that who you're waiting for?"

Amy nodded and forced a smile and not wishing to engage in further conversation she retreated to a table in the dimmest corner of the pub. She had full view of the door and everyone in the bar. Greg followed with the drinks and placed them on the table. She moved the glass of red placing it opposite her and gratefully sipped her chilled white wine and waited. Her mind was in a spin as she tried to analyse all that had happened since Electra's death. She ran over the events in her mind trying to make sense of everything. She glanced at her watch. Jon had been gone nearly fifteen minutes. She hoped he wouldn't be much longer. She didn't have long to wait.

The pub door opened and Jon sauntered in. He spotted Amy, walked across the floor and joined her. He indicated the drink, "Thanks."

"Pleasure," she answered perfunctorily and waited for Jon to speak. She took a huge mouthful of wine. "Well?"

Jon frowned. "It's not good. I'm sure my place is bugged and I had no joy with the PC. As soon as I linked-up, everything I tried to download from the office just deleted before my eyes."

"What about Rumble?"

"I didn't think you'd care."

"I care. I'm not completely heartless, I just pretend to be," Amy mused.

"I knocked on Mike's door. Thought if I bunged him a few quid he'd help out. There's a new tenant. It seems Mike's dead."

"How?"

"Some sort of overdose. He actually died in here. Funny, I didn't take him for a druggie." Jon paused, "In fact, he was the guy hauled out on a stretcher one night when I was working."

"Is it connected?"

"I don't know. I hope not."

"So, what about Rumble?"

"With Mr. Blight until I can collect him. I told him I was going away for a few days."

"You'd better drink up," said Amy finishing her wine. Jon threw her a questioning glance. "If your place is bugged, then…"

"They won't be long," Jon concluded and downed his drink.

Amy and Jon quickly gathered the laptop and briefcase and moved to the pub door. Jon looked out cautiously and saw the black van loitering in the street like some alien machine. He pulled back into the doorway, hurriedly. He caught hold of Amy's hand and yanked her back inside the pub, almost forcing her into a run as he crossed to the landlord, Greg. "Hey, Greg! Is there a back way out of here?"

"Fire door out past the Gents. You okay, Jon?"

"If anyone asks… You haven't seen me."

Greg nodded, "No worries, mate." Amy and Jon scuttled out of the back.

Biff and Ron had let themselves into the building and they ran up the stairs to Jon's flat. They removed their guns and looked around, carefully covering each other's backs. Biff opened it up and they entered. Biff crossed to the PC and felt it, "Still warm. He's not been gone long."

"Try the pub?" asked Ron.

"Right," agreed Biff. They shielded their firearms and retreated.

Amy and Jon sprinted around the corner and hailed a double decker bus that was approaching a stop. They jumped aboard when the door opened. The driver asked, "Where to?"

"Terminus, please," asked Jon.

The driver punched out two tickets and took Jon's money. The two filmmakers climbed up the stairs to the top deck and sat on the vacant back seat. They watched a myriad of shops go by their lights blazing invitingly. Amy was becoming more fidgety, "We can't ride around all night," she grumbled.

"If they're watching my place, then they're bound to have tabs on yours, too."

"Agreed. But at least if we had my car we'd be mobile."

"Mine is stuck in the community car park. It's too close and too dangerous to get it. Where is yours?"

"In a lock-up I rent close to home."

"How close?" questioned Jon.

"I think we could get to it safely. They shouldn't know about it. I only started renting the garage last month."

"Hmm. Never take anything for granted," muttered Jon philosophically.

"We need cash, desperately. How much have you got?"

"Very little after that hotel," said Jon turning his mouth down.

"Let's get my car, find a motel and take it from there." She peered out of the window. "We're coming to Alexandra Road. It's only five minutes from there. Come on."

They alighted from the bus and walked down the road. "Where's the nearest Internet café?" asked Jon.

"Why?"

"Do you always have to answer a question with another one? Bear with me."

"Do I do that? Answer a question with another?"

"Yes."

Amy suddenly connected with Jon's line of thought, "Oh, I get it! We can use it without being bugged. Nice one."

Carol was dressed casually in jogging bottoms, a sweatshirt, baseball cap and trainers. Her hair was stuffed inside her hat and her face devoid of makeup. Her eyes were glassy and her expression fixed. She strode out purposefully along the bank of the river. She looked like a woman on a mission.

She began to jog and no one gave her a second look. She passed other runners on the path and her breathing was measured and even. She speeded up and her breathing became heavier. She reached a tree on the path and stopped. Overcome by a surge of grief she slumped down and swore, "God Damn!" She laid her head in her hands and wept. She cried for Karl, and she cried for herself. Her mobile phone rang and jolted her to her senses. She snatched at her phone with trembling fingers and answered, "Yes?"

Carol listened and her eyes glazed over. She stood up and brushed herself down and marched toward the entrance to a marina. Without a glance back, without hesitation she punched in a key code and opened the security gate. She strode on, turned along a jetty and headed for a boat moored at the end of the pier. She jumped onto the back of the Lady Giselle and fiddled with the lock on the door and entered, closing it fast behind her and settled down to wait.

Carol explored the berths and hid. She was sitting in a cramped position in a shower room off a small cabin. She checked her watch. According to her instructions her target would be boarding shortly. She took a deep intake of breath. She hoped it wouldn't be long.

The boat rocked as someone stepped aboard. There was more movement as two more people climbed aboard. Carol stiffened. She prayed that neither her intended victim nor his guests would enter this birth. She had deliberately picked the smallest in the belief that the larger cabins would be taken first. The engine grumbled into life and the boat began to chug its way out of the marina.

Someone had put the radio on; a music channel was playing one of Electra's songs and Carol heard male voices. It was all as she had been led to believe. She just had to wait. The boat cleared the Thames barrier and began travelling out to sea.

On deck, Birchell was enjoying a drink as he piloted the boat. His son, David chinked glasses with him. "Where are we going? And why tonight?" David questioned.

"I have to get out for a little while. I need a break. We'll anchor up a bit further out in the North Sea. We're well stocked up, and then we can head around the coast for the Channel Islands. Our final destination is the Med for a few months."

"Can't you tell us what's going on, Dad?" questioned his other son, Andrew.

"Not yet. We just need to watch our backs."

"Yours? Or all of us?"

"Mine for the moment. That's why I can't say anything. Pour me another drink."

The boat cruised on and began to travel around the British coastline staying reasonably close to shore. A small pilot boat followed at a safe distance and watched their progress.

They travelled for over two hours and moored up in a small bay. David worked in the galley and prepared some plates of food, which he took on deck as Andrew replenished everyone's glass. Birchell moved onto malt whiskey. His son, David advised, "Please, Dad, don't mix it. You know what that stuff does to you."

"Right now, I don't care. If you don't like it don't watch."

"At least eat something."

Andrew passed his father a plate and Birchell took a chicken drumstick and gnawed on it before tossing the bone into the water. Birchell studied the faces of his sons who looked filled with concern, and relented, "Okay, boys I'm sorry. I'll stick to the wine. Let's open another bottle and eat this veritable feast that David's served up. I need to relax and unwind. At least, I should be safe out here. I'll reveal more to you tomorrow but for now… let's party!" He turned up the volume on the music.

Father and sons continued eating and drinking into the early hours. Carol remained hidden. Andrew was the first to announce, "I'm bushed. I'm going to grab a bed and sleep. See you both tomorrow." He descended to the lower deck and selected one of the spacious cabins and flopped on the bed. He was in a snoring sleep in just a few minutes.

David spoke up, "Think I'll retire, too." He yawned loudly, "Do you want me to clear this up?"

"Nah! Leave it till the morning. It's not going anywhere," said Birchell wryly.

David grinned and hugged his father goodnight and he, too, went below to crash out in one of the luxury cabins.

Birchell took out a cigarette and lit it. He gazed up at the night sky, littered with stars and sighed. There was a slight noise behind him. Birchell spoke, "Forgotten something?"

There was no answer and he turned and came face to face with Carol. His eyes opened wide in surprise, "You…" he didn't say anymore as the knife she was wielding plunged into his heart. Carol caught him as he staggered forward and she flipped him backward over the rail and his body splashed into the cold black waters below. Carol tossed the knife in after him and watched as the body sank.

She wiped her bloodstained hands on her sweatshirt and moved to the prow of the vessel, where she stood outside on the front as the small pilot boat silently came alongside. Carol was helped off and into the small craft, which sped away.

Andrew stirred in his sleep and sat up. He rubbed his eyes and a feeling of unease crept through him. He arose and looked in the cabins on the lower deck. He couldn't see his father and returned to the top deck to look for him. It was with horror he saw the blood spatters covering the cream leather and the bloody smears on the rails. He shouted in anguish, "Dad!"

The following morning just after dawn Amy and Jon were uncomfortably asleep in her Mini, parked in a Shopping Centre Car Park. Jon moved and nudged Amy's arm, which hit the horn that blared out, suddenly waking her. "This isn't any good. I haven't slept at all," she complained.

Jon was quick to refute this, "You've been snoring like a little porker."

"I have not!" argued Amy.

"I had no idea there were such a variety of sounds that a human being could make," returned Jon.

"And what about your choo choo train?" accused Amy.

"What?"

Amy launched into an impression of Jon asleep breathing in and blowing out through his mouth in a puffing action.

"Get on!" he chided in disbelief.

"I'll get some cash," announced Amy feeling as if she had won that round. She struggled to extricate herself from the Mini, and scrambled out from the cramped car but nearly fell as her leg had gone to sleep. She made a face and stamped her foot hard hopping around on the tarmac outside the vehicle trying to rid herself of the numbing pins and needles.

Amy smacked her lips and twisted them in an unpleasant grimace as her mouth tasted sour. She rummaged in her handbag for some chewing gum and popped one in her mouth, which she chewed with relief. She limped toward the cash point and took out her banker's card, which she inserted in the flashing slot and tapped in her pin number. Instead of receiving cash the machine swallowed her card. A message appeared on screen: 'Refer to the Bank'.

"Bugger!" exclaimed Amy and ran back to the car.

A cheer went up in the black van that had been parked outside Jon's house. "Got a trace! She's just tried to use her cash card… Silly girl." The black van started its engine and pulled away heading for the Shopping Centre Car Park.

Amy and Jon reversed quickly out of the parking space and fled the place. Amy was driving as Jon was on full alert checking the traffic and other vehicles on the road. Amy was still railing against the loss of her card, "There were plenty of funds. Ibrahim's cheque was in there."

"We'll try my private account. But first, let's get some breakfast and clean up. My mouth feels like the cat's litter tray," groaned Jon.

Amy swung the car around and pulled into a twenty-four hour supermarket, where she parked the Mini. "They do full English here for two ninety-five …. They also have a loo and sell toothbrushes and paste."

"Done!" enthused Jon.

They both left the Mini and pushed through the double doors of the supermarket. Amy headed straight for the café while Jon picked up a basket and grabbed a daily paper. The same headline shrieked across all the tabloids and broad sheets, 'NEWSPAPER MAGNATE ROBERT BIRCHELL DROWNS IN FREAK BOATING ACCIDENT'. His face appeared in a large photograph next to the article, with a sub heading, 'Body Not Found.'

Jon moved around the relatively empty store and picked up some toothbrushes, toothpaste, soap, flannels and a couple of towels. He tossed them in his basket and made his way to the check out. He paid for his goods and joined Amy in the café.

As soon as he appeared she removed her jacket and laid it on the chair. He dumped his shopping and they went to the counter to order their breakfast. Jon ordered the full works while Amy was more conservative with tea and toast.

"You ought to have more than that," said Jon. "You don't know when we'll get to eat again. Come on, Amy. Have something more."

The café assistant looked at her and Amy submitted, "Oh, go on then, I'll have the same." She turned to Jon. "Wouldn't do me any good to live with you. I'd be the size of a house in no time."

"Nah, you wouldn't. You'd be gorgeous," replied Jon.

"Are you flirting with me?" asked Amy batting her eyelashes exaggeratedly.

"Moi? No. Didn't I tell you? I'm gay," he teased.

"Thought so… that's why you have resisted me and have a male cat." Their breakfasts were passed over the counter to them and they pushed their trays to the till.

"I'll get these," said Jon. "May as well clean myself out!"

They strolled back to the table and began to tuck in. "I didn't realise how hungry I was," murmured Amy between mouthfuls.

"Thought so, when did you last eat?" asked Jon.

"Too long ago, obviously," said Amy forking another piece of bacon into her mouth.

Jon's tone became serious, "Now, I think we need to get to an Internet Café as soon as possible."

"The nearest one's about two blocks from here. Not far."

"We can't use any of the office PC's or mine at home. Apart from being watched, I think they've bugged them."

"But, just who are they?" asked Amy. "Who is it we are we running from?"

"I don't know. We've stumbled onto something that puts us in the firing line and until we can put all the pieces together. We're in trouble."

"We can't fight Government forces," agreed Amy.

"I don't think it's just Government forces."

"What if we turn ourselves into the police?"

"No. I believe that really would seal our fate. We'd disappear forever. Someone is blocking our every move. Before long, we won't officially exist. What then?"

"Jon, what are we going to do?'

"I don't know. I really don't know, but when we've finished our breakfast, let's get to that café."

"Use my laptop."

"Not this time. Just in case."

"It can't possibly have been got at," protested Amy.

"Humour me. Let's play it safe."

"When we've done I need to get cleaned up. Sleeping the night in the car is not the healthiest way to spend the night."

"Then I have gifts," grinned Jon and he showed Amy his purchases.

"Oh, Jon. You're a star! Thank you," gushed Amy.

"You go first and I'll watch your coat," said Jon. "And I'll have another cup of tea."

They finished their breakfast and Amy made her way out to the public toilets, where she washed as much as was acceptable in public and scrubbed her teeth much to the amusement of various customers coming in to use the facilities. She sighed, "Ah, nothing like a fresh mouth!"

A woman, responded, "No, I agree. What was it, love? A night on the tiles and got to get to work? I know what that's like."

Amy grinned, "You wouldn't believe me if I told you but now… at least I feel human again."

The woman disappeared into a stall and Amy left the Ladies with a distinct spring in her step feeling fresher and more in control.

Jon had left the café, done his ablutions and was waiting outside with her coat.

"I suppose if the worst came to the worst, we could always use this place as a stop-over point. Sleep in the car park, wash and breakfast here," mused Jon.

"Forget it! We're going to do something about this conspiracy, whatever it is, and we're going to win."

"I just love it when you get assertive," laughed Jon.

"Hold that thought. But, remember dominatrix I am not!" she quipped.

They reached the car and set off for the café. "There's a car park around here somewhere. I just know it," thought Amy aloud.

"Over there. That pub car park. That'll do won't it?" suggested Jon.

Amy nodded and swiftly parked in the back of The Green Man pub. They scanned the area around them. This was now becoming second nature. They began to walk toward the Internet Café. They glanced up at the name, 'On-line'. It was just opening up as they entered. They paid for an hour and selected a PC away from the window.

The café was quiet; only one other person had entered and was now online. Jon settled himself at a PC and began to type. He hacked into a classified address taken from his printout. "That should do it... Now then..." And he scrolled through the ensuing data and information.

Chapter Eleven

Hidden Ally

CLAIRE WAS ON THE top floor of the multi-storey car park. She climbed onto the railing above the concrete wall without looking down and altered the angle of the security camera so her own motor was not in shot. Breathing heavily from her exertions she jumped down and hurried to remove the envelope from the boot of the car and placed it on the back seat of the vehicle. She slapped a resident's permit on the dash, stowed a mobile phone in the glove compartment, along with another envelope, locked the car and walked away from it toward the stairwell and lift to take her to the main entrance.

Claire glanced about her to ensure she was unobserved. The place seemed deserted. She ran down the stone steps wrinkling her nose in distaste at places where someone had used a landing as a urinal or worse. She took a deep gulp of air when she arrived at street level and watched the passing traffic waiting for a cab that was free to hire and looking for business. She crossed to her regular newspaper vendor.

"Usual, love?" asked the old chap.

"Please."

The newspaper seller picked up a paper and flipped it into three and passed it to her. Without another look at it she pushed it into her bag and fished in her pocket for some change and paid him. She scanned the road both sides still looking for a taxi.

She didn't have long to wait. A black cab with its hire lights on, was heading toward her. She flagged it down.

The journey passed uneventfully and Claire was lost in her thoughts. There was an innate sadness about her, but a steely determination, too. The taxi drew up outside the disguised Homeland Security Offices of MI6 where she worked. She paid the driver, took a deep breath and ran inside the building.

After wishing the Security Officers, who checked her pass, good morning she stepped into the lift and got out at her floor and made her way to the office. She looked around the room. Two other workers were in place. There was no sign of Max or Jack. Claire sat at her desk and pulled out her paper. She gasped in shock. On the front page was the story of Birchell's 'accident'. With growing horror, she read the news item. His words echoed in her head, 'It's just a matter of time. How and when? That's the mystery.' She thrust down the paper and booted up her PC.

The black van was on patrol with Biff driving and Ron in the front passenger seat. Steve and Alan were on duty using the high tech surveillance equipment in the back.

Steve called out to Biff, "Someone is using classified codes to access the Mind Control Programme. And it's not from an official source."

"Kill it and put out a trace," ordered Biff. "Notify Max and his team."

The information was immediately transferred in a coded alert to Claire. She tuned in to the online movement and paused uncertainly wondering what to do. She suspected it was the filmmakers. She licked her lips nervously and taking a chance she made a decision. She hooked onto the same signal and began to type quickly and with extreme urgency.

Max and Jack arrived in the office. They strolled in chatting affably. Claire turned and spotted them and hastily cleared her screen. Jack plonked a dozen free range eggs on the desk next to her keyboard.

"There you go. They're the best, the largest. Some may even be double yolkers," he announced cheerfully.

Claire nervously ran her fingers through her hair. She hurriedly deleted her history. Jack and Max looked at each other in puzzlement as if to say, 'What is she up to?'

Claire rose from her PC and tried to show that she was poised. She gave a half smile and said lamely, "Hit the wrong button."

She hoped Max would accept her explanation but a part of her felt he didn't. She knew he couldn't be exactly sure of what he had seen, but she realised that her actions could look suspicious to him.

Jon and Amy seated in the café were studying, with growing alarm, the accessed file on screen when to their amazement the information deleted before their eyes. "Aw…What?" exclaimed Jon.

"It can't be…" added Amy.

A message came up on his PC and flashed an alert, 'GET OUT NOW. GO TO LEVEL THREE TOP FLOOR GEORGE STREET CAR PARK. GO!' After what they had been through they didn't need to be told twice. They stood up and moved to the exit. They looked out and saw the black van speeding down the road approaching the café. They turned back and headed for the back of the premises.

Amy asked the waitress behind the counter, "Ladies loo? Gents?"

The waitress gestured with her head, "Out back."

Jon and Amy scrambled to the toilets. They each entered their respective gender's toilets and locked the doors inside. Jon pulled open the window, stepped on the lavatory seat and wriggled through the gap into the yard below. Amy was scrambling out of a very small window and nearly got stuck. "I knew I shouldn't have had that breakfast," she complained.

"Hush up!" ordered Jon. Give me your hands. He tugged and she finally popped through the gap and landed on her tummy outside, on top of the waste bins. Jon gave her a leg up; they shinned over the fence, and dropped down the other side onto the road. As they landed there was a massive explosion. The ground shook and sirens were heard. The Internet Café had been bombed.

A policeman just going off duty stopped in his patrol car and parked up outside the Green Man Pub. He went around the back to the Gents' toilets that were outside in the beer garden and passed through the rear car park. He noticed Amy's Mini Cooper and paused. His toilet stop forgotten he walked around the vehicle and checked the licence plate. He took out his notebook and checked a number he had scrawled in haste from a police message and immediately alerted his superiors on his radio.

"Suspect vehicle wanted in the Hit and Run on Friday. It's in the back car park of the Green Man Pub, Clapham. I've checked the bodywork, there's no evidence of an accident. What do you want me to do?"

"Location has been noted. Continue with your duties, someone will be out to tow the car shortly. We will send an unmarked car to wait for the suspect's return. You can leave the scene. We will deal with it."

The policeman acknowledged and made his visit to the Gents, returned to his vehicle and left the scene as instructed. He was relieved that he didn't have to stay, it had been a long night and he was looking forward to getting home and falling into bed. Although, he had heard some sort of sonic boom and sirens in the distance, he hoped he would get home before someone redirected him elsewhere.

As soon as the Police car pulled out of the car park and into the traffic the black van drove to the pub and raced around the back. Obeying instructions Steve stepped out from the back and planted a GPS tracking device underneath the back bumper. Then sped away and parked at a safe distance from the pub to watch. The café had been virtually destroyed but the operatives didn't know whether Jon and Amy had escaped or not. They were prepared to wait and see.

Claire felt increasingly uneasy in the office and tried to regain her usual calm demeanour and poise. She picked up her jacket, which she wrapped around a small package she had brought with her and then moved to the door. "I'm going to pick up some doughnuts, run a few errands. You guys want anything?" she asked.

Max checked his watch and eyed her critically. "Bit early for that isn't it?"

"It's all right. I'll work through lunch. There're a couple of things I have to do. Besides, I need change for the eggs," she said, trying to keep her voice level.

Max nodded as if he was unperturbed. As soon as she went out of the door he signalled to Jack to follow her. Max picked up the newspaper from her desk and read the article that Claire had been reading. A thoughtful expression settled on his face.

Amy and Jon ran in a blind panic to The Green Man Car Park to Amy's car. Her hands were shaking so much that as she fumbled with the lock, she dropped the keys twice. She eventually opened the door and they scrambled in. She drove off at pace, with tyres screaming.

"Calm down, Amy. Slow down. We don't want to attract any attention."

"That was meant for us," she sobbed.

"I know…. Those poor people."

"What do we do now?" said Amy, as tears streamed down her face.

"Head for the car park … Do you know where it is? This George Street."

Amy nodded, she checked her mirror and swore, "Oh my God. Look behind."

Behind them was a black van following them about three cars back travelling at a steady pace. "Look! A black van. Is it them?"

"I don't know. Can you lose it?"

"I can try."

Amy shifted the Mini into third gear and pulled out to overtake the car in front. Jon watched the vehicle behind. "It must be them. He's pulling out after us."

"I can see," cried Amy, her eyes flicked back and for to the mirror and the road. "How? How did they find us? And my car?"

Amy speeded up. She drove as fast as she dared in the suburban roads and raced through a light as it was turning to red. The black van was forced to stop and wait. Amy took advantage of this she turned down a side street and off into another and parked with the engine running but hidden behind a builder's skip on the side of the road.

The black van was in full pursuit and turned off. It whizzed past the first side street, then stopped abruptly and reversed back its wheels spinning and turned into the same street. By this time Amy and Jon had moved off again.

"There must be some sort of tracking device here somewhere. We need to get out of range," shouted Jon. He twisted around in his seat watching the traffic behind him.

"I don't think I can drive that fast," Amy murmured.

"Just get to that car park," urged Jon.

Amy manoeuvred the Mini, "Then what?"

"I'm thinking."

"Well, I hope you get the germ of an idea soon!"

"Shit!"

"What?"

"The black van. It's behind us again."

Claire was exiting a bakery, carrying a bag of goodies. She scanned the street around her and caught a glimpse of Jack watching her from across the road.

She started to half run and half walk down the avenue. She quickened her pace, flagged down a black cab, got in and it drove away. She looked back out of the window and saw that Jack had emerged from his observation post. He ran down the street trying to find a taxi to hail, in order to follow her but there was not one to be seen.

Max was wearing headphones sitting at a screen in communication with the operatives in the black van. "Keep after them. And this time, don't lose them," he commanded.

A crestfallen Jack entered the office, and Max looked up.

"Don't tell me you lost her?"

"She got the doughnuts then hailed a cab. I couldn't follow her."

"Never mind. She'll be back. But for how long I don't know." Max looked meaningfully at Jack.

"Christ, Max! Not Claire?"

"Deal with it… We all have to."

"But, she hasn't paid for the eggs yet," Jack said lamely.

"It won't be immediate… but it will be soon."

Amy hurtled down a tree-lined avenue. She glanced in her mirror, "Damn, damn and damn again! They're still with us."

"Drive faster."

"I'm doing the best I can."

"Not good enough."

"Okay, smarty pants. What else do you suggest?"

At that point a lorry began to pull out from the kerb and Amy swerved around it. Cars honked angrily at her as she strayed out of her lane. The black van became stuck behind the lorry and Amy took full advantage. She dodged, twisted and turned in the Mini and raced down the main thoroughfare, turned back on herself with a U turn and into George Street.

"You realise, of course, that this could be a set up and in here we're trapped," observed Amy.

"We have no choice. Step on it!"

Rubber burned and tyres screamed as she entered the multi-storey car park. They careered around the twisting spiral of a ramp to the third level and onto the top floor. As they turned into the space a woman stepped out and waved them down. She was of slim build with short fair hair. The two filmmakers looked at each other.

"Do you think she's the one…" Jon didn't finish the sentence.

"Only one way to find out," said Amy, who stopped and parked next to her. Cautiously, the filmmakers stepped out of the car.

"Are you…?" asked Jon tentatively. "Are you the one who's been helping us?"

"Yes. You have to trust me."

"What do we call you?" asked Amy.

"Claire."

"Claire…?"

"Just Claire. Here, take this car it's safer." Claire handed them a set of car keys. "Is there anything else you need?"

"Money. Our business accounts have been shut down. We've nowhere to go," explained Amy.

"You'll have to get out of the country," declared Claire.

Amy and Jon looked at each other in dismay. "How do we do that?" pressed Amy.

"Is there anyone who can help you? Someone you can trust."

"Ibrahim Khalid. He's been bank rolling us," claimed Jon.

"You'll need new ID's. I have that in hand, as you will see. I'll call you and explain."

"How?"

"I will, believe me; most of the work has been done. Now, hurry."

Amy opened the boot of her Mini and took out Jon's briefcase and her laptop bag, then hurriedly got into the front passenger seat, with Jon driving. He started the engine, reversed out of the parking space and drove off at speed. They raced down the ramps and fled into the street and away.

Claire took the small package she was carrying and unwrapped it. She attached it underneath Amy's Mini. She sped away and ran down the stairs of the car park. She saw the approach of the black van and darted back out of sight. The vehicle entered the multi-storey and headed for the first ramp. Claire watched them go by unobserved and then detonated the device under Amy's Mini.

Inside the van Steve had remarked, "They're parked. Keep an eye out."

Suddenly, there was a huge explosion, which rocked the black van. The trace on the computer screen vanished. "Bugger!" yelled Steve. "What now?"

Amy and Jon were driving at a steady pace unsure where they were going or what they would do. Amy glanced behind her and on the back seat of the car was a large thickly stuffed envelope. She had to undo her seatbelt to get at it. She grabbed it and swivelled around and began to look through the contents. She gasped in astonishment, "I can't believe what I'm seeing."

"What? What is it?"

"More on this mind control programme… Remember Christopher Lomax?"

"Who wouldn't? Electra used his execution as a basis for one of her biggest hits."

"The Shortest Day," affirmed Amy.

"What about it?" questioned Jon, curiously.

"According to this, Lomax was revived and used in the programme. He underwent plastic surgery."

"And?"

Amy showed a picture of Paul Grayson, which Jon snatched a look at. "No wonder he didn't know his own name." The realisation of the man's identity caused him to swerve violently.

"Watch out!" shrieked Amy. A car honked crossly at him as he strayed across into the oncoming traffic. "Where exactly are we going?" she asked once she had recovered from the near miss of an accident.

"I thought we'd try a Travel Lodge near Heathrow."

"We've got to get some cash and clothes. I'm beginning not to like my own company," she said sniffing herself.

"They've tampered with our business account. What about our private ones?"

"Too risky," asserted Amy.

"For you, maybe. I have one in my pen name. That may be safe. It's worth a shot."

"Let's do it, but park the car somewhere safe where it won't be connected to us."

"Just in case?"

"Just in case."

Chapter Twelve

Hunted

EVER WATCHFUL, CLAIRE WENT into High Street to a mobile phone shop and bought a cheap pay as you go phone. She used a false name and address to register the item, as this was the mobile she would use to contact Ibrahim and explain the peril of the filmmakers' situation. She daren't use her own as she was certain it would be tapped. Now, she had become frustrated in trying to get through to him. Even though she had his private number she was forced to go through a host of people before she was allowed to speak to him. And now that she had him on the other end of the line, she was having a hard job convincing him that she was telling the truth.

"So, there you have it. They are in serious trouble," concluded Claire.

A pause. "It all seems a little convenient," replied Ibrahim guardedly.

"Dammit! If you don't believe me try contacting them yourself... You'll find officially, they don't exist."

"I might just do that"

"And how are they supposed to manage?" demanded Claire.

"Just supposing I do believe you, and I'm not saying I do, what do you want me to do?"

"Get them enough cash to get them out of the country for a few months and I'll give you information, which you can use to out this conspiracy."

"So, you agree there is one?"

"I have to go."

"Okay. Get to the Hilton tomorrow afternoon at three. A room will be booked in the name of Blake. You'll hear from me then."

Claire replaced the receiver, looked about her, picked up her bag of doughnuts and a dry cleaning bag and strode toward the underground.

Ibrahim stared at the phone, Carol watched him from the bedroom door. He picked up the phone book, searched through it and found the number of Monumentous Films. He dialled. He didn't have long to wait.

A telephone receptionist answered in coolly efficient tones, "Reid, Charters and Pearce Construction...."

Ibrahim put down the telephone. He was now very concerned and listened to his inner voice, which was telling him the woman on the end of the phone had spoken the truth. His face was troubled. He suddenly became aware of another presence. Feeling he was being watched, he turned around and saw Carol. She smiled and walked toward him.

The cameras continued to serve, delivering every detail to those who needed to know.

Jon was completing a transaction in the very prestigious Coutts Bank. The teller counted out two thousand pounds, which Jon put away in his wallet. Amy sat on a comfortable leather seat and watched him in awe. She was clearly impressed with the bank and its plush surroundings.

Jon walked back to her and Amy rose. The teller behind the counter observed them move toward the front door. She kept her eyes on the filmmakers, picked up a telephone and made a call. "I've just paid Jon Curtis AKA Jon Chandler two thousand pounds."

"Was he alone?" asked the voice on the other end of the line.

"No, he was in here with a woman."

"So, they are both alive... Shut down and close his account, transfer any funds to escrow. If they return, notify me and stall them."

Jon and Amy were oblivious to what was been said. They were just delighted to have some cash. "When you said you had another private account, I never imagined it would be Coutts," said Amy.

"Well, I always intended to be rich and famous one day... Jon Chandler noted author and playwright."

"Is that your pen name?"

"It was my mother's maiden name," explained Jon as they left the building.

The operatives and agents were in the black van awaiting further orders. Alan and Steve on headsets received instructions. Alan shouted across to Biff and Ron, "Coutts bank. Now!"

The black van turned haphazardly and sped off.

Amy and Jon were now safely back in the car. Amy was struggling with a large ordinance survey map trying to find a quick route through to Heathrow. She spread the map out to such an extent that the paper obstructed Jon's vision and he had to stick his head out of the window to see where he was going.

"Amy!" he exclaimed crossly.

"Sorry!" She battled with the huge swatch of paper trying to reorganise it. They progressed further down the street. Amy was still fighting the map and Jon kept driving with his head stuck out of the window when he saw the black van approaching from the opposite direction. He quickly ducked his head back inside the car as the black van hurtled past.

Jon punched the paper with his fist. Amy had no idea what was happening and squealed in annoyance and fright. He hissed at her, "Get down!"

Just then a phone began to ring. Amy looked at Jon.

"Don't look at me. It's not my ring tone."

Amy searched about her for the source of the sound and opened the glove compartment. There was a mobile phone in there with another envelope. She answered cautiously, "Hello?"

"They're on to you. Someone at the bank. You can't go back there. You have got to get new ID's," warned their female deep throat, Claire.

"But how?" questioned Amy.

"The packet I left you with the phone. The instructions are in there."

"Then what?"

"I'll meet you tomorrow," Claire asserted.

"Where and when?" demanded Amy.

"I'll call you. That phone is safe to use but don't over use it. Oh, and don't use your laptop. It's got a trace. I'll email you an eradicating programme when you have cleared the country. I've deleted the GPS on the idle machine. It's fine as long as you don't start it up."

Claire terminated the call. Amy looked stunned and then burst into life. She tore into the envelope.

"What is it?" asked Jon.

"It's a list of names and birthdays. Infants who died young…"

"So?"

"So, we use one of these to get ourselves a birth certificate and apply for a passport."

"Okay, so the sooner we find somewhere to stay, the better and then we can forward plan."

"There should be a Travel Lodge through the next roundabout on the left," said Amy interpreting the signs.

Jon continued, following Amy's directions. He drove on until she excitedly pointed it out. "There! There! Over there!"

Jon smartly turned the car into the car park and stopped. "Okay. Let's hope they have room at the inn," he joked. "We better get our story straight."

"Yes. Our names and address," replied Amy.

A few moments later they were at the desk and signing the register as Mr and Mrs Murphy from 5, Broome Close, Stevenage. The desk clerk didn't bat an eyelid and checked them in to room seven.

"Seven is my lucky number," smiled Amy, looking up at Jon.

"Thank God for that. We need a barrow load of luck and more," said Jon, unlocking the room.

They entered the plain, clean and functional room. "Well, the Hilton it ain't," grinned Amy. "No champagne... Fancy a cuppa?"

"Please, I'm gasping. There's nothing like a good cup of tea. It helps put things into perspective."

Amy filled the electric kettle and twittered on as Jon sat on the bed watching her. He studied her shapely form, the curves of her hips, her pert bottom and neat tiny waist. She turned from the dressing table housing the tea things and giggled mischievously. He didn't hear what she said but studied her huge eyes and dark curling lashes, her soft, inviting lips, and her upturned nose. He admired her thick, glossy hair that showered her most perfect shoulders. She stopped speaking and stared back at him. He then realised that she had asked him a question, "Sorry? What? What did you say?"

"I said, we even have biscuits. A veritable feast, no less. Do you prefer ginger nuts or custard creams?"

"Um, whatever. You choose. Ladies first," Jon answered. He shook his head as if trying to clear his mind from the thoughts that were tumbling through his head, the passion of which unnerved him.

Amy noticed the change in him; his studied gaze, and she became aware of a prickling of electricity that pulsed through her. "What? What is it? What have I said?"

Jon patted the bed next to him. "Come, come and sit here. We need to talk."

Across town, Claire safely entered a small local library and retreated to the reference section and sat at a table at the back. She was alone and unobserved. She checked both of her phones and switched them off before putting them away carefully.

She lifted up her backpack and pulled out two big packages. Claire thoroughly checked the contents of each one and wrote covering letters to accompany them. She chose her words carefully and her nerves became more and more apparent. She knew she had to get this done now before it was too late.

The library CCTV monitored her as she worked.

With a shaking hand she sealed the first package and made it doubly secure with strips of parcel tape and then she took her pen and began to address it. The addressee was the editor of a national paper; a popular broadsheet that Claire felt would be able to use the contained information. She checked the postcode from a reference directory and added it.

Sighing heavily, she repeated the exercise with the second package. This one was assigned to a firm of solicitors, Greig, Dunbar and Wilks. She sat there a few moments longer trying to compose herself and quiet her churning emotions. Claire knew she had to get control of herself if she was to pull this off. She stood up, stuffed the packets back into her rucksack and left. She ran down the stairs out of the library and headed for the nearest Post Office and joined the very lengthy queue, where everyone stood in line and cameras watched them.

"Cashier number eight, please," intoned the recorded voice and slowly she moved up the queue until she was summoned to cashier number five. Claire placed the first packet on the scales, then the second and paid to have both delivered by recorded delivery.

The girl behind the counter dropped the parcels into a thick canvas sack. Claire smiled and walked away. She had done it. Her shoulders went back, her head lifted up and there was more of a purpose and steely determination in her step, but a sense of euphoria, too.

Amy sat with Jon on the bed. "So, you wanted to talk. Talk."

"Yes, we will, but first… I'm going to take a shower."

"Thanks, you need to!" exclaimed Amy.

"Cheeky! What about yourself?" responded Jon.

"Eau de unwashed woman and aroma de stale pub clothes. I thought it was your favourite," chirped Amy.

"In a former life maybe." Jon paused and gazed at her once more. He leaned in toward her. "What do you say?"

Amy cheekily leaned in toward him and became playfully teasing. "What do I say about what?"

Jon's demeanour changed as the reality of their situation kicked in telling him that now was not the time. "Nothing. It doesn't matter."

Amy put her hand on Jon's thigh to stop him moving away, and lowered her voice seductively, "No. Go on."

Jon stared at her hard. Amy started to remove her hand realising the intensity of the moment. He grabbed both ends of the scarf she was wearing and pulled her into him. She didn't resist. Their passion became more urgent. Jon took off his jumper and she feverishly undid her blouse. His eyes drank her in and she suddenly became modestly shy.

"You're beautiful," whispered Jon.

"You never noticed me before," replied Amy.

"I never allowed myself to notice you before."

"It screws up working relationships."

"We know each other better than that," said Jon.

"Do we?" asked Amy huskily.

Jon stopped himself from going any further. He rose and moved to the bathroom door. "No, you're right. This is neither the time nor the place."

Amy stopped him, "Jon?"

He turned back to her.

"If not now, then when?"

Jon looked at her pleading eyes and unable to resist her any longer he returned to the bed and straddled her, smothering her with kisses. Amy's face filled with absolute joy.

They caressed and kissed and with a passion divined from their desperate situation, began to make love with dramatic fervour. Their bodies melded together and became slick with sweat. Neither wanted the moment to be over.

Overcome with their strengthening loving desire the tempo changed and slowed. The thrusts became gentle, deeper and more satisfying. Jon was gratified when Amy trembled in orgasmic delight and only then did he allow himself to let go. For a first time it was tender, loving and immensely fulfilling.

Jon rolled off her and flopped onto his back. "I need a shower."

"Me too."

Jon caught her hand and pulled her to her feet. As their bodies met he could feel his passion rising again. They went into the bathroom and Jon started up the shower. The hot water soon flooded through and the room began to fill with steam. They both stepped into the shower stall and lovingly soaped and explored each other's bodies. Their sighs mingled with the splashing of the water, their breath disappeared into the clouds of steam. Jon took her again and Amy groaned in pleasure as he lifted her up and she wrapped her limbs around his waist. This time the climax built more slowly and they deliberately delayed the moment causing a heightening, urgent need that culminated in a flooding, melting ecstasy that made their eyelids flutter and their bodies shudder.

Amy unwrapped herself from him and Jon lovingly washed her body, shampooed her hair and cleansed Amy's most intimate and private parts and he sighed in pleasure.

Amy stepped out of the shower and wrapped herself up in a thick fluffy towel and retreated to the bedroom, where she dried herself and her hair. Not wanting to put on her stale clothes she slipped naked between the sheets and switched on the television. Jon's cheerful whistle resonated into the room and Amy smiled as she idly flicked through the channels and clicked on the late night news.

She sat up in shock as she saw Jon's face staring out at her. She turned up the sound.

"... is a suspected terrorist working with an animal rights group. Earlier today he stole a cat from a military facility in Hertfordshire. It is believed the animal is carrying the deadly Ebola virus. Do not confront this man, if seen go directly to your local police station."

Amy shouted to her partner, "JON!"

Jon switched off the running water and emerged towelling himself dry. He saw Amy's horror struck face and sat by her on the bed. "What is it?"

Amy explained what she had seen and Jon's face became serious. "What do we do?" asked Amy.

Jon spoke matter of factly, "We change our appearances."

"Okay, how?"

"You'll have to go out. Get to an all-night supermarket."

"Aw, what? Where?"

"Ask at Reception. I daren't be seen."

"I have to wear those stinky clothes," complained Amy.

"Get new ones and we need a pair of scissors, hair dye and underwear."

"And washing powder."

"There you go."

"Have we got enough money?"

"Here," Jon took a wad of notes from his wallet. "We are going to have to be careful. This won't last long."

Amy took the cash and slapped it on the bedside table. She reluctantly got out of bed and began to dress, frequently interrupted by Jon who made it very difficult for her to leave. She gave him a kiss and departed the room and headed for Reception. The girl was disinterested in Amy's request but pointed out that she only had to walk through the car park to the end where there were steps that led to a path going directly to a twenty-four hour Sainsbury's and a small shopping plaza.

Amy dashed off following the girl's instructions and came across the superstore. She grabbed a trolley and went up and down the aisles as quickly as possible, gathering a number of items, washing powder, new underwear for both of them, a couple of shirts and trousers for Jon, and tops and slacks for herself, hairdressing scissors and hair dye, and two matching holdalls. She dropped in a couple of salad plates from the deli and some other selected food items.

Amy hurried through the checkout and back outside. All the time she was watchful and careful to look inconspicuous. She carried her orange plastic bags briskly back to the Travel Lodge and was relieved when she was back inside the room.

"Okay," said Jon. "Get cracking and cut my hair."

"I've never cut anyone's hair…. Then again, how hard can it be?"

Jon sat and wrapped a towel around his shoulders and waited for the first cut.

Amy lopped a chunk of his long flowing locks. Jon winced as his hair fell to the floor.

"Ouch. That hurt, didn't it?" said Amy sympathetically.

"Worn my hair long for…" he calculated on his fingers, "Eleven years." Amy wielded the cutters again, and another lock fell. "Just do it," he ordered. "It's got to be done."

Amy chopped and trimmed and tidied until his hair resembled someone in the forces. Jon studied his new look in the mirror disapprovingly and Amy continued, "Actually, it doesn't look half bad… Now for the hair dye."

Jon was pasted up with a purple brown foam. Amy timed the colour's development for thirty minutes then rinsed the mixture off. She looked at her handiwork. "Your own mother wouldn't recognise you, now. Damn, I wouldn't recognise you. Some designer stubble will complete the look."

Jon studied his reflection critically, "I need to pad out my cheeks a bit, change their shape."

"And how are you going to do that?"

"Not sure, use a wad of cotton wool?"

"Like Marlon Brando in the Godfather?"

"It's a thought."

"How will you speak or eat?"

"Good point. Maybe not! Okay, your turn now."

Amy grumbled as she sat in the chair, "I hate short hair. It doesn't suit me at all and I can't hide behind it."

"That's what you do when you hang your head forward. You stop people seeing what you're thinking."

"Caught me," Amy admitted and winced as Jon began to hack at her lustrous locks.

Jon pulled at a swatch of her hair and cut and cut and cut. He shaped and feathered and concentrated hard. He brushed the hair forward and gave her a fringe.

He looked critically at his handiwork and smiled, "It looks good, even if I do say so myself. It suits you."

Amy rose and walked to the mirror. She studied her very elfin look from every angle and eventually pronounced, "Actually, it does look quite good. Well done! Now for the dye. Will you like me blonde?"

"You know what they say, blondes have more fun," said Jon.

"It would be good to have some fun again. Okay, let's do it!"

Night had drawn in and Mr. Blight, a kindly, and lively man in his sixties was filling Rumble's dish with some food. Jon had left his precious pet in his caretaker's care and Mr. Blight was taking the job seriously and enjoying it. Rumble was rubbing himself around Mr. Blight's legs and purring loudly.

Mr. Blight leaned down and smoothed the cat. He smiled at Rumble and chatted away to the cat clearly delighted with Rumble's company. "Well, Rumble while you have your supper I will make myself a nice cup of tea." He pottered about and filled his teapot then poured himself a strong mug of tea.

He wandered back into his sitting room and made himself comfortable before settling down to read the paper. Rumble padded through and sprang onto his lap and began to purr. Mr. Blight's face creased in pleasure as he fussed the gentle tabby and white cat.

He switched on the television and his jaw dropped as he saw the news item on Jon. "Well, I'm blowed!" he exclaimed. "I can't believe that." He turned it off in disgust and looked at the affectionate cat sitting on his lap, "Ebola virus," he snorted. "Nah! It's just not true."

As if to concur, Rumble nudged the man's hand for more fussing and petting and Mr. Blight happily obliged.

Chapter Thirteen

On the run

AT THE HILTON HOTEL, Claire waited impatiently for Ibrahim to arrive. She paced the room nervously, frequently crossing to the window and checking the vehicle and people movement to and from the hotel. Her raincoat lay on the bed alongside a thick padded A4 envelope.

She was distracted and on edge. She knew she needed to calm down and she was very aware that she was playing an extremely dangerous game. Claire was now in over her head. There was no going back. But, for how long could she remain undiscovered? She thought of Birchell and shivered. These and other thoughts rambled through the trellis of her mind. None of them were comforting; Claire was aware that she was on borrowed time like Birchell and she wasn't quite sure how she felt about that.

There was a knock on the door.

The sudden interruption of her thoughts brought her back to the present. Claire hurried to the spy hole and peeped out. She saw the distinguished figure of Ibrahim Khalid standing outside and hurriedly opened the door to admit him.

"Were you followed?" questioned Claire.

"I am not an object of interest, yet, Miss…? I don't yet know your name."

"I don't suppose it matters anymore," said Claire resignedly. "It's Claire, Claire Williams."

"You promised to help me," pressed Ibrahim.

"Yes, the filmmakers desperately need money to survive; they cannot access their own accounts. They have all been blocked. They are being hunted like common criminals."

"So you said."

"They have made it impossible for them to stay here. According to the authorities, they no longer exist. Jon and Amy have to leave the country and they need money to do it."

"And what do I get in return?"

"Then you have checked that I am telling the truth?"

"Monumentous Films is now a construction company and none of their telephone numbers are working. So, yes I believe you."

"We must be quick. It won't be long before they realise my involvement. Do you have the money?"

Ibrahim reached into his inside pocket and removed a bulging envelope. "I trust this is enough for their needs?"

"Yes, thank you," said Claire with relief. "Here!" She passed him a piece of paper with a phone number. "This is a new pay as you go mobile phone that I obtained for them. Try to hold off using it unless absolutely necessary. If you do need to call them it must be from a pay phone or somewhere anonymous. I think your personal and business lines are hacked."

"Is that all?"

"No," she picked up the envelope from the bed. "This is some of what you need. Amy and Jon have more. You will have the truth behind Electra's assassination. And take these." She passed him two flash drives, "Get these to Wikileaks. I daren't hang on to them anymore."

"But it's not all here?" quizzed Ibrahim.

"No, but it is enough. You will be able to pool your resources with the filmmakers and have the entire picture."

Ibrahim opened the package and his eyes grew wide as he saw the information on the Brandenberg Sect and why they wanted rid of Electra. He hurriedly replaced the papers and turned to Claire.

Claire glanced at her watch. "I must go. I daren't stay any longer. Thank you, Mr. Khalid."

"And how do I get in touch with you if I need to?"

"You don't. I'll get in touch with you. That's if I'm around long enough to do so."

"Aren't you being a little melodramatic?"

"Melodramatic? Electra is dead and so is the person who provided me with the information you now have."

"And my son, don't forget Ahmed." Ibrahim scrutinised Claire's face.

She turned to him, "I'm sorry. I knew nothing about it… if I had…"

"What?"

"I don't know… I hope I would have been able to do something."

Ibrahim took a deep breath and swallowed hard. He attempted to stop his eyes from welling up.

"I have to go. Please. I really cannot stay. I'm sorry." Claire picked up her things. She shoved the money into her bag and left hurriedly. Ibrahim sat heavily on the bed. He opened the envelope again and began to look through the contents in more detail. What he read was shocking.

Amy, with her new elfin haircut now turned blonde was at the counter of the offices of Births, Marriages and Deaths. She waited patiently but kept her eyes open and her wits about her. A small Welsh woman returned to the counter carrying two birth certificates. "There you go, Miss May," and she beamed at her.

"Thank you," gushed Amy. "How much?"

"Thirteen ninety-nine each. I make that twenty-seven pounds and ninety-eight pence," came her sing-song tones.

Amy took out thirty pounds from her purse and paid the very pleasant clerk. "Passport Office next stop," she said.

"And have a lovely holiday. I would love to travel more. I do envy you."

"Yes, it will be exciting. My first time out of the country," she lied.

"Don't forget to take mosquito repellent," added the kindly lady. "And remember if you travel to America or any of its territories you will need an ESTA."

"What's that?"

"A form you have to complete for entry into America as they no longer have the waiver visa. It will cost you fourteen dollars. You just need your details, name, address where you are going to stay and so on."

"Right, yes, I will, thank you." She smiled at the woman again, picked up her change and left the office.

Jon was waiting for her outside. He certainly looked vastly different. His long flowing hair now ruthlessly cropped short and dyed dark brown gave him a whole new persona. Gone were his comfy corduroy trousers to be replaced by smart jeans and open necked shirt. He was sporting designer stubble. And his appearance definitely resembled that of an off duty soldier.

"Come on, we need to get photos."

"And get to the Passport Office."

"Yes, and if we are travelling to the US we need an ESTA. We will need authentic addresses to go with our identity and an address in the US."

"How can we do that if we don't know where we are going?" queried Jon.

Amy shrugged, "Don't ask me. One more thing to figure out."

The couple hurried to the main thoroughfare to hunt for a photo shop that did accredited passport photographs. Half an hour later, they were still looking.

"We need a post office or big supermarket," said Jon becoming irritated with the task.

"No!" asserted Amy. "They just have to be a little bit off and they get rejected. Trust me I know. Ah! Over there! Look!"

On the other side of the road was a small camera shop with a board outside advertising and guaranteeing passport style photographs. "In there." Amy grabbed Jon's hand and they dodged the traffic on the busy road to reach the outlet and dived inside.

Amy addressed the shop assistant, "We need passport photos. Can you do them now?"

"Certainly," The young man replied. "Step through to the back of the shop and I'll call Pete to take them."

"Will we have to wait for the prints?" queried Jon.

"In this day of technology? No. It's pretty instant."

"Oh, good."

True to the young man's word, the job was speedy and painless and they left with their pictures.

"We'll have to countersign each other's forms," observed Amy.

"We can do that – what do you want me to be? Your dentist?"

"We'll work something out," laughed Amy.

"Right! Next stop, passports," ordered Jon. "Let's go."

"We need to get ourselves an ESTA how do we do that online without a bank account?" asked Amy.

"Maybe we can pay at the Passport Office?"

"Either that or the U.S. is off the list," concluded Amy.

"Globe House, Ecclestone Square, here we come," affirmed Jon.

Max Stafford was in an irritable mood. He had Biff on screen and was venting his anger on the operative. "They can't have disappeared off the face of the earth."

"There's a team watching Miss Wilde's address and we are around the corner from Curtis' pad. If they try to return, we'll have them."

"I've got all major airports and ports covered. If they haven't gone already? … No, that's impossible. They can't hold out forever," grumbled Max. "Sooner or later they will have to break cover. Their money won't last forever."

Chapter Fourteen

Escape

AMY AND JON WERE sitting unobtrusively in the darkest corner of the bar of The Lazy Landlord. Amy had collected the drinks and so far she had gone unrecognised by the barman, Greg. She sipped a mineral water. "This is madness."

"I can't just leave him there. It would be like a betrayal. Especially after that news item. Those people could kill him. I can't risk it."

"How can we take him abroad?" argued Amy.

"It's not a problem taking him out. Only if we return," reasoned Jon.

"They'll be expecting you to get him. It's not safe. Has he got a passport?"

"Passport, microchip, the lot."

"Yes, but in your name, your address."

"I'll work something out…" he paused. "Look, I just want to see that he's okay, that's all. I thought we could drop him off at my sisters."

Defeated, Amy gave in, "Okay, I'll go and get the car and park on Burrows Street."

"Behind the house?"

Amy nodded. "How long will you be?"

"Give me ten minutes." Jon checked his watch and stood up to leave.

Amy stopped him, "Jon?"

He turned to her, "Yes?"

"Be careful."

Jon leaned over and kissed her. "Don't worry and remember if I don't get back to you within half an hour, follow our plans and go on without me." Jon left, and Amy moved to the back exit.

Jon hurriedly crossed the road, looking about him all the time. He headed for his building and unlocked the main door and tentatively walked upstairs anxious not to alert anyone. He passed Mr. Blight's door and noticed the light spilling out from underneath. He could hear the sound of the television. Jon tiptoed past and continued up to his floor.

Hardly daring to breathe, Jon tried the key in his lock. To his relief it still worked. He entered quietly without switching on any lights. He opened the hall cupboard and removed a pet carrier and left. The door clicked shut softly behind him.

In the black van Steve alerted Biff, "Someone's moving around in Curtis' flat, in the hallway."

"Curtis?"

"Can't tell… no lights"

"Enhance the picture. Infra red."

Steve did as he was asked, "It could be. I'm not sure."

Alan chipped in, "Whoever it is has got short hair."

"So, maybe he's cut it. Get around there." Biff ordered.

Jon crept back down the stairs with the pet carrier. He tapped on Mr. Blight's door. The door opened and Blight looked out. He didn't recognise Jon and stared at him blankly. "Yes?"

"Mr. Blight, I've come about Rumble."

Rumble heard his master's voice and came running. The cat took a giant leap into Jon's arms and nuzzled him. Mr. Blight looked on in astonishment, "Jon? Is that you? They said you were a terrorist and that Rumble…"

Jon cut in, "I know. It's not true. I can't explain now, but I will…"

"I knew it couldn't be true…. Are you taking him, then?" he asked with a hint of sadness in his voice.

The sound of the main door to the building crashing open filtered through to them and feet could be heard pounding up the stairs. Jon pushed past Mr. Blight and into the flat. "Please, can I come in?" he said with urgency.

Jon gingerly closed the door and leaned against it still holding Rumble and basket with his fingers held close to his lips in warning to Mr. Blight. They both heard feet running past the door.

"Are they after you?" asked Mr. Blight looking concerned.

Jon nodded. "Can I use the fire escape?"

Mr. Blight pointed out the back. "Don't worry, son. I won't say nothing."

Jon put Rumble down and opened the pet carrier. He picked his cat up and popped him inside then headed for the fire escape. Mr. Blight watched them go regretfully. He knew he would miss the affectionate cat, dreadfully.

Mr. Blight sighed and settled himself back down in front of the television. His gaze drifted to the cat bowl and he wistfully stared at the basket on the floor. To his shock his front door was forced open and the lock broke. Biff and Ron rushed in aggressively.

Mr. Blight rose crossly. "Here! What do you think you're playing at?"

Ron demanded threateningly, "Curtis. Where is he?"

"You've missed him," said Mr. Blight with a hint of pleasure in his voice.

"Where? Where has he gone?" pressed Ron.

"You won't catch him. He's too clever for you," goaded Mr. Blight.

Ron jerked his head to the back of the flat ordering Biff, "Check the fire escape."

Feeling bolder, Mr. Blight continued, "I'll have the law on you, terrorising old folk."

"I don't think so," replied Biff and he levelled his gun at Mr. Blight and pulled the trigger. Mr. Blight fell back onto the settee, his chest pouring with blood. Ron looked at Biff in dismay then they both dashed for the fire escape.

Jon was just stepping off the bottom stair when he heard the gunshot. He froze for a moment, instantly knowing what had happened. Then, he gathered himself together, steeled himself and ran off into the enveloping night.

He heard a shout behind him as Biff and Ron begin to descend the iron staircase after him.

Jon's breath was ragged as he raced to Burrows Street. Amy had been watching in the rear view mirror. She had the engine running. Jon scrambled in complete with Rumble as Amy tore away.

"Go, go, go!" gasped Jon. "We don't want them getting your licence plate number."

Amy drove like the wind while the car bleeped at her that the front passenger's seat belt was undone. "For God's sake, do your belt up. The beeping is driving me mad," complained Amy. Jon was struggling to sort himself out with the seat belt and the pet carrier. "What's the time?" questioned Amy.

She glanced at the dash as Jon threw her a look and declared, "How the heck do I know, tied up like this?"

"Oh, my God, it's five past ten," shrieked Amy.

"So?" asked Jon.

"We need to step on it. Claire's phoned. We're to meet her by the Bandstand in Hyde Park. In one hour."

"I've got to call an ambulance. I think they've shot Mr. Blight."

"What?" asked Amy in horror. "The phone's in the tray."

Jon picked up the mobile from the centre tray in the car.

"What about being traced?" warned Amy. "They're bound to get a record of your number when you ring the Emergency Services."

"I'll use my spoof card. That should work. I can't leave the old man dying or injured." Jon began to fiddle with his phone. He pulled up the application and entered the number he wanted to call and entered a fake number to appear as ID. He then selected his voice to be disguised on the other end as female. It took seconds.

Jon looked across at Amy and she nodded, "Go on, we have to do it. Tell me, what's a spoof card?"

Jon dialled nine, nine, nine. "I'll explain later.... Hello? Ambulance, please."

Jon relayed the information and hung up quickly.

"Damn, which way? How do we get to Hyde Park? I'll have to go through the Congestion Zone."

"You needn't worry, you won't get the charge," joked Jon.

"No, Claire will."

"Turn right here," advised Jon and Amy dutifully manoeuvred the car.

"Ah! I know where we are now," Amy drove as quickly as she dared through the streets until they eventually arrived at Marble Arch car park. They drove into it and collected a ticket.

Rumble mewed plaintively in his crate. "Okay, Rumble, not much longer. Then we'll stop."

Amy spotted an unallocated space almost immediately and reversed into it. "Come on," she urged as she noticed Jon's hesitancy in getting out.

"I can't leave Rumble here."

"You'll have to."

"What if we don't come back?"

"Don't be such a pessimist. We'll tell Claire, just in case."

Jon fussed over his cat that looked totally miserable in the carrier with whiskers turned down. "I won't be long, I promise," murmured Jon softly.

"Honestly, I swear that cat is the most important thing in the world to you. Still, it's part of why I love you."

Jon grabbed her hand. "And do you?"

"What?"

"Love me?"

"I didn't mean to say that," Amy backtracked.

"But you did," persisted Jon.

Amy studied his earnest expression and looked him squarely in the eyes. "Yes, I do," she said simply.

His reaction surprised her as he jumped out of the car and punched his fist in the air. "YES!"

Amy clambered out of the car. Jon bade a final goodbye to Rumble who still looked less than impressed and she locked the motor. They dashed out to the street and crossed to Hyde Park and hurriedly made their way to the bandstand where Claire was waiting and looking anxiously about her. She checked her watch it was late, coming up to 11:15 p.m.

Amy and Jon were panting by the time they reached Claire. She handed them a thick envelope of money, "Here, take this. It's from Ibrahim." She passed them a bundle of files, "And this is from me. It's all I could get on the Mind Control experiments and Electra. But it's not complete. There are still things I don't know."

"Thanks," said Jon appreciatively. "This will really help."

"And one more thing. You're wanted for attempted murder," she addressed Jon.

"Attempted murder?" exclaimed Jon in shock.

Amy, however, understood, "Mr. Blight."

"How is he?" asked Jon concerned.

"Not good. He's in a coma on life support. It all ties in with this terrorist propaganda story they are putting in the press, but if the old boy comes round…."

"They'll finish him," murmured Amy.

"Right," acknowledged Claire with gravity. She handed Amy a printed list. "These are all the flights from Heathrow tomorrow with seats available. I can't help you anymore. Ibrahim has your phone number; he also has some of the classified information. Now go. You must hurry."

Claire watched them as they swiftly departed the bandstand and were soon swallowed up into the night. She waited a while for them to clear before moving off herself and heading for her own transport.

Amy and Jon sped away through the park as fast as they could and back to their car. She dutifully paid at the pay station and they set off once more. "See Rumble, I said we wouldn't be long," said Jon gently.

"How much money do we have?" asked Amy.

Jon opened the stuffed envelope and began to count he almost stuttered his answer as Amy waited, "I hope we don't get mugged. There's nearly a quarter of a million here."

"Bloody hell!"

"My sentiments exactly. We'll divide it up or it could be a problem getting through Security tomorrow. At least it's in fifties, that will make it easier when we go through the body scanners."

"Where to now? The motel?" questioned Amy.

"No, we've one more stop to make. I have…"

"I know…" interrupted Amy and they chorused together, "A germ of an idea." They both laughed.

"Well, spit it out. I can't drive around all night and I'm tired."

"My family is bound to be watched as is my sister; they'll expect us to try and get help with them."

"So? What are you trying to say?"

"I can't take Rumble there."

"You should have thought of that before…"

"I know, but the threat was that they would snatch Rumble saying it had the Ebola virus and he would never be seen again. They'll use the cat against me. We need to visit Ibrahim," Jon said decisively.

"Now? At this time?"

"Yes, he'll see us. He's bound to after giving us this," Jon fanned the money.

"Okay, I hope you're right. Which way now?"

The little car whizzed through the streets of London until they came to a quiet street in an exclusive area where Ibrahim Khalid had his luxury two-storey apartment.

They managed to find a parking space on the street. "That was lucky, someone must be looking out for us." She jerked her eyes heavenward and crossed herself. "I've just had a thought... I hope he's not being watched, too," she muttered.

"They can't be everywhere," said Jon.

"Huh! They seem to be..." Amy retorted.

They walked back along the tree-lined avenue to the exclusive building, stepped up the shingle drive to the entrance and pressed the bell. The guard on the security desk shuffled to the door and unlocked it admitting them. They hurried through with Rumble in the pet carrier.

"Bit late to be making house calls, isn't it?" said the security guard, critically.

"We wouldn't normally but this is an emergency," smiled Amy trying to appease the disgruntled guard.

They started for the elevator. "Hold on. I can't just let you up. Who do you want to see?"

"Ibrahim Khalid," beamed Jon, copying Amy's pleasant demeanour.

The guard whistled low and long between his teeth and inspected his list. "Got no mention of anyone visiting Mr. Khalid, tonight." He checked again. "Nope. Nothing."

"Please, Sir. If you could just ring his quarters I know he will see us. It is important or we wouldn't be here," pressed Amy.

"I know he doesn't like to be disturbed," said the guard softening.

"We'll make it worth your while," said Jon waving a fifty-pound note in front of the man.

"I can't be bought, you know," said the guard crossly.

"No, no. No one is suggesting that. It's just a small reward for helping us out. Please, Mitch," pleaded Amy reading his name badge.

The guard grunted and reluctantly picked up the phone. "Who shall I say is calling?" he looked quizzically at them.

Amy was stumped and began to flounder. Jon blurted out, "Chico Towns and Lady Antebellum."

Amy threw him a cross-eyed look as if to say, 'What are you doing?'

The guard dialled Ibrahim Khalid's apartment number and spoke quietly, "Yes. I am sorry to disturb you, I have two people at Reception who insist on seeing Mr. Khalid. A Chico Towns and Lady Antebellum."

Mather, Ibrahim's bodyguard and aide, had answered the internal line and replied, "I'm sorry, there are no scheduled appointments this late, Mitch. Apologise and send them on their way."

Ibrahim came to Mather's side. "What is it?"

Mather put his hand over the receiver and explained, "Someone downstairs trying to see you."

"We're not expecting anyone, are we?" questioned Ibrahim.

The guard downstairs listened and responded, "Yes, I will..." He looked across at the filmmakers. "I'm sorry. It's late and Mr. Khalid's aide says he is not expecting anyone."

"No!" butted in Jon. "He is not expecting us."

"Then I can't let you go up."

"But he will see us..." persisted Amy. "Tell him it's something monumentous."

Ibrahim instructed Mather, "I'm curious, let me take the call."

Mitch spoke quietly into the phone, it was clear that Ibrahim had come on the line himself. He turned to the filmmakers again. "I'm sorry, he's not prepared to see anyone."

"Tell him in those words," urged Jon, "That it's something monumentous."

Mitch looked back suspiciously. Amy smiled pleadingly again, "Please... It's a matter of life and death."

Jon followed on with a different tack, "And if Mr. Khalid was to find out that you were responsible for losing him millions of pounds..."

"Please, Mitch," Amy reiterated. "Just use those words."

The guard acquiesced and they heard him say, "They say it's something monumentous."

The reaction on the end of the phone changed dramatically as Ibrahim ordered Mitch, "Please, send them up, now."

Mitch replaced the receiver looking puzzled. "It seems to have done the trick. Take the lift. Floor three."

"Thank you," gushed Amy and they both dashed to the lift. They pressed the button and entered. Jon selected floor three. The elevator ascended and opened out onto a plush carpeted corridor and Ibrahim's main entrance. The door opened before they had an opportunity to knock or ring. They were welcomed in immediately by Ibrahim in his night attire.

"Come in, come in. What has happened?"

"You've seen the news?" asked Amy.

Ibrahim acknowledged that he had with a nod of his head "I did." He then asked, "You got the money?"

"Yes, thank you. I don't know how we would manage without your help."

"I think you agree that there is a conspiracy?" pronounced Ibrahim.

"You bet," answered Jon.

"You will still work on getting this out to the public at the right time when you have completed your film and investigations?" requested Ibrahim.

"We have to or we will never have our lives back," agreed Jon.

"We also need to keep our options open about where we can travel so we need to apply for an ESTA. Can we do that through you?"

"Of course, over here." Ibrahim led them to the computer in his office and they logged onto the official U.S Site.

They entered their new identities at Ibrahim's address and Ibrahim paid with his credit card details, which were all accepted much to their relief.

"Smart move entering one of the hotels that you know well in New York," said Jon appreciatively. "Not that we had to give a destination on registering."

Ibrahim printed off the ESTA approval for their records and passed them to Amy. "Ah, now that's over would you like a drink?"

"I would love one," accepted Amy. "Just what I need. You'll have to drive," she ordered Jon.

"Story of my life," said Jon.

"I must say that you have done a good job with altering your appearances. Very effective. What would you like, Amy?"

"Do you have any dry white wine?" she asked.

"I possibly do, but I have some champagne open, will that do?"

"That would be perfect," sighed Amy.

"Do sit down... I expect you wonder why a man of my religion would drink alcohol?"

"Not at all, each to their own," said Jon diplomatically.

"It is useful for business and I admit to liking some of the fine wines... but there, no one will take me to task for that, I'm sure," said Ibrahim as he poured Amy a glass. "Jon?"

"I'll just stick to orange juice, please."

"As you wish. I must say you took a chance coming here, although I'm not aware of anyone watching me I have been told that there is a possibility that my outside phone line and mobile could be tapped," added Ibrahim as he handed Jon a glass of juice and then sat down. "So, tell me, why are you here?"

"I know it's an awful cheek, but it's not only us whose lives are threatened but my cat's life, too. I wondered if you would help me by looking after him, after Rumble? Please?"

"A cat?" said Ibrahim surprised. "You want me to look after your cat?"

"Yes, please."

"And your cat is called, Rumble?"

"Yes," said Jon sheepishly.

"Why Rumble?" asked Ibrahim, smiling.

"Because he has the biggest rumbling purr you've ever heard," added Amy. Ibrahim laughed.

"If you could just keep an eye on him until we're settled," said Jon.

"And then send him on to us," completed Amy.

"All right. You have my private number?"

"We have this apartment number," said Amy.

"Yes, it's on the files we have," added Jon.

"I will give you my personal phone line that only I answer." He stood up and went to his bureau and took out a card. "My personal line and email communication. I will also take a leaf out of Miss Williams' book and purchase a pay and go phone. As soon as I have this, I will ring you with the number we can then speak freely without fear of being monitored. So, only use my direct line in an absolute emergency."

"Thank you," said Amy as she swallowed down her champagne. She glanced at the time. "We must go. We've been here too long already."

Carol's voice called down from up the stairs, "Ibby?"

Ibrahim called back, "I won't be long." He rose, "I'll see you to the door." He walked to the front door and opened it.

Jon passed across the pet carrier. He looked sadly at his beloved Rumble that mewed sorrowfully at him.

"Don't worry, Rumble will be safe," soothed Ibrahim.

Jon and Amy started to leave as Carol started to walk down the stairs tying her robe. She moved into the hallway toward the door and Ibrahim, just as Amy turned back and gave Ibrahim a kiss. "Thank you. You may have saved our lives." Ibrahim flushed with pleasure at the touching comment.

Amy caught a glimpse of Carol before the door closed. There was the flicker of something, a memory in the back of her mind, which was just too fleeting to grasp. Amy headed for the elevator with Jon. They sped down and hurried out into the foyer where Mitch was waiting ready to let them out.

They ran to their car, checking about them in the street for any signs of the evil black van, which seemed to Amy to have a power of its own. Jon examined their car to see if it had been tampered with. It hadn't. They were safe and so they made their way back to the Travel Lodge and parked up for the night.

They fell in through the room door with obvious relief. Amy flopped on the bed, "At least Rumble's going to be all right."

"Yes, and we need to form some sort of game plan for tomorrow. But, now… Now, I want to turn my attention to you."

Jon lay down beside her and they began to kiss. It would be a while before they would get to sleep or make any plans of action. For now, they were only interested in each other. "I'm going to make the most of this while I can," whispered Amy.

"Me, too," admitted Jon as he nuzzled her neck. "Come here, Miss Wilde, I think you are a little overdressed."

Chapter Fifteen

Retribution

CLAIRE PULLED HER COAT around her as she hurried down the street to MI6. She was nervous and jumpy as she entered the lobby. Her ID was routinely inspected and Claire crossed toward the elevator trying hard to keep a grip on herself. She managed to smile at one or two people that she knew.

The receptionist spotted her and called her over, "Claire! Wait up! I have a message for you."

Claire moved back to the reception desk. "Yes, really?" she asked struggling to keep her voice even, knowing she'd never had a message left for her at Reception before.

"Don't go to the office. They're in the lab. You're to go straight down."

"Oh, okay. Thanks," murmured Claire. Her heart was thumping. Claire knew full well that below the seedy tech lab in the basement there were underground interrogation rooms and other things that she dared not think about. At that minute she thought of walking out and running away as far from the place as possible, but as she glanced about her, she recognised a couple of armed MI6 agents waiting at the entrance and watching her. She turned and walked quickly to the lift and with trembling hands she pressed the call button. The lift was already there. It was empty as the doors opened. Claire stepped inside. She struggled to still her heaving breaths and could feel her stomach twist in knots and bile began to rise into her throat. She had to remain poised, even if only on the outside. The doors closed on her and she reached for the buttons.

Max and Jack were watching Claire in the lift on a high angled CCTV camera. Claire stood back in the corner after considering and then ignoring her orders.

"She's pressed for the fourth floor," observed Jack.

Max shook his head regretfully. "She's sealed her fate. Why, oh, why didn't you do as I asked, Claire?" he asked sadly. His voice became more efficient and brusquer as he ordered, "Do it."

Jack looked unhappily across at Max who reiterated, "Do it!"

Jack reluctantly stretched forward and pressed a key on the control pad in front of him.

The lift crunched and groaned. It stopped and started again. Claire's face registered panic as she realised that the lift was travelling the wrong way. It was going down. With growing alarm, Claire repeatedly punched the stop and alarm buttons. They didn't respond. The lift continued to plummet down below the basement and sub-basement and further. Claire froze and a sob escaped her lips. She had been 'got.'

On the CCTV screen in the lab, Max and Jack watched Claire break down. She slumped to the floor of the lift that was dropping at an ever-increasing speed. Max and Jack could see the elevator descend deeper past the floor they were on. Claire's terrified and anguished cries could be seen but not heard. The lift filled with crackling bright blue light as electricity pulsed through the elevator carriage. Claire was hit with enough volts to incapacitate her. Her hair sizzled, her eyebrows were singed and her body began to convulse. The full extent of the terror she was experiencing was clearly visible and Jack was unable to watch anymore. He leaned forward and turned off the monitor.

Max studied Jack. "Getting squeamish?"

"It's not that… Claire was a friend and colleague… I didn't want to see her fry. Or anything else that I know will be done to her."

"Give it ten minutes, then report the accident with Maintenance and the Electricity Board. The elevator will need fixing. Claire will be disposed of once we have our answers, which should be more readily available now, don't you think?" Jack didn't respond. Max glared at him. "Don't go soft on me now, Jack. I did warn you. You knew this was coming."

Jack nodded his acknowledgement and turned away. He was unhappy with the assassination and it was difficult to disguise his feelings, but he knew he had to. He didn't want to end up like Claire.

Amy and Jon parked in the airport car park. They grabbed their overnight bags, laptop and briefcase, locked the car and made their way to the terminal. They walked in a business like fashion through Terminal Three whilst keeping a watchful eye out for police and security officials.

"As I said last night, I'd rather go to some place where they speak English."

"Let's try Canada. There's a flight to Toronto at twelve."

"Right. Let's go for it!"

They walked briskly toward the Air Canada desk and waited impatiently behind the privacy line while another passenger was being dealt with. All the time they stood there they were on the alert. Eventually the traveller moved on and they proceeded to the desk and spoke to a member of the ground staff at the check in.

"Hi, we'd like two tickets to Toronto, please"

"I'm sorry. There are no seats left on that flight."

"What about in First Class?"

"I'm sorry, no. There's another one at six tonight. All our other scheduled flights are full. I could put you on standby," offered the woman.

"Thank you, but we'll see if we can get there another way." Amy's face registered her disappointment.

"You could go via New York, if you can get a connection," advised the official trying to help.

"Thanks, we'll check it out," said Jon brightly. They walked away.

"What about it? Do you fancy a trip to the Big Apple? There's a flight there on the list."

"Okay. Let's give it a whirl," agreed Jon. They crossed to the American Airways desk. Fortunately, there was no one in the queue. "Do you have any seats available on the 11:05 to New York?"

The female advisor checked her screen, "You're in luck. Two people in Economy?"

"Please," affirmed Amy.

They presented their passports and the advisor checked they had permission to travel. Her eyes widened in surprise when the tickets were paid for in cash. Nevertheless, she issued them with their boarding passes. "Boarding is at 10:15. Check the display for the number of the boarding gate. Don't you have any luggage to check in?"

"No, just hand luggage." They indicated their holdalls.

"Are you carrying any liquids, electrical items, sharp or prohibited goods?"

"No."

"Did you pack your bags yourselves?"

"Yes."

"Could anyone have tampered with your bags or asked you to carry anything for them?"

"No."

"You will have to put your laptop inside your bag before boarding and your briefcase, Sir," she nodded at Jon. "You are only allowed one piece of hand luggage."

"No problem. Thank you."

They walked away toward Security and joined the queue, which fortunately was not too long and moving reasonably quickly. Amy removed her laptop from its bag took off her shoes and jacket and placed them in the tray to go through the X-ray machine. Jon did likewise. They both stepped through the body scanners and made it through to the other side. Jon decided to empty his briefcase of all the papers and files and he shoved them in his carry-on bag. He ditched the briefcase in a bin.

"Bit of a waste," he muttered. "But I can always get another."

They were unaware of Ron trawling the check in desks questioning all the ground staff. He arrived at American Airlines and questioned the official that sold Jon and Amy their tickets.

Max and Jack had arrived in the airport and came through the revolving doors. They both had radios and earpieces. They searched the area with their eyes. Max acknowledged Steve and Alan who were dressed as Security Guards. They in turn greeted another man in plain clothes. It was Biff. Biff scanned the airport crowds in the immediate vicinity and he spotted Ron striding toward him who gestured to the American Airline Desk.

Ron exchanged a few words with Max before he and Biff scrambled through the growing queue at Security. They flashed their badges at the gate and were admitted. The area was now milling with people. They looked around hunting for Jon and Amy. They now had a full description of the filmmakers and what they were wearing relayed to them through their earpieces.

Max engaged in conversation with the female advisor. "Excuse me, I understand that you have served two wanted suspects in a serious crime."

"As I told the other gentleman, it was unusual to receive cash for the tickets."

"I need the information on the flight and the names they are travelling under."

The woman hesitated, "I don't know if I can do that."

"Look, this is a case of national security. Here, my authorisation." Max showed his identification, which appeared to satisfy her. "I want you to look at these pictures and select the nearest of these computer-generated images to the people that you served." He showed her pictures of Jon and Amy with different hairstyles.

The woman pointed at two photographs. "That's them."

"Great. Can you tell me what they were wearing?"

The check in clerk described as best as she could remember how they were dressed. Max continued, "Which flight are they on and under what name are they travelling?"

The advisor tapped a few keys and pulled up the list of passengers for the flight to New York. She turned the screen toward him so he could read the list himself and she indicated the two names.

"Thanks." Max strode off and pushed through Security. He met Jack who was waiting on the other side, near the Duty Free. "They've changed their names. Miss Susan May and Mr. Gregory Davis."

"But how?" said Jack incredulously.

"One guess…"

"Claire!"

"We know what they look like and we know their new names. Should be a breeze," smirked Max.

Jack pointed at the departure information board, "Flight gate is up. Let's go."

Amy and Jon were on route to the boarding area when Jon noticed a security guard studying a photo printout. He pointed directly at the couple.

Jon hissed at Amy, "Run! We've been clocked."

They began to run back the way they had come. Amy called in desperation, "Where to?"

"Split up. I'll meet you…"

"Oh yeah?" she called anxiously.

Jon glanced across at the Brasserie Pub, "There! The pub in about fifteen minutes."

"That's if we don't get caught first," muttered Amy.

"If one of us does the other must go it alone."

Amy threw a helpless look at Jon believing their situation to be hopeless and then ran as though her life depended on it.

The security men that had alerted other agents to their quarry now gave chase. When the couple parted and each went in a different direction it momentarily confused their pursuers. They had to pause to decide, which one to follow and by which time Amy had disappeared from view.

Amy hurried down the lengthy corridor toward the main shopping area and dived into the ladies' lavatories. Fortunately, and unusually, the place appeared to be empty. She selected a closet, ducked inside and locked herself in. Her heart was pounding, her stomach churning and her breathing laboured. To say she was in an acute state of fright would be an understatement.

She opened her small overnight bag and rummaged through it. Amy hastily removed her jacket, stripped off her top and changed it, stuffing the other in her bag. Next, she changed her jeans for a pair of lightweight Capri pants and swapped her trainers for sandals. For a second she wondered if she was right to change her footwear but then decided that she needed to look as different as possible. Out came a scarf, which she tied bandana style around her head, hiding her hair.

Amy struggled to close the zip on her bag and swore vehemently as she battled with the wayward fastener. Once done, she emerged from the closet as would a butterfly from a chrysalis and looked utterly transformed. She ambled out of the Restroom and crossed to Accessorize where she purchased a large colourful shopper in which she placed her laptop, a mid-length wig in another colour and a pair of sunglasses. Next stop was the newsagents and bookshop, where she chose a novel and two newspapers. She queued and paid like any other ordinary passenger and popped them in her shopper.

Amy leisurely strolled to the large television screen that announced the departures and she ran her eyes down the list before she crossed to a bank of seats, which gave a good unrestricted view of the area and sat. Amy removed her novel and pretended to read, whilst checking the time and keeping on the alert for her pursuers and any sign of Jon.

Max arrived with two agents at the New York Boarding Gate where bona fide travellers waited. He spoke to one of the crew, "When does this plane board?"

The steward told him, "We'll be boarding in forty minutes. If you just want to wait with the other passengers we'll make an announcement when we're ready."

Max showed his ID and explained, "I'm not travelling. Two of your passengers are wanted by Interpol. I'm assigning two agents to remain at the gate area and be vigilant. Here." He flourished the photographs of the filmmakers and indicated their names on the list. "If you see them or hear from them, please contact one of my men immediately." He gave the official a card with a central number, which the steward took and placed in his pocket.

Jon was being pursued by Biff and had been unable to shake him off. He had now found his way into the children's play area. "Oh, shit!" he exclaimed involuntarily.

Acutely aware of the danger of the situation not just for himself, but also for the children playing happily Jon did not know what to do. He knew at any moment Biff would be upon him. He stood and dithered.

A small, bonny little black boy with his thumb in his mouth watched Jon curiously. He popped his thumb out and grinned toothily showing the loss of a few milk teeth. He said in all innocence, "Do you want to play, Mister? It's great fun." He pointed at the huge playpen mass of coloured balls and as if to prove it he dived in headfirst and disappeared amongst them. When he surfaced he grinned again. "Come on!" he urged, "It doesn't hurt, honest." He watched Jon some more who seemed to be concentrating on the approaching mass of people. "My name's Oliver. What's yours?"

"Jon," he answered distractedly. Jon hesitated but then saw Biff in a crowd of travellers and he was headed in Jon's direction. Throwing caution to the wind he dropped his bag on a seat and dived into the balls by the small boy and scrambled around in them trying to swim out of sight.

Oliver giggled delightedly and threw a couple of balls where he supposed Jon might surface as Biff entered the children's play centre. His hand rested on the bulge in his jacket as he searched around with his eyes. He caught sight of Oliver pointing and laughing at a very adult male foot in a shoe that was only just visible as it poked through the balls.

Biff immediately dived in after Jon, much to the joy of the children at play who were totally unaware of the danger that they were being exposed to. Biff waded through the balls and hauled Jon up; they began to wrestle. The tussle attracted the attention of the other children who believed it was a game. The kids applauded and cheered. Biff grabbed Jon by the jacket and Jon wriggled out of it leaving his coat with Biff, who looked at it in a disgruntled fashion.

Jon climbed the play ladder and entered the hollow tube and slid down the other side into another bunch of balls. Jon shouted across to Oliver, "Hey, Ollie! My friend loves being jumped on. Do you want to have a go?"

Biff scrambled after Jon and crawled through the tube. He unsheathed his gun as he slid down the slide and tumbled into the pit of balls. Once there, he was suddenly besieged by children. The little ones swarmed all over him. Aware of the seriousness of any incident or accident in this sensitive area he tried to replace his firearm but instead the children tugged and pulled at him so much that he lost his jacket and gun, the barrel of which was just visible and beginning to sink in the mass. Biff went right under the balls with about six children on top of him. Jon stretched across and snatched the weapon before it disappeared and jumped out of the balls. He immediately posted the gun in a red letterbox at the side of the play centre.

Jon shouted across to Ollie who was now riding Biff like a bucking bronco. "Hey, Ollie! Can you keep him there for me for a count of a hundred? We're playing hide and seek."

Oliver grinned at Jon and stuck his thumb up. All the children clambered over the struggling Biff, now drowning in the balls. The children began to chant, "One, two, three…"

Jon picked up his bag and made his escape. He ran through the airport and passed a broom cupboard, the door of which was slightly ajar. He flicked it open. Hanging inside was a jacket, which he snatched and pulled on. Surprisingly it fitted.

Amy had made her way to the boarding area of a plane travelling to Croatia. She eyed the passengers sitting on the seats waiting to travel, a number of young couples with children, a few single gentlemen that looked as if they were on a business trip. There were some obvious holidaymakers and an elderly married couple that were quietly sipping a cup of coffee. Amy targeted the pensioners. She hoped and prayed that her ruse would work.

Jon reached a seating area and sat down with his back to the corridor and paused to gather his thoughts. He needed more of a disguise. Now they knew what he was wearing and his changed hair colour. He scanned the shops on the shopping plaza until he saw what he was after. He sauntered deliberately slowly into a shop selling gaily, brightly coloured apparel, hats and accessories. He chose a very loud shirt that was screaming with colour, bought an outrageous pair of platform-soled shoes that added a good two and a half inches to his height, and a pair of flared black trousers. He glanced at his watch, time was going on and he knew he had to find Amy, but first he wanted a few more things. He strolled across to the hairpieces and wig section and selected a long red wig.

The assistant watched him amused at the items he was gathering. He finally picked up an outlandish piece of headgear and went to the till to pay. The sales assistant smiled curiously, "Fancy dress?"

"Going to a seventies Mexican stag do," he lied as he paid for the items.

"Boarding pass?"

"Blast, it's with my friend," he responded flashing her a huge smile. "Safer with him than me, I'm bound to lose it."

"You'll have to pay the tax, then."

"Can't be helped. Hey, I want to have a bit of fun with my mates do you have a changing room?"

"Sure. Just through there."

Jon disappeared inside and fitted the wig and hat on his head. He changed his shoes, shirt and trousers, replaced the jacket and emerged looking like a renegade from the seventies that had been caught in a time warp. He waved cheerily at the assistant, who laughed. "Will they let you on the plane like that?"

"Oh, I'll take it off before we board. It's just a bit of fun," he explained.

"Well, you look hysterical. No one will know you," she said.

"That's the idea," Jon murmured as he left the store.

Amy was now in deep discussion with Emily and Wilf, the two pensioners she had singled out earlier. She was putting on a wonderful display of emotion and the tears began to roll down her cheeks, "So you see, if my fiancé and I can't get on this plane we'll miss our wedding and everything."

Emily studied her husband's face. "What do you think, Wilf?"

Wilf was dubious, "Oh, I don't know. This was supposed to be the holiday of a lifetime."

"Please," pleaded Amy her eyes brimmed with tears. "With the money I'll give you, you could have three holidays."

The couple used to playing by the rules looked uncertain. "It's a lot of money," said Wilf, as he thought aloud.

"So many people will be disappointed and you could get the next flight. You could even travel, first class," coaxed Amy.

Wilf and Emily looked from one to the other.

Amy was now getting very desperate, "Please. I'll give you anything. Anything you want."

"What about our baggage?" asked Wilf. "We've checked in two cases."

"I'll collect them and send them back to you. They are labelled, aren't they?"

"Well, yes, but…"

Emily interrupted, pointed at the laptop in the colourful bag. "What's in there?"

"My laptop computer, top of the range. Take it," she urged.

Emily hesitated, "It would make a lovely present for our granddaughter."

"It's yours!" exclaimed Amy handing over the laptop and the money. Amy hugged her and kissed her. She grabbed the boarding passes and tickets and ran off in the direction of the Brasserie.

Wilf eyed his wife. "If you'd have held out you could have had her watch an' all," he said critically.

"Don't be mean. Remember what it was like on our honeymoon?" Emily gave Wilf a kiss.

"Well, we'd better get ourselves organised with another set of tickets first," said Wilf sagely.

"There's no rush, now. We can get the tickets later. Let's find a quiet spot with a table," commanded Emily.

"Yes, and see how this thing works," Wilf agreed.

They walked through to the duty free shopping area and found a corner with a table and sat down. Emily opened the laptop bag and removed the Apple computer.

Amy forced herself to walk calmly to the Brasserie. She looked around for Jon, and for a moment she didn't see him, in his different jacket, red wig and huge sombrero. He ambled across to her and she had to suppress a giggle, "We have to hurry. We've got ten minutes to board."

Jon looked apologetic, "I've lost the passes."

"No, not to New York."

"Where then?"

"Croatia."

"What?"

Amy grabbed Jon's hand and they headed for the gate. They looked such an odd couple that no one took any notice of them or rather they avoided them!

"How are we going to do this? We are not the people named on the boarding cards; our passports don't match," queried Jon.

"There shouldn't be any more passport checks unless it's the airline's policy. Follow my lead. I'll be so busy chatting to the flight staff as they check us through they won't notice. I've done it before."

"What?"

"Trip to Greece, my passport was a couple of days out of date. I chatted away and blagged my way through. It wasn't spotted until the journey home by the Greek authorities. By then it was too late, I'd had my holiday. They just waved me through. Trust me."

"Oh, I trust you. It's everyone else I'm worried about."

Biff was now minus his jacket. He waded through the balls and children and scrambled out up the ladder to the top and struggled to his feet. He was absolutely exhausted and had a look on his face that registered total disbelief as if he could not imagine what had happened to him or how it had occurred. He picked up a jacket from the floor, which had been tossed out by the children.

Still dazed Biff put on the jacket but it didn't quite fit. He felt in the pocket and pulled out a coloured ball, which he tossed back into the play pit. He reached in further and took out two boarding passes. A look of elation crossed his face as he realised what he had in his hand, "Bingo!" Biff made his escape from the play area and stumbled onward to find Max.

Amy and Jon were sitting in the boarding lounge by the departure gate. The seats were called out in batch numbers. They waited nervously, hoping desperately that there wouldn't be another passport check. First class passengers had boarded as had mothers with babies and children. The stewardess announced through the microphone, "Now boarding Premium Economy passengers through to fourteen to seventy."

"That's us!" exclaimed Amy eagerly. They jumped up and joined the line filtering through the gate. Amy watched the actions of the two staff checking the passes. One relatively young stewardess was merely tearing the tickets and returning the stubs with the seat number. The steward on the other side was taking a little more time. Amy joined the first queue. The line of people moved relatively quickly and when Amy and Jon arrived at the gate.

Amy chattered incessantly, "We are so looking forward to this trip. We haven't had a holiday in years. The last one was in Mexico eight years ago. My husband has been itching to wear this hat ever since." She continued to babble trying to engage the woman with her eyes.

The stewardess appeared anxious not to get caught up in conversation and smiled back, "I hope you have a wonderful time." She ripped the tickets, posted one half in the collecting box and gave them the stubs.

Amy and Jon moved through the gate, down a short corridor to the plane. They were directed to their seats. Jon popped their bags into the overhead locker and they sat down trying to settle themselves and buckled their seat belts up for the journey.

"I wonder what the food's like," mused Amy. "I'm starving."

"Wine and champagne is complimentary," said Jon as he watched a steward coming down the aisle handing out a welcome aboard drink.

"Good, I could do with a drink."

"Me, too. But I'll be happier when we're in the air."

They sat nervously awaiting the rest of the passengers to board the plane and find their seats. Jon jiggled his knee while Amy twiddled her thumbs. They kept checking their watches. So far, so good; Amy said a quiet prayer that their luck would hold.

Max and Jack were waiting at the New York flight check in desk in the boarding lounge, watching the last passengers go through the gate. Biff came running up, wheezing and out of breath, "Where are they?"

"I don't know," replied Jack.

"The plane is grounded. They won't get far," said Max.

"I had him," grumbled Biff.

"But, you lost him…" complained Max.

"Not my fault," said Biff. "If you'd have seen what happened…"

Jack cut him off, "Well, it won't be long and we'll soon have them. The place is crawling with agents and they're not on any plane that we know of."

"You're sure?" questioned Biff.

"No boarding passes have been issued in any of their names," replied Jack.

"Apart from these," grinned Biff, holding the two boarding passes up for inspection. "And as they are in my hand, they're band-jaxed," he said triumphantly.

Max shushed them as he listened to a message being relayed on his earpiece. He grinned broadly and turned to his men, "Got them!" he sneered, "She's using her laptop." He tutted sarcastically, "Silly girl."

Amy was feeling a little more relaxed and took a manila file from her colourful shopper. The flight staff, airhostesses and stewards were circulating, checking the passengers had their seats in the upright position and that seatbelts were on and luggage safely stowed. Jon removed his sombrero. It dragged the red wig with it, which Amy snatched up and placed in the bag.

"Paper, Sir?" asked the attractive stewardess.

"Please," said Jon, holding his sombrero on his lap.

"Would you like me to stow the hat for you, Sir?" she asked.

Jon happily passed her the hat from his lap, which the airhostess struggled to force in the overhead locker. She eventually succeeded in closing it. She then passed Jon a newspaper.

Amy had begun flicking through the files that Claire had given them. She muttered, "We've got most of this, but there's a list of targets, too. It's horrendous. Look!" She pointed out a name, "Ibrahim Khalid is on the list. We'll have to warn him," said Amy her forehead furrowed with concern.

"Not until we get to a safe place, then, of course, yes, we will call him."

Jon shook out the newspaper and began to browse through it, "Maybe we can hook up with some human rights groups or neutral Government representatives. Just give them the lot. Get some real weight behind us… Maybe even to another country's militia or…" He stopped suddenly as something caught his eye in the paper. "Jesus, will you look at this…"

He showed Amy the paper and scan read the news item aloud, "Decapitated body found in the Thames. The victim is unidentified so far. Signs of electrocution and torture. Police believe it is a possible ritual killing. A woman in her late thirties. Bloody hell!"

"Oh my God," exclaimed Amy.

"What? What is it?"

Amy handed Jon the file she was perusing, in the back of which was a note. Jon read it, 'Just to let you know that I know this file exists. If it has got into the wrong hands then I can guarantee that its courier is no longer with us. The longer you have the file, the less valuable its contents will become and the less time that you have left.'

Jon looked with alarm at Amy who whispered, "She's dead. Claire's dead."

"The body in the Thames, I bet that was her."

The steward made an announcement that passengers and crew should prepare for take-off and the plane began to taxi toward the runway. A safety video played on screens with equipment demonstrated by one of the hostesses.

The seat belt lights were lit and in flight staff rechecked that everyone had buckled up and was safe.

The pilot's voice boomed out, "Crew prepare for take-off." The staff retreated to their assigned places and fastened their seat belts as the aircraft prepared to fly. They reached the main runway, the engines went full throttle and sped down the concourse.

To Jon and Amy's relief the plane soared up into the sky and continued to climb. Amy settled back contentedly to enjoy the flight.

"We're not home and dry yet. I'll feel safer once we've landed and gone through customs."

"Don't be such a pessimist, Jon. You always imagine the worst. Think positive."

"I try, but it's hard. What if they find the old couple with the laptop? It won't take them long to discover what flight we're on. It could be recalled. Or we could be apprehended at the other end."

"Right now, I couldn't care less. If it happens, it happens but I tell you now. I won't go down without a fight. I will pass these files to another member of the public and make an announcement on this plane if need be and tell our whole story."

"They'll think you're off your head."

"Maybe, maybe not. What is the old saying, 'There's no smoke without fire,' someone will take notice – all it needs is one person."

"There's another saying, 'There's safety in numbers,' we need more than one person in the loop."

"Do you think they've realised yet, which flight we're on?"

"So far so good. Long may it continue. I'm going to rest a moment," said Jon. "I'm whacked."

Amy studied the confidential list of Sect members and a name caught her eye. "I don't believe it," she muttered under her breath, "Malcolm West." Suddenly, things began to slot into place. She shoved the information back into her bag and looked out of the window at the clouds beneath her, as the plane climbed, a worried expression on her face.

The elderly couple were absorbed and busy with the laptop. They hadn't noticed that they had been surrounded by security guards and plain clothed officers and agents. There was the sound of a number of guns being cocked. The old couple looked up. All they could see were the barrels of the firearms pointing at them. They slowly raised their hands in shocked surprise.

Max lowered his weapon, stamped his foot and swore in exasperation.

"What is it?" asked Wilf in a tremulous voice.

"That laptop, where did you get it?"

Emily answered and kicked Wilf under the table. "Why do you want to know?"

Irritated Max responded, "Madam, we believe that you have appropriated the laptop belonging to a known terrorist. We need you to tell us how you came by it."

"Fair and square," replied the old lady. "It's a present for my granddaughter."

"But how?" pressed Max.

A crowd began to gather around the officers and the old people. One person called out, "You ought to be ashamed of yourself, frightening old folk."

Another shouted, "Leave them alone, bullies."

Even more irate Max raised his voice, "We can always do this somewhere else."

"By what authority?" questioned Emily getting bolder.

More bystanders stepped forward to watch the exchange. Emily announced, "A young lady wanted help, she needed money and asked us to buy her laptop, which we did. It was a bargain, just a few hundred quid. This here's top of the range." Emily was becoming more fired up.

"But…" interrupted Wilf. Emily kicked him again.

"Yes, Sir? Perhaps you can tell me the truth."

"We are. It's what she said," confirmed Wilf.

"I'm sorry but I'll have to impound that machine," insisted Max.

"No, you won't; we paid good money for this," and so the wrangle continued.

Max addressed the growing crowd, "Did anyone else see this transaction?"

A man, who was part of a touring rugby team, raised his hand, "Just like the lady said. She paid a young woman money and the lass pocketed the cash and went toward the Emirates Desk."

Max gestured to Jack and Biff to get across to the airline's desk.

Max instructed two guards to stay and watch the couple while he followed his agents across to the Emirates Check In desks. He swore when he saw that the desk was some distance from where they were.

Wilf whispered to Emily, "Why are you saying all this?"

"Because I liked her. I'm not about to ruin her wedding and honeymoon. And I don't like them. Something's not right about this. If there was a terrorist running loose, the whole airport would be under siege with announcements and everything, yet nothing has been said. Remember what the police did to my brother. They carted him off into a holding cell, for something he hadn't done and he died in their custody. Oh no, I'm not going to help them and nor are you."

Wilf nodded, "So, what do we do now?"

"I suggest we sit tight and when the time is right we make a break for it."

"With the laptop?" questioned Wilf.

"With the laptop," affirmed Emily. "There's something on here that we need to see. Something they want. In fact, we'll close it up now and open it up when we are away on our holiday. They won't trace us in another country so easily." She shut the laptop down and packed it away. They would have to pick their moment, when and how that would be the difficulty.

There was still a crowd around them. The two agents stood guard watching them. The man, Jimmy, who had shouted at Max in the old couple's defence, pushed through and sat with them at the table. "Is it right? What that bloke said?" he asked.

"Just a front, I bet. They want this computer for a reason. But they're not going to get it," pronounced Emily.

"I'm no lover of the cops," he said. "How can I help?"

"We need to get away before that other one comes back that you sent to the Emirates desk."

"He'll be a while," laughed the man. "It's right at the other end of the airport."

"Can you do something to get rid of those so and so's? So, we can get away?" asked Emily, indicating the two agents on watch.

"Maybe I can, keep your eyes peeled. When you see me keel over into them, take a chance and run. I'll get my mates to crowd around and stop them following you. Got it?" he winked at Emily who flushed with pleasure.

"Hear that, Wilf? He's going to help us."

"The name's Jimmy. Good luck." With that the man stood up and joined the rest of the members of his rugby team that were watching curiously. They huddled together, scrum like, as Jimmy explained what he wanted them to do. All in agreement, they grinned and edged closer to the guards whose attention had been taken by a scantily clad, nubile young woman strolling past.

A couple of the rugby players whistled after her and she shook her long hair appreciatively and smiled. Jimmy stepped closer to the guard and crashed into one clutching his heart and groaning loudly. He fell against him and the two guards knelt down to see what they could do to help. The rest of the team crowded around and prevented them from seeing Wilf and Emily who picked up their things and scuttled away and disappeared into the crowds.

Jimmy received a signal that the old people had gone and suddenly recovered. "I must have stood up too quickly, low blood pressure does that. It makes you faint. Sorry."

His friends pulled him up, one said, "We'll get to the medical centre and have you checked out. Come on." The team drifted away with Jimmy. The guards looked around to see that Wilf and Emily had vanished.

The old folk had hurried back through the shopping concourse, down the escalator, and managed to get through the security gate and back into the main body of the airport. They raced outside to the taxi rank and climbed aboard one to head home. Emily turned to Wilf in the back seat. "That's the best fun I've had in years. I could do it all over again."

"I don't think my heart would stand anymore excitement," replied Wilf. "But it was good, I'll grant you that. I'd love to see their faces when they see we've gone," he chortled.

"And now, let's get home and plan another trip. First class for you and me," beamed Emily.

Jon and Amy engaged their seatbelts as the warning light came on and the pilot announced that they were now descending to Dubrovnik airport. Here they would discover their fate. Would they make it through customs or not? Had the authorities discovered yet which flight they had taken?

The plane landed smoothly in brilliant sunshine. Jon collected the hand luggage from the locker and looked at the sombrero. "Are you taking that?" quizzed Amy.

"Perhaps, not. It does get in the way a bit," said Jon sensibly.

"Take it and bin it when we get off," advised Amy.

Jon tugged it out of the overhead locker. It looked somewhat the worse for wear and the straw had broken and cracked in parts so he squashed it up and held it in his hand.

They exited the plane and walked along a gangway and into the airport where Jon trashed the hat. They joined the queue at Passport Control and waited nervously. Amy looked at the armed guards and soldiers that cast an eye over the arriving passengers. "Keep calm, Amy. Keep calm," she told herself.

"It will be okay," said Jon. "Be positive."

It was their turn to walk to the immigration desk. The border control officer studied their photos and then their faces. "On holiday?" he asked routinely.

"Yes, we plan to tour around your beautiful country," praised Jon.

The officer smiled and stamped their passports. "Have a good time."

They each breathed a huge sigh of relief as they walked away and into the arrival hall with the baggage carousels. They waited for Wilf and Emily's cases to appear, watching carefully as other passengers removed their luggage until there were only a few bags left circling around. An airport official lugged the remaining cases off and stood them in a line and Amy crossed to inspect the labels. She found them and relieved they collected them and walked to the exit. They stepped outside into the dazzling sunshine and heat to look for a taxi.

"Let's ask the cabbie if he can recommend any self-catering accommodation, or if he can take us to a tourist office where we can book somewhere," suggested Amy.

"We are going to need a car. We can't use taxis all the time."

"And we can't hire one without driving licences and credit cards."

"I've got my driving licence," said Jon.

"So have I but it's in my real name not Susan May."

"We've still got our real passports. I reckon they know our false identities now anyway. Heck that goon at the airport grabbed my jacket with the boarding passes."

"Then we'll have to buy one."

"What?"

"A car. But first we need to change money. Have you seen a bureau de change anywhere?"

"We passed a booth on the way out near the exit door," remembered Jon.

"Let's get back there; we can't operate without kunas."

"You go and change some cash I'll wait in the queue."

Amy dashed back. She soon emerged smiling triumphantly and joined Jon who had moved up the line at the rank. "We are now solvent."

A cab pulled up, the cab driver scrutinised the pair. "French?" he asked.

"No, English."

"Great. Where to?"

"You speak English," said Amy surprised.

"Moved here ten years ago. My wife is a Croat. Where are you headed?"

"Maybe you can help us?" Amy launched into an explanation of how they had arrived on spec and wanted to tour the country. "So, do you know of any self-catering accommodation that may be available?"

"I know just the place, hop in."

They clambered in with the bags and the cabbie chatted almost non-stop in a chirpy, friendly manner and put them at their ease. He drove them to a holiday park with self-catering chalet bungalows. They expressed their thanks and took his card in case they wanted his help again.

The manager of the concern was equally friendly and also very helpful and they soon settled into a tastefully smart log cabin, which they booked for a month and paid for in cash.

"Tell me," asked Amy as they were being shown around. Is there anywhere I can get a Croatian sim card for my phone?"

"Yes, and where could we hire a car or motorbike?" asked Jon.

The manager was only too delighted to help them and promised to furnish them with a local pay and go sim card that he kept on sale behind the counter at Reception.

It all seemed to be going very well and for once they were not running for their lives.

Later that night they would need to organise themselves and plan their next move. They intended to finish the film and release it to the world.

Ibrahim was aware that he was now being kept under surveillance. Every time he left his home he was followed. He knew from Claire that his phone was tapped and his emails hacked into. He determined to thwart these forces somehow. He was keen to contact Jon and Amy but had no idea where they were.

Carol was becoming emotionally torn. Her rigorous training and tragic loss had thrown her into Ibrahim's arms and she now had a conflict of interest that she needed to keep to herself. Her training had been strict and regulated. She knew what she was supposed to do. Her next assignment was to assassinate Ibrahim when she received the directive. But, Carol no longer felt that she could do this. In fact, she admitted to herself that she didn't want to.

Chapter Sixteen

Clean up

AN ELDERLY, FATHERLY LOOKING solicitor opened the door of his office at the start of another day. He took off his hat and coat and hung it on the coat stand by his office door. Waiting on his desk was a large package sent by recorded delivery. He examined at the handwriting. Something flickered deep in his memory.

His secretary popped her head around the door, "Parcel on the desk, Sir. It's been stuck in the mailroom for days. A junior had to sign for it. And we've been receiving some strange phone calls this morning. We think they may be something wrong with the phone lines."

"What do you mean, strange calls?" asked Mr. Reginald Greig.

"Hang ups. Oh, and someone asked for you by name and when I said you were out and asked what it was about they ended the call."

"Right. Thank you, Jeannie."

"How was the dentist, Mr. Greig? I hope you didn't have to have too much done."

"Root canal, not pleasant. I'll survive," he smiled at his secretary. "I could murder a cup of tea."

"Coming right up."

Reginald picked up the packet and took his paper knife and cut through the tape binding it closed. He took out a number of files and a couple of CD's, which he placed in his drawer. A note fluttered to the floor, which he retrieved. "Claire Williams, I knew I recognised the writing. Well, well, well," he murmured softly.

He read her letter –

'Dear Reginald,

I didn't know whom I could trust. And then I thought of you, our loyal family solicitor. I don't want to place you in any danger but I need to entrust these files somewhere for safe keeping that can be acted upon when the time is right.

Put the CD's somewhere safe and separate from the files. Take the time to read them and you will see the material is not only of a very sensitive nature but also top secret. I know you will be appalled as I was that such things could happen in our country.

Destroy or hide this letter.

I don't know if I will be alive long enough to see this through. If you haven't heard from me in three days from the delivery of this package you must assume I am dead.

I hope you will know what to do with the contents and make sure this gets to the right people. You are not the only one who knows of the existence of these files. The more people that know the better and the more we can get it out there in the public domain the more chance we have of getting the truth out there.

I hope to speak to you later and then I will explain further what we need to do.

Best as always,

Claire (Williams).

Reg placed the letter in the drawer under the CD's and picked up the files.

Jeannie entered with his morning tea and placed it on his desk. She barely glanced at the papers he was ploughing through. "Call me if you need anything." Reg answered with a nod of his head and she slipped out quietly.

Reg sat down and put his feet up and began to read the information in front of him. He shuffled through the comprehensive notes and top-secret files. His eyes widened as he began to digest what was in front of him. He couldn't believe the information on MK Ultra. He took his glasses off and rubbed his eyes. "Just what does she expect me to do with this?" he muttered aloud.

Reginald Greig paged his secretary, "Jeannie, can you hold all calls and cancel my appointments?"

"Sir?" queried Jeannie.

"Something important has cropped up and I need time to think," he concluded. He turned another page and read, 'The Electra Conspiracy'. He picked up his tea and took a mouthful when he heard a kerfuffle outside his door.

"I'm afraid you can't go in there," admonished his secretary, Jeannie.

Greig put down his cup and looked toward the door, which burst open. Ron and Steve entered with uniformed police.

"I'm sorry, Mr. Greig," said an ashen faced, Jeannie.

Reginald Greig's jaw dropped at the intrusion and Ron's next words, "Mr. Reginald Greig, I am placing you under arrest. The contents of these files are confiscated and your business is to be shut down pending further investigation."

The solicitor looked aghast. His face registered stunned amazement.

Handcuffs came out and were placed on his wrists. "Jeannie, call my solicitor. This is urgent. Do it now," he instructed.

Ron picked up the brown paper package and the files from the desk. He searched the desk surface and asked suspiciously, "No covering letter?"

Reginald Greig, answered, "No. None. Just these papers, which I have barely started to examine. I have no idea who sent them." Jeannie looked on in fear as her boss was herded out. "Please, Jeannie, I need a lawyer."

Across town in a busy newspaper office, the tabloid's editor Raymond Baldwin was engrossed in what he was reading. The outer packing of Claire's package was on the desk at his side. He, too, had received a letter and CD's, which he had already fortunately filed away in one of his cabinets.

The outer office was a flurry of activity, with journalists moving to and fro between desks, some on the telephone, others writing their news items at computers. The outer door opened and Max entered with Jack. Max pointed at the Editor through the glass and they made their way past the workers to Raymond Baldwin's door. They didn't knock. They walked straight in.

Max stopped at the desk, "Hello, Ray".

A fleeting glimmer of alarm flashed across Raymond Baldwin's eyes as he recognised his visitor. "Hello, Max."

"I'm afraid you can't use any of that," said Max in measured tones. He indicated the files with a flick of his eyes. "The story is not in the nation's interest."

Jack removed the file from him, which was relinquished without fuss.

"This file is impounded. And if you try to print anything or pursue this story…" admonished Jack.

"…The newspaper will be shut down," finished Max.

"You can't do that," protested Ray.

"Oh, yes, I can," asserted Max. "We have ways and means."

"And what if I disobey?"

"You don't want to do that. I would hate anything to happen to you or your family," said Max, the inference was obvious.

"Are you threatening me?"

"No, I wouldn't put it like that. Let's say I am advising you that none of this is in the nation's or anyone's interest."

"Isn't that for me and the general public to decide?"

"Not in this case," said Max raising his voice a little. "You had better forget what you've seen and speak about it to no one or I will not be responsible for the repercussions."

Max and Jack confidently left the newspaper offices with the package and retreated outside.

"How many more of these do you think she's sent?" asked Jack.

"From the information from Claire's tracking receipts from the Post Office, only two."

"What now?"

"We wait, Jack. We wait. Ms. Wilde and Mr. Curtis are bound to slip up sooner or later and when they do, we'll be there. Better get back to the office we still have a couple of loose ends to tie up."

"The old couple?"

"That's one of them."

"And the others?

"The photographer in the White Fiat Uno. He has to go. He's been making noises about exposing the conspiracy. His drinking has loosened his tongue. Member of the Sect or not, he has outlived his usefulness. He has worked on one too many assassinations and then there's Ibrahim Khalid. Don't forget him."

Jack shook his head. His face and expression said one thing but his heart and mind were telling him something else. He mooched back to the car and waited for Max to get in and began the journey back to MI6.

Max continued to talk, "The photographer…"

"Which one?"

"Anderson."

"From the tunnel?"

"From the tunnel," confirmed Max. "As I said, he's talking too much. He's been heard bragging that he was at the crash site."

"So?"

"We need to shut him up and quickly."

Jack prevaricated, "But, I thought he was a useful operative, as well as a Sect member. You've used him a number of times before," Jack remarked.

"Yes, but he's becoming blasé. If we don't want the truth to come out, he has to go. Get rid of him."

"But…"

"Are you questioning me?" Max was becoming angry. "I'm not asking you to pull the trigger yourself. Organise it. The man spent time, a few hours on Ahmed Khalid's yacht photographing the playboy and Electra just days before the reception. We don't want people putting two and two together."

They continued the rest of the journey in silence until Max turned on the CD player and one of Electra's songs filled the car. The song with five repetitive notes played underneath the vocals. Jack drove like an automaton. "Electra," he breathed.

"Just because she's gone doesn't mean I didn't appreciate her music," said Max.

The security building came into view and Jack drove into the underground car park and stopped. "Get on with it, Jack and that's an order," roared Max as he left the vehicle.

Jack, glassy eyed shook his head as if trying to clear it. He proceeded to the seedy basement tech lab and summoned Biff whose face popped up on screen.

"James Anderson has been shooting his mouth off. Stop him doing it anymore," ordered Jack.

"On whose authority?" queried Biff.

"Max has a directive from the top," replied Jack.

"Where is the target?" questioned Biff.

"Somewhere in the New Forest, Burley Village."

"Do I look for his car? Does it still have a trace for GPS?"

"It was re-sprayed and sold, according to the police it has never been found. Deliberately so. It had to be got rid of. So, it is sitting in a crusher somewhere being recycled."

"We will have to isolate our man somehow and get him into a secluded part of the forest. That could prove to be tricky," said Biff.

Jack had an idea. He spoke to Biff on screen, "I will tell him he has another magazine assignment. He'll turn up. His ego wouldn't allow him to turn a celebrity job down. You'll see."

Biff acknowledged and the screen went black.

The black van set off onto the road almost immediately and was now travelling to Burley. The operatives had the address. The agents followed directions and entered a clearing surrounded by a thick wooded area in the forest. They parked out of view and were careful to remain hidden. There they waited. Time ticked on.

Darkness began to descend and in the pervading gloom and the quiet of the forest settling down to sleep, a car engine was heard approaching the road that led to the clearing and picnic area. Biff was immediately on the alert. He slipped out of the van, with Ron and they stayed under cover as the vehicle rolled up and extinguished its headlights. The car engine idled for a few moments before being switched off. James Anderson stayed in his car.

Biff signalled to Ron and they slipped out of hiding. Biff jumped into the front passenger seat and Ron into the back.

"Hello, James."

"What the…?"

There were two shots to Anderson's head. The photographer slumped forward onto the steering wheel and the horn blared out. Biff pulled him back and quiet was restored. He grabbed the car keys and the operatives exited the vehicle.

Biff wanted no mistakes made. The hit had to be certain. He retrieved a can of an accelerant from the back of the black van and liberally sloshed it over the car. He locked the car doors, tossed a lit match into the mix, which instantly ignited the fuel. He watched the greedy flames grow as they bubbled and blackened the paintwork and spread. The heat was searing.

Afraid that the plume of smoke that billowed up into the star filled sky would soon be noticed, Biff and Ron returned to the van and they reversed out from behind the trees, passed the burning vehicle and drove back onto the road.

Wailing sirens were heard in the distance, as fire engines raced to find the source of the smoke. They eventually arrived, at the scene and began to extinguish the flames, afraid that the fire could spread to the trees and cause infinite damage to the forest and wildlife.

Once the vehicle was reduced to a smoking hulk, one of the firemen tried to open the driver's door. Finding it locked, cutting equipment was used to release the badly charred body inside. He noted the two bullet holes in the head and that there were no car keys.

This was not a suicide as some of his men had supposed. It looked more like an execution.

Chapter Seventeen

Further developments

THE BURNT ORANGE SUN bathed the rustic taverna, near Split, in its golden glow. It was going to be another beautiful sunset. Amy and Jon sat sipping wine with the remains of a meal in front of them. The filmmakers were relaxed and looked rested and content.

Rumble sat in a pet carrier on a seat between Ibrahim and Jon. They all raised their glasses in a toast. "To success," announced Amy.

Ibrahim added, "And the truth." They all sipped from their glasses.

Jon's hair was beginning to grow back and just skirted his shoulders and he had regained his natural hair colour. He shook his head and murmured, "I still can't believe that Malcolm West was involved in all this."

"He was a major player," asserted Ibrahim. "And yet he continues to walk free."

"Not for much longer, I'm sure. He used Electra by putting the triggers in her songs… Unforgiveable."

"I know," agreed Ibrahim. "But the film is almost ready for release. I have the copies safe. It is entered into all of the major film festivals and will get its first outing a Venice. This is brilliant news."

"It's a pity we were just too late for Cannes, but there… You know, I would just like to go home," said Amy.

"It's not safe yet. You are still wanted by the authorities. But, don't worry, I will continue to support you financially," confirmed Ibrahim.

"But, what about you? You are on their hit list. You've seen the evidence yourself," said Amy a look of doubt crossing her features.

"I'll be fine. They wouldn't dare touch me, because of the publicity it would bring. I am convinced that I am safe for now. That is as long as we can get the film into distribution and it is shown to the masses and I have people working on that around the clock."

"Where are you going now?" asked Amy.

"I think I may change my main residence. I am thinking of selling up my UK home and moving to Switzerland. I have bought property near Zurich. You will be free to visit me there."

"What happened to your plans to do an exposé through Wikileaks?" asked Jon.

"It looks like the owner of the website is a victim of some sort of conspiracy himself. He's trying not to get himself extradited on some alleged sex charge. I believe he's been granted asylum at the Ecuadorian Embassy. So, we're still working on that. It will happen eventually and to allay your fears I am sure that I am safe for now. Please don't worry."

A racy red convertible sports car sped up the drive to the restaurant driven by Carol. She was wearing shades and a headscarf. She called out, "Ibby, we're going to be late! Come on."

Amy glanced at Carol and struggled to think why she looked a little familiar but she was distracted from this thought as Ibrahim rose. He embraced Jon and hugged Amy, kissing her fondly on both cheeks. He stepped back and studied both of the filmmakers with tears in his eyes. "Thank you, both of you. My heart is full. Because of you the world will know the truth and no one can stop it getting out now. They would have to kill me first and that won't happen, not now." He looked at Rumble in his pet carrier and addressed the cat, "Bye, dear Rumble. You know, I never thought that I could get fond of a cat."

"Ah, but not any cat," said Jon. "This one is a super cat!" They all laughed.

Carol called out again, "Ibby!" She stood up at the wheel and gestured him to come. She watched them all saying their goodbyes again.

"I must go. I will be in touch." Ibrahim walked away and climbed into the low-slung car. Carol waved goodbye at the filmmakers as she manoeuvred the car and turned it around. They sped away down the road.

Amy turned to Jon, "I can't help thinking that I've seen her somewhere before."

"Probably that night at Ibrahim's apartment."

"Maybe, but I'm certain it was somewhere else…" Amy trailed off.

"Don't worry, you'll remember when you least expect it," soothed Jon.

Amy smiled and shrugged it off. She laughed and turned up her face to kiss Jon. They were comfortable with each other and clearly happy that their relationship had progressed.

"I fancy another glass of wine. Oh, Jon I am so relieved that it will soon be all over. That really is something to celebrate."

"We have done our best. Wilf and Emily have the story, too. When is it they are coming out?"

"In two weeks, June 16th. If it weren't for them we wouldn't be here. A holiday with us is the least we could do for them."

"I'm just amazed they escaped with your laptop."

"Soon to be returned laptop," smiled Amy as she poured them both another glass of wine. "Cheers!"

Back in England a faceless journalist wearing a gold ring with an embossed lion's head was working long into the night as he prepared an obituary. The date on the column read, June 16th. The headline blared out, 'Ibrahim Khalid dies tragically in a cliff fall whilst holidaying in Croatia.' He glanced at his desk calendar June 2nd and reached for a file on Ibrahim Khalid.

It was happening all over again.

Author's Acknowledgements

THIS BOOK IS DEDICATED to all those who support and encourage me, especially my loving husband, Andrew Spear who persuaded me to write full time.

I must mention my lovely son, Ben Fielder who shares my passion for writing and thanks for all the excellent discussions and ideas we share together.

To my commissioning editor Sarah Luddington who is a tower of strength and valuable mentor.

Thanks to some special people in my life, Pamela Hamer, Dawn Wheeler, Sue Taylor, Barbara Davis, Gail Angove and Karen Gulliford.

My lovely FB friends from around the world, who have bought all my books, read them and wanted more.

Future titles will hopefully include, Return of the Tide the sequel to Against the Tide, a fifth in the Llewellyn family series, a sixth in the Detective Inspector Allison series. Please feel free to contact me on my Facebook Author's page:
https://www.facebook.com/Elizabeth-Revill-221311591283258
If you like my books please click 'Like'. Thank you.

Other books by the author

The terrifying Inspector Allison
psychological thrillers:

Killing me Softly,
Prayer for the Dying
God only Knows
Would I Lie To You

Llewellyn Family Saga:

Whispers on the Wind
Shadows on the Moon
Rainbows in the Clouds
Thunder in the Sun

Against the Tide
Turn of the Tide

Stand alone novels:

The Electra Conspiracy
Sanjukta and the Box of Souls
The Forsaken and the Damned

THE CIRCUMSTANCES SURROUNDING THE death of Princess Diana were nothing if not controversial. Conspiracy theories abounded from claims of Government plots to much, much more. Rumours raged after her death and the press was very keen to play up to this. Many television programmes sought to investigate the truth behind her death and although many doubts were cast on the accident, none came up with a totally satisfactory explanation to this tragedy.

I always admired Diana and thought her untimely death was a great loss to society, so much so that I did some digging and investigating myself. This led me on to discover any number of claimed 'conspiracies' out there from the death of Marilyn Monroe, John Lennon and JF Kennedy to the landing of men on the moon. It was all fascinating stuff.

This gave me an idea, I wondered if it were possible to use some of these theories, fictionalise them, take them further dramatically by incorporating threads of other conspiracy claims, and weave them into a novel.

When I read about the secret Bilderberg group, and the claim that they controlled the fate of the world and the experiments performed in the USA on the military in years gone by, a glimmer of an idea began to grow. I knew that there had been a thought provoking movie, "The Manchurian Candidate" on this subject but I deliberately didn't watch it until I had written my story. I saw it very recently and was literally enthralled.

Electra is my idea of the music world's counterpart to Diana. I wondered, 'What if...?' My imagination knows no bounds and from that small seed, The Electra Conspiracy was born. I hope you've enjoyed it.